More praise for The Professor of Immortality

"The Professor of Immortality is a tragicomedy about the paradoxes of trying to be a decent human, and—maybe even trickier—of trying to be a decent mom. It's also page by page a joy to read. Eileen Pollack is one of the smartest, funniest and most companionable novelists out there." (Rivka Galchen, author of *Atmospheric Disturbances*)

"In this exceptional novel, Eileen Pollack writes with great immediacy about the impact of grief on a parent's perception of the world. Tender, wry, full of unexpected revelations, The Professor of Immortality gripped me from the first scene, and the urgent questions it poses have stayed with me." (Idra Novey, author of *Those Who Knew*)

"Wrapped in some stimulating intellectual discussion about what the future might bring, The Professor of Immortality is an old-fashioned suspense mystery, which will have you wondering along with Professor Sayers, whether any of the world's verities remain true." (Donald H. Harrison, editor of San Diego Jewish World.)

"The Professor of Immortality is an original work of fiction, an engaging domestic drama and a critical questioning of significant and diverse contemporary issues, especially the need for more women to feel welcomed in the mathematical sciences." (Joan Baum, WSHU Public Radio)

Also by Eileen Pollack

Fiction

The Bible of Dirty Jokes
A Perfect Life
Breaking and Entering
In the Mouth
Paradise, New York
The Rabbi in the Attic
Whisper Whisper Jesse, Whisper Whisper Josh: A Story about AIDS

Nonfiction

The Only Woman in the Room: Why Science Is Still a Boys' Club
Woman Walking Ahead: In Search of Catherine Weldon and
Sitting Bull
Creative Nonfiction: A Guide to Form, Content, and Style

THE PROFESSOR

of

IMMORTALITY

a novel by

EILEEN

POLLACK

DELPHINIUM BOOKS

THE PROFESSOR OF IMMORTALITY

For information, address DELPHINIUM BOOKS, INC.,
16350 Ventura Boulevard, Suite D
PO Box 803
Encino, CA 91436

Library of Congress Cataloguing-in-Publication Data is
available on request.
ISBN 978-1-883285-93-7
20 21 22 23 LSC 10 9 8 7 6 5 4 3 2 1

First paperback edition

Jacket and interior design by Colin Dockrill

For Noah

The Professor of Immortality

. . . Gets out of Bed

For most of her life, Maxine has assumed anyone who *couldn't get out of bed* must be in the grip of a severe mental illness. In college, while her classmates slept off their hangovers, she leapt up eagerly to take a shower, get dressed, and set off to the dining hall. How could she not look forward to the secrets of relativity due to be revealed that day in physics? The magic of linear algebra in math. *Middlemarch* and *Jane Eyre* in English lit. Even at the modest public university she found the wherewithal to attend, any student who accomplished the not-so-difficult task of getting out of bed could learn to play the harp, fence, skydive, sculpt, paint, speak Mandarin, or design a submarine.

Later, at MIT, she felt lonely and overwhelmed. But then she met Sam, and every fresh day provided an opportunity to get to know him. Sam might not have been perfect, but he had been perfect for her. Unassuming. Slight. With pale red hair and a sparse, soft beard. To her mother's generation, such a man might have been considered too "sensitive." Too easily mistaken for a homosexual. Now, Maxine's female students seem to believe mild, technologically proficient guys like Sam won't boss them around. Cheat on them. Drink too much beer and yell profanities at the television when their team misses an easy lay-up or blows a touchdown. Such women find younger versions of Sam to be attractive for the same reasons they enjoy shopping at a thrift store: coming home with a plaid polyester housedress shows their more original taste in fashion.

But Sam has been dead eight years, and Maxine hasn't been able to find anyone to date or sleep with, let alone to replace him. The eighteen-year-olds who make up the majority of Ann Arbor's population are like stem cells: put any two in a Petri dish, squirt on nutrient solution, and each will take on the characteristics of the other. But by the time any two adults have reached their fifties, each has differentiated to such an extent that asking one to share the other's life is like asking a heart cell to morph to become a liver cell or part of an eye.

Her friends insisted she try online dating. But in a city so small, she might as well have stood on Main Street with a sign around her neck: MIDDLE-AGED PROFESSOR, REDUCED FOR SALE. When she finally gave in and posted her profile—by then she was fifty-four and desperate—all she found were a few burly inhabitants of outlying towns, where the most common male pastimes seemed to involve speedboats, guns, and Harley-Davidsons. Of the three "matches" she agreed to meet, the first didn't show up, and the second turned out to be a wealthy, combative lawyer who, when she revealed she directed something called the Institute for Future Studies, laughed and asked her to predict whether she would become his fourth and final wife, or his fourth divorce.

And yet, the night before, she had somehow found the courage to meet the third candidate with whom the wizards at Match.com had paired her. For a while, she and this man—a sweet but self-deprecating preschool teacher—made conversation about the weather. Then he asked what she did at the university, and Maxine tried to describe the courses she taught, her role in riding herd on a bunch of scientists studying the effects of computers on human psychology and behavior. "Digital" this. "Voice recognition" that. Cochlear implants. Fake electronic eyes. Prosthetic limbs. Prosthetic bodies. Nanobots that might repair malfunctioning blood cells from inside a person's marrow. Maxine's own area of specialization was the study of immortality.

By the time she had explained all this, her date had devoured most of the pizza they had ordered, while Maxine's own slice had grown greasy and cold on the plate before her. "What about you?" she said. "It must be wonderful being around young children all day. They *are* the future, aren't they?"

"Yes," he said. "I love watching children play. But it's nothing like studying immortality." He excused himself to visit the "little boys' room," then slipped out the back without paying the check or telling Maxine goodbye.

No wonder she can't get out of bed. Not to mention her son has stopped calling her or responding to her emails. For the past seven months, she has had no idea where he is.

She drags herself to the bathroom. For most of her life she appeared far younger than she was. Her hair, still black and long, shows only a few silvery strands, like the tracks dividing the songs on an old LP. But eight years of grief for Sam, along with the more recent worry about her son, have exacted their toll. When did she grow so haggard, the lines around her lips and eyes so drawn?

She splashes cold water on her face, then trudges downstairs and chokes down her calcium and Omega-3. In the old days, when Zach was so thin she couldn't find jeans narrow enough to stay on his hips, Sam had cooked them all elaborate breakfasts—oatmeal thick with raisins and dates; omelets loaded with mushrooms and parmesan; pecan-studded waffles smothered in apple-and-brown-sugar syrup. She could fix those same breakfasts for herself. But every raisin and date would remind her of the sweetness that has gone out of her life. Instead, she pours a bowl of the same dry Special K she ate as a child. (Her father used to tease that she was the only girl who ate cereal without milk. "Why don't you just chew on the box?" he joked.)

Still, she hasn't deprived herself of the *Times*. How would it look if the Director of Future Studies couldn't summon the interest to find out what happened the day before, let alone gain insight into whatever new catastrophes might be brewing? She opens the front door and darts out, barefoot, into the gray Michigan dawn. The blue plastic bag lies in a gutter filled with muck. She looks up and down the block. If her neighbors read the *Times*, they read it on their computers. She understands the allure of not needing to go outside in one's pajamas. But the gritty feel of the paper and the burnt-toast smell of the newsprint kindle the excitement she experienced as a child, sharing it with her father. Her job had been to bring in the bottles of milk the dairyman delivered, along with the *Times* and the *Fenstead Press*. On cold winter mornings, great yellow plows bleated past on the street, piling up snowbanks Maxine and her friends would later excavate into tunnels. In the spring, dew glistened across the lawn, patterned by the tracks of birds. She would scurry inside and hand the paper to her father, who fixed them both breakfast, then read aloud to Maxine about this discovery or that invention, the way the government had passed, or failed to pass, some regulation that made it easier for little guys like him to earn a living.

The first Sunday Sam slept over—this had been when she

was a graduate student at MIT and Sam a post-doc—Maxine cooked him eggs, then passed him the front section of the *Times* and listened happily—well, not happily, but with the knowledge she was falling in love—as he raged against the corruption that had caused a factory in India to collapse, killing hundreds. They married and moved to Ann Arbor, Sam as a highly recruited associate professor in the Program for Global Initiatives, Maxine with a junior appointment in the Residential College. Zach was born, and by the time he was in elementary school, the three of them would sit around the table eating Sam's ambrosial omelets, chattering blithely, and grabbing whatever section of the paper someone had just set down.

Then, when Zach turned fourteen, he decided his father, in the guise of alleviating poverty, was importing the miseries of the First World to the citizens of the Third. "You're just bringing them the pollution we have here! They'll end up a bunch of industrial clones like we are!" Sam had allowed Zach to express his views. But the fights became unpleasant. Zach would reach a point where he grew so frustrated with his father, he would sit simmering in silence. His eyes would bulge, and you could see he was arguing in his head. If only he would come out and curse them. Hurl a chair. Dump his omelet on the floor. Anything but hold in that anger.

This went on for two years, until Sam died, after which Zach's moods grew incomprehensible. He and Maxine would sit hushed in numbness, the paper untouched between them, as if, should either unfold a section, they would be opening a Pandora's box of arguments. Then Zach seemed to decide his father had been a saint, devoted as he had been to the welfare of people so much less fortunate than himself. To atone for having given him such a hard time, Zach cooked up the idea of going on a hunger strike. If the adults in Ann Arbor refused to acknowledge that children in other parts of the world were starving, Zach would demonstrate what a starving child looked like. Maxine coaxed him to eat. But he refused so much as a Cheerio. He created posters showing the malnourished children in Malawi and tacked them to telephone poles around town. He gave an interview to the local radio station. Other parents complimented her on having such a good-hearted, strong-willed son. But she could tell they were grateful their own children were more oblivious.

By the third day of his hunger strike, Maxine was frantic. "Please," she begged. "I admire your values. But you're already so thin! You'll get sick. You'll pass out on the street." She prepared his favorite meal—vegetarian chili and cornbread—and insisted he come to the table. But he sat with his hands folded, even as his mother consumed two portions. She wanted to hold him down and shove cornbread in his mouth, but she couldn't very well do that, could she?

"Don't worry," her friend and coworker Rosa Romanczuk assured her. "Zach isn't Bobby Sands. He'll eat when he's good and hungry." But Maxine suspected her son was fully capable of starving himself to death. She cried. She wrote a check to UNICEF. And another check, for twice that amount, to CARE. She persuaded Zach's classmates' parents to donate money. But asking your friends to write checks to UNICEF so your son won't starve himself to death isn't like asking them to buy thin mint cookies.

On the fourth day, Zach wobbled home from school, sat down to do his homework, then laid his head on his arms and cried. "I'm so weak," he said. She interpreted this to mean he was weak from hunger. Then she realized he was beating himself up for not being able to carry through on his promise. She microwaved a Trader Joe's lasagna intended to feed a family of four. Zach wolfed it down. She returned to the kitchen to heat up another.

Then, just as he was gaining a few pounds, Zach read an op-ed piece by a professor of ethics at Princeton who argued that since each of us is born with two kidneys, we are morally obliged to donate the spare to someone who might die without it. At sixteen, Zach was too young to have the surgery without her permission. But he was so single-minded she was afraid he would slice out his own kidney and advertise it on the Internet. She spent days trying to convince him she would never survive the loss of her only child on top of losing his father. Reluctantly, Zach promised he wouldn't donate his kidney until he turned twenty-five, by which time she hoped he would develop a modicum of the selfishness that protected most people from the advice of childless Princeton philosophers. Recently, Zach had turned twenty-four. Maybe he couldn't bring himself to wait another year. Maybe he had signed himself into a hospital to donate his kidney and didn't want his mother to find out and stop him.

It wouldn't be the first time her son had run off to commit an act of charity. When he was seventeen, Zach had left a note and hitchhiked to Louisiana to help the victims of Hurricane Katrina. As angry as she was, Maxine knew his leaving had been her fault. He had seen her watching the news and crying. "We don't do that in America!" Maxine had ranted. "We don't abandon old people and black people and people in wheelchairs to drown, then leave their corpses beside a highway!" In Louisiana, Zach spent ten days heaving sodden mattresses and moldy carpets from people's houses before returning to Ann Arbor to begin his junior year of high school. Maybe she had been too lenient. But it wasn't as if she had discovered a cache of automatic weapons in his room.

Besides, after Zach got back from Louisiana he buckled down and accomplished everything a high-school junior needed to accomplish to get into college. Five years later, he earned his degree in environmental engineering from MIT and accepted a job at a classmate's start-up in Palo Alto. Maxine assumed she could let down her guard.

Then, the previous summer, Zach had turned sullen again. Withdrew. When she begged him to come home to visit, he mumbled some excuse. She called his cell. The number had been disconnected. She remembered his housemate's name and contacted the young man via Facebook. Apparently, Zach had given away his terrariums, his bicycle, and his books, then gotten in his car and driven off. A week later, Maxine received a postcard. The front showed Fisherman's Wharf. On the back, Zach had printed in awkward block capitals, as if he were his own kidnapper: I NEED TO GET AWAY. I WILL BE IN TOUCH WHEN I CAN.

Maxine had taken the note to the police, strangely embarrassed by her son's childish writing. (The year Zach was in third grade, his teacher had neglected to instruct her pupils in how to write cursive. Maxine had been upset, not knowing that within a few years, writing by hand would be obsolete.) But the cops weren't willing to send out a bulletin about a healthy, white, middle-class, twenty-something-year-old male who needed a break from his mother and had been considerate enough to send a postcard. Maxine's mother keeps demanding she hire a detective to find her grandson. But Maxine worries Zach will never forgive her if she tracks him down.

Or maybe she is afraid of what the detective might discover if they do find Zach. Every morning, when she reads the newspaper, she isn't sure if she is searching for disasters her son might be working to alleviate, or disasters he might have caused.

She bends and scoops the *Times* from the leafy muck, then carries it inside. Muddy water drips to the hardwood floor; a person doesn't need a degree in Future Studies to predict she will forget and step in that puddle later. She eats her dry Special K and scans a story about whether the Obama administration should repeal the Bush-era tax cuts. An online retailer admits its customers' financial data has been hacked—Jesus, Maxine thinks, it's 2012 and Visa and Mastercard still haven't figured out a way to safeguard their data? In Brazil, a battle has erupted between a group of peasants and the mercenary thugs hired by the government to evict them. Children have been shot. A man has been forced to eat the brains from the clubbed head of his brother. Maxine can't summon the compassion her late husband or missing son would have wanted her to feel. In the old days, a person would have been aware only of the tragedies in her own hometown. Now, she is expected to grieve for the entire world. Our hearts aren't designed to absorb so many strangers' pain, she thinks. It's like trying to pour Lake Michigan into an espresso cup.

She is about to turn the page when she realizes she has skipped the day's biggest headline. TECHNOBOMBER DEMANDS MANIFESTO BE PRINTED: *Threatens More Carnage if Call for Revolution Isn't Heeded.* Apparently, the serial terrorist the FBI long ago dubbed the Technobomber has demanded the editors publish his ravings. If they don't, or if the revolution he is calling for doesn't begin soon enough, he will escalate his campaign and send more bombs. What shocks Maxine is that the editors have caved in to the bomber's demands. What can be gained by stirring up more trauma for his victims? Four or five years ago, a professor at her own university received a package he assumed to be a manuscript from a fellow scientist. As he tugged open the wrapping, the package blew up in his face. He lost the sight in one eye and three fingers from his right hand. Maxine never cared much for Arnold Schlechter. But she hates to think he will need to spend the rest of today recounting his injuries to reporters.

Then again, as the director of an institute that purports to study the same future the writer of this manifesto is determined to prevent, Maxine might be spending her own day fielding calls. The *Times* has printed the document in a separate section. The densely packed paragraphs seem forbidding. Already she is running late—she has a meeting to lead in another hour. And some dread she can't identify, as if she might find her own name, or her son's name, or her late husband's name, amid those densely packed paragraphs, causes her to put off reading it.

She spoons up the last mouthful of Special K and washes down the tasteless paste with coffee. She slips the manifesto in her backpack, then pads across the living room to go upstairs. As she does, she steps in the muddy ooze that dripped from the paper earlier. Maybe, she thinks, it is time to give in and join the rest of the world in reading the *Times* online.

. . . Drags Herself to Work

As much as she used to love walking to work with Sam, that's how much she dreads the same walk now. Each morning, when she opens the front door, she turns in the hope of seeing him there behind her. Pulling on his blue watch cap. Zipping his orange anorak. Taking one last sip from his coffee before setting down the mug. Then they would wait for their moony, methodical son to gather what he needed for that day's activities and come dreamily down the stairs.

Once, when she scolded Zach to hurry, he said, "Mom? How can a person *hurry*? When you're going somewhere, there are a certain number of things you need to do. You need to brush your teeth. You need to eat breakfast and get dressed. It's not as if you can leave out any of those steps." When she realized he wasn't kidding, she said, "Oh, honey. You do all the same steps, but you do them faster." His expression revealed the fear she might try to make him. Instead, she suggested they get up a few minutes earlier, a solution Zach met with obvious relief. Asking a child like Zach to hurry would be as heartless as turning up the speed on some antique automaton, then watching it fly into a frenzied dance and grind to a crippled halt.

Every morning, the three of them would make their way to Zach's elementary school, she and Sam cheered by the round yellow Pokémon character on their son's backpack as he bobbed before them, as if leading them in a song. A block from school, Zach allowed them to kiss his hatted head, then scampered the rest of the way himself. Now, when she sees the other mothers kissing their sons, she needs to avert her eyes.

She drags herself up the hill to campus. It's the middle of April, but already her neighbors' tulips have bloomed and turned brown; the lilacs droop like bridesmaids who are wrinkled and drunk before the bride walks down the aisle. She ought to be alarmed. But since Sam died, she hasn't been able to muster much concern about global warming. A futurist who doesn't care about global warming! Ordinary people might be excused for their inability to comprehend the devastation that four—let alone six—degrees of elevated temperature will wreak on the planet. But a scientist ought to be doing everything in her power to raise the alarm. Is she truly that selfish? Apparently, she is. She is too dispirited to keep up with the new technologies. The future has left her behind, and she can't summon the energy or concern to follow it.

Panting now, sweating, she considers removing her jacket, but her backpack would make the required contortions too daunting. She passes a fraternity house, the muddy front yard bloody with red plastic Solo cups that will survive by centuries the students who chugged their contents. The institute she directs is housed in the basement of what used to be the business school until a billionaire alum donated the money to erect the concrete-and-steel monstrosity her husband dubbed the Death Star. This allowed the Institute for Future Studies to occupy the moldy subterranean floor of a building so outmoded that anyone who plugs in a laptop and a coffeepot at the same time risks plunging everyone into the Dark Ages. At the start, the provost provided the IFS with ten years of funding. But that decade soon is up, and if the institute doesn't develop additional sources of revenue, it will be forced to shut down. The obvious place to turn is the Department of Defense. But the faculty would be required to devote their energies to inventing shinier, more lethal weapons, or predicting the next outbreak of geopolitical chaos. They could rake in millions by hiring out their economists to predict whether consumers who live hundreds of years will be likelier to buy adult diapers or memberships at golf clubs in the Bahamas. But if they allow themselves to be seduced by consulting fees, won't the payments influence their predictions? As she pushes open the frosted glass door stenciled with the university's maize-and-blue logo, she feels inclined to accept the most obvious prediction concerning the program she founded and directs: namely, that it is doomed.

Then she sees her friend and chief administrative officer, Rosa Romanczuk, who, at sixty-three, might never find another position at the university, certainly not at a level that will allow her to continue paying her sons' tuition at MSU, and Maxine knows she needs to continue struggling. Rosa is as curious about the future as Maxine. But Rosa believes less in the powers of the medical establishment to extend human life than in the certainties of reincarnation. Maxine would never have hired Rosa if she had known. People have a low enough opinion of her institute without discovering that its chief administrator believes in casting horoscopes.

And, until she met Rosa, Maxine pitied anyone who believed the position of the stars could affect our lives. By what mechanism might such an influence be conveyed? How could the soul survive the body? In what vessel might it hover until it found another being to inhabit? What Maxine never realized was that people like Rosa pitied people like her for being narrow-minded. Scientists thought only the weakest, most ignorant minds fell prey to the supernatural. But in knowing Rosa, Maxine has come to see that only the most deluded believe in pure reality. Our senses can detect the merest shadow of what is out there. When electromagnetic waves were the latest theory, none other than Pierre Curie pronounced this method of transmitting energy the means by which we might communicate with the dead. He turned out to be wrong. But Maxine continues to be amazed that electromagnetic waves exist. Or that beings on other planets might use these invisible waves to signal they are out there. Entire new worlds might lie curled up within dimensions beyond the four we humans are able to experience. We are like cartoon creatures who, when a hand reaches down to penetrate our flat-paper world, perceive five mysterious black holes through which we are unable to travel. We come up with equations that describe their impenetrability. Then we congratulate ourselves on knowing everything there is to know about the universe. Maxine might not believe in reincarnation. But her colleagues study the possibility of uploading a human mind into a computer and allowing that consciousness to survive its body's death. Isn't it a matter of time before we are able to transmit our thoughts from a chip in one person's brain to a chip in someone else's? To maneuver a car by thinking? How would such displays have been interpreted by our ancestors if not as telepathy and telekinesis?

Besides, Maxine can forgive anyone who has lost someone she loves for believing the loved one isn't gone. When she got the call Sam had fallen prey to the West Nile virus, Rosa helped arrange the funeral. When Sam's mother accused Maxine of not being a good enough wife to keep her husband home where he wouldn't have been susceptible to a rare tropical disease, all that prevented her from grabbing her mother-in-law by her withered throat was the look Rosa shot her across the room. *This woman has lost the same dear man you lost. This woman has lost her son.*

Rosa didn't try to convince Maxine time would heal her wounds. What she said was that at some point, the torture would become more bearable. When other well-meaning people said this, Maxine could disregard their platitudes. But here was a woman who had suffered the same agonies Maxine was suffering. The night after the funeral, while Rosa was putting away leftover platters of turkey and cheese, she told Maxine she had been married to a businessman who, while negotiating a deal in Los Angeles, had gone for an evening jog. Fevered and confused, he had been taken to an emergency room. Misdiagnosed as a homeless black drunk, he had been left raving in his bed until the bacterial meningitis was so severe he couldn't be saved.

Absurdly, Maxine asked Rosa how she could continue to believe in astrology if she hadn't been able to predict her husband's death.

"Oh, honey," Rosa said. "Death is too much of a mystery, even for me. There isn't just this one future, and I see it, and I tell you what's going to happen. Living that way would ruin your life. You would always be walking with your eyes around the next curve. All I can predict is the next transition. That's what you scientists are always studying, isn't it? One particle becomes two other particles, and those particles become two others. All this being and becoming." Rosa flapped her multiringed hands. "I knew some very big change was coming for my Celestine.

But I thought he was going to give up trying to revive black businesses in Detroit. I thought he was going to buy a chain of Burger Kings and ask me to move with him to the suburbs."

Rosa tore off a swatch of plastic wrap and used it to cover a tray of smoked salmon. "I can't say you will ever recover from this. But one day, you might not feel you are betraying Sam because you enjoy something he is never going to enjoy. You won't be kicking yourself for whatever mean thing you said to him. For not allowing him to make love to you that last morning you saw him alive, before he flew away on his travels. For not being there beside him as he lay dying, lonely and delirious. You will still be very sad. But you will understand how lucky you are compared to all the people who never were loved by a man the way you were loved by the man you loved."

Rosa, thank God, never offered to read Maxine's Tarot cards. But in the months that followed Sam's death, Maxine was tempted to ask. It was remarkable how quickly she became a convert to the supernatural. In the middle of the night, when she couldn't stand the loneliness a moment longer, she would get up from her bed and google Sam's profile, which was still on his department website. Then she googled the video of him speaking at a symposium on low-cost technologies to prevent premature infant deaths. Then the guestbook Sam's mother had set up through the funeral home. She listened to an interview Sam had given for a radio show in Minneapolis. The intelligent rasp of his voice (*a synthesis of innovative materials will allow the purification of water even in the harshest environment . . .*) allowed her to believe she might break in to the interview and ask her dead husband questions. After all, once someone achieved non-materiality, what prevented him from traveling around the ether, putting in appearances at will? When Maxine found an article about a project Sam had funded in Rwanda and read how the solar-powered lights allowed commerce to flourish even at night, lowering the rates of rape and theft, she enlarged the photo of the newly lit market, hoping to learn that Sam, instead of dying, had migrated to this new locale.

More recently, she had taken to googling Zach. She checked his friends' Facebook pages in case one of them tagged her son. She typed in every combination of phrases that might lead to Zach's mug shot. Or, God forbid, his obituary. She sent emails to the company where Zach worked before he quit. Because the messages didn't bounce back, she fooled herself into thinking they might have reached him.

Which is to say that even if Rosa Romanczuk purported to tell the future by studying the vertebrae of dead cats, Maxine would be grateful for her presence behind the front desk this morning. The institute's receptionist is on maternity leave, and Rosa is taking her place, talking on the phone while tick-tocking her elaborately scarved head to signal her impatience with whoever is on the line.

"Yes, yes, yes," Rosa says. "*The Washington Post* is a very important newspaper. Even here in the Midwest, we know that. Yes. I know what a deadline is. But Professor Mickelthwaite is speaking to a reporter from NPR, which isn't such small potatoes either. I promise, he will call you as soon as he hangs up from this other gentleman." She jots a number on her pad and circles it in pink ink, each circuit lessening the probability the number will be conveyed to Professor Mickelthwaite.

Rosa hangs up. "You are not offended?" she asks Maxine. "I could have waited until you got in, but the calls were piling up." She lets fall a rainbow of neon-colored Post-its, each embossed with its own pink-gelled number and a name.

"No, no," Maxine says. "I'm fine with Mick fielding the reporters." She hates talking to the press. And to deprive John Sebastian Mickelthwaite of the opportunity to respond to a journalist's request for an interview would be like dining on a bloody steak in front of an emaciated old lion.

As it happens, her colleague does wear his abundant white mane in the same leonine manner of such well-known hucksters as Buffalo Bill Cody, Mark Twain, and Colonel Sanders. Maxine has never seen him without a colorful cravat. Each spring, he trades his fedora for a woven panama. He drives a low-slung sports car he assembled from a kit. (The vanity plate reads THWAITE, so anyone behind him might think the owner is lisping a command to sit patiently while he proceeds down Main Street at whatever ceremonial pace he likes.) He earned his degree from Yale in an era when all you needed to gain admission was a name like John Sebastian Mickelthwaite. You could graduate with a degree in the Philosophy of Science without knowing much about either subject, qualify for a Rhodes by lettering in squash, then spend the rest of your life elocuting in plummy tones, as if your vocal cords had contracted a chill in the damp halls of Oxford and you never shook it off.

In his early years, Mickelthwaite had written a tome called *The Birth of the Modern World*, which every book club selected as that month's offering. Radio and television hosts invited the author to speak to the anxiety of an age in which the atomic miracle that powered America's cities might turn those same cities into ruins. Such celebrity earned Mickelthwaite the role of scientific advisor to a roster of presidents that included Richard Nixon, Gerald Ford, and the elder George Bush.

But times have changed. As deferential as the presidents of Harvard and MIT once were, only Michigan will employ him now. Even here, Mick has been consigned to teach an introductory course filled with freshmen more impressed by their professor's flowing white locks and ability to relate anecdotes about "Jack" and "Tricky Dick" (whom they grow less able to identify as the years go on) than any insights he might offer as to the epistemology of scientific knowledge. Beneath his bluster, Mick must know he has sunk below whatever regally appointed office he occupied as adviser to so many presidents. He leaves his door open so everyone can hear him talking about the million-dollar consulting fees he has been offered. The invitations to fly to Stockholm or Berlin. The solicitations of advice from monarchs whose kingdoms he can't reveal. But Rosa has told Maxine that whenever such conversations appear to be taking place, no buttons on the switchboard light up.

Rosa motions Maxine to wait. "With all the reporters, I forgot to tell you, your mother also called. She wanted me to remind you she has an appointment to get her hair washed and set tomorrow morning at ten, but you need to get her there by nine because the time zone in the basement is different. And you need to bring the tweezers with the fine point, not the blunt end. And the shade of mascara she keeps telling you to buy. And the tissues with the lotion already in them—the regular tissues make her nose rough and red." Rosa consults a second Post-it. "Oh, and she's gotten some very good news about the lawsuit. She can't find the letter, but she wants you to look for it when you come."

Maxine takes the Post-its, careful not to betray her impatience with her mother. Poor Rosa. Her father, a runner for the Polish mob in Detroit, disappeared when Rosa was five, after which her mother abandoned her to a cadre of undependable aunts before jumping down an elevator shaft. If Rosa hadn't developed such exquisite intuition as to which grown-ups she could trust, she wouldn't have survived her childhood. How can Maxine begrudge the need to tweeze a few stiff hairs from her mother's chin?

Besides, Maxine is terrified her mother will die. No one loved Maxine's father as much as Maxine and her mother loved him. No one loves Maxine's son with nearly the same intensity as Maxine's mother. What will she do when her mother succumbs to Parkinson's? To whom will she turn when another month passes with no word from Zach? For that matter, who will bother to comment that Maxine might find more success attracting a second husband if she put more effort into styling her hair, wore more figure-flattering dresses, and bought a brighter, more seductive shade of lipstick?

Strangely, her mother seems unaware she is dying. She can't get out of bed. She is in danger of choking on her own saliva. Yet she frets that she will outlive her money and be tossed out in the street. "Mom," Maxine assures her, "I would never allow that to happen. If worse comes to worst, you can come live with me." But how can anyone be so oblivious to her own demise?

Then again, hasn't Maxine fooled herself into believing scientists will soon confer on the human race—at least, those rich enough to afford it—the benefits of immortality?

"What ho, fair damsels!" Mick stands beside them, glowing with the satisfaction of a man whose ego, for once, has been sufficiently fed. "I might advise you two young ladies to exercise especial caution not to open any packages about whose provenance you are not absolutely sure."

The concern on his face is real. As long as a woman demonstrates the deference he considers his due, Mick will roar and bare his claws if anyone dares to harm her. Add to that his kindly heart, which had been pierced by a loss so sharp it would make even the most courageous beast roar in pain, and Maxine warms to her pretentious colleague. A decade ago, Mick, who already had lost his wife to cancer, lost their only child to delusions and paranoia. Despite the finest care, his daughter had left home and pinballed around the country until she was found battered to death in a Cleveland alley.

About a month after Sam's death, Mick had parked his sportscar in front of Maxine's house, then waited while she pulled a sweatshirt over her pajamas. "Come," he ordered. "I will brook no excuse." When she protested she couldn't leave Zach alone, he assured her a boy of sixteen would be only too glad to spend an hour in his house alone. Reluctantly, she accompanied him to his car. There, she discovered the human animal is incapable of despair while being driven in a convertible whose top-of-the-line stereo is blasting into the crisp October air the sublime and soaring chords of Ralph Vaughan Williams's *Lark Ascending*. They stopped at the cider mill in Dexter for hot, fresh donuts, which they ate beside the river, wasps zinging around their heads. When this reminded her of the time she and Sam and Zach had sat on this same log, nibbling donuts and sipping cider, her colleague allowed her to lean against his stiff Harris tweed jacket and have a good cry.

If that weren't enough, after Zach departed for MIT, Mick showed up wearing a multipocketed J. Peterman coat and leather gloves and set about raking the leaves Zach would have raked if he'd still been home. When the first snow fell and Maxine glumly went out to shovel the walk, she found Mick finishing a path to the garage. The thought crossed her mind that he was buying her affections. But Mick never cashed in on his favors. When he passed Maxine in the hall, he lifted one bushy eyebrow, as if to inquire whether her son had seen fit to provide evidence of his existence. When she shook her head no, Mick took her hand and gave it an optimistic squeeze.

Besides, she can easily summon compassion for a man who has sunk from attending a White House conference chaired by George Herbert Walker Bush to the monthly airing of grievances around a particleboard table in a mold-infested basement at a meeting convened by her.

. . . *Leads a Meeting*

When she enters the conference room, the thirteen men who comprise the faculty of the Institute for Future Studies seem to be playing musical chairs. Each chooses a seat as far from his enemies as possible. Which means they will be glowering at those same enemies across the table. The mood is even more embittered by their inability to comprehend why Maxine is directing the program when they are so much smarter.

If she were a man, they might pay her the compliment of scheming to overthrow her. As it is, they imagine her role to be secretarial and besiege her with requests for new computers or complaints about their offices being too hot or too cold. Or they treat her like their mother, rolling their eyes when she pleads with them not to overspend their travel limits or to please mop up the coffee grounds in the sink and the sauce spattered inside the microwave.

You might think a field as progressive as Future Studies wouldn't be retarded by the sexism of the past. But if any discipline attracts fewer female scholars, Maxine doesn't know what it is. Maybe women are too preoccupied helping their children master the new math or making sure their elderly parents don't go tumbling down the stairs to worry about robots taking over. If a man with flowing white hair and a paisley scarf claims to foresee the future, he is invited to pontificate on the news; a woman with the same credentials is accorded the respect of a palm reader at the country fair. Of the two female professors Maxine implored to join her institute, the first snapped: "Do you know how many years I've needed to be taken seriously? If I move to something called Future Studies, I'll get laughed off the invitation list for every physics conference in the world." The other woman's husband received an offer from a university in Colorado, and even though she preferred to remain in Michigan, she didn't want to split up her family.

As to professors of color, they served on so many committees to promote diversity they had little spare time in which to stray across the boundaries of their fields. The future in which most people eventually found themselves living would be determined largely by straight white men.

And yet, watching Alphred Kisbye battle Tobin Brazelton to snag the last chocolate-filled croissant as opposed to, say, the almond, Maxine feels overcome with tenderness. Who but these men—crumbs in their beards, dabs of butter on their lips—are willing to use their intellect not for private gain but to head off the catastrophes that might dim the prospects of generations they won't live to see? Maxine recalls the pride that buoyed her heart when she secured funding to pay their salaries. The *Times*, in its fall 2003 education supplement, had devoted seven full paragraphs to what the reporter called "Professor Maxine Sayers's important and far-seeing innovation." And yet, in the nine years since then, the future has become old hat. What grows stale sooner than the future? Even as a child, holding her father's hand as they skipped through the turnstile of the 1964 World's

Fair in Flushing, Maxine sensed that calling an exhibit "Tomor-rowland" was childish. Or maybe Tomorrowland remains as shiny and new as ever; the problem is she no longer has a father with whom to skip through the gate.

Tobin Brazelton tosses the day's newspaper on the table. Tobin is the institute's expert on Terror Management Theory, which postulates that every human institution—religion, sci-ence, art—was created to distract us from the reality that we each must die. "I see our favorite sociopathic Luddite is at it again," Tobin says. "Next time I submit an article to a journal, I'm going to threaten to blow up their offices if they don't accept it."

Everyone starts talking at once. If the revolution the Tech-nobomber is trying to incite doesn't begin immediately, will he attack Google first, or Facebook? Which computer sci-ence department will be his next target? Their own university already has suffered one such act of terrorism; shouldn't they be on high alert?

"Hey, Maxine," Tobin says, "don't you teach that novel the bomber quotes in his manifesto? The one by Conrad? Come to think of it, I've heard you espouse many of his same convic-tions."

She feels as exposed as if she had proceeded directly from her shower to this conference room without putting on the gray wool skirt and cream silk blouse she selected to lend herself an aura of authority. Again she is struck by the irrational dread she is somehow to blame for the bomber's tirade.

"I'll tell you what," says Alphred Kisbye, one of the three AI guys on their faculty. "The person I feel sorriest for today is that bastard Schlechter."

Despite herself, Maxine also feels pity for Arnold Schlechter, the bomber's third victim and a member of their own university's computer science faculty. But her compassion is balanced by how deeply she dislikes the man. The first year she and Sam lived in Ann Arbor, they couldn't attend a party without encountering Arnold Schlechter. And each time they met, Schlechter acted as if he and Maxine had never been introduced.

What diminishes her sympathy even more is that after Schlechter recovered from his injuries, he published a book about the pernicious effects of liberalism on academia, blaming the nation's ills on feminists, blacks, gays, journalists, working mothers, atheists, and vegetarians. Worse, when Maxine reached the part in Schlechter's book in which he quoted from the letter that had arrived in the same day's mail as the package that had blinded him, she was horrified to catch herself agreeing with the bomber. "You're not as smart as you think you are," the madman taunted. "If you were, you wouldn't have opened a package you weren't expecting from someone whose name you didn't know solely because that person seemed to work at an Ivy League university."

Incited by Schlechter's claim that in the technology-driven future, no one would be left behind because any reasonably intelligent, college-educated person would be able to master the new machines, the bomber scoffed: "What about people who aren't 'reasonably intelligent'? Or who can't afford to go to college? Have you ever stopped to think some people might not *want* to compete in a world in which computers have deprived everyone of his privacy and condemned most of us to sitting for hours hunched over a keyboard performing repetitive tasks, or carrying out simulations that masquerade as authentic human life?" What angered the bomber even more was Schlechter's belief that such a world had become inevitable. Really? A world in which no normal human wished to live had become *inevitable*?

If so, it was only because nerds like Arnold Schlechter caused it to seem inevitable. If all the people who didn't want to go along with the so-called "inevitable" computer revolution were to rise up and eliminate the computer scientists, there would be no "inevitable" revolution in computer science.

That was where Maxine got off the bus. Unless you were willing to execute everyone who had a technical degree, or, like the tyrant Pol Pot, everyone who wore glasses and could read, you couldn't put a halt to progress. You predicted what could be predicted. You prophesied. You warned. You made aware. You shielded the most vulnerable citizens from the harshest effects of the innovations that stood to benefit the majority. You made sure the human race didn't devolve into two species—the effete, atrophied Eloi, who knew how everything worked, and the sad, brutish Morlocks, who served the Eloi. You didn't allow society to be ruled by arrogant jerks like Arnold Schlechter. But you didn't send them packages that resulted in their losing an eye and three fingers of their right hand.

By now, everyone is arguing whether Schlechter should be pitied for the deluge of interviews he will need to endure that day, forcing him to relive the moment he pulled that tab and was blinded by a flash, his hand shredded by fragments of a lead pipe inserted in a hollowed-out ream of inkjet paper, or whether he should be disdained as a reactionary troglodyte who would capitalize on this platform to spout his elitist white male propaganda.

Maxine tries to bring the meeting to order. "Everyone! Please!" Each man in the room considers himself a feminist, yet none seems able to pay attention to the female voice. "Carleton," she says, "why don't you start us off with an update on your project?"

Carleton Marius, whose colleagues in English used to scorn him because his specialty is science fiction, now finds himself in demand as the only member of his department who can navigate the websites needed to post a syllabus, apply for a grant, or submit a letter of recommendation. His lectures on the mythos of *Star Wars* and Harry Potter are far more popular than his colleagues' seminars on the deconstruction of the Spenserian sonnet. A disheveled, Lear-like man, Marius is convinced he came up with the idea for the Institute for Future Studies, then graciously stepped aside so Maxine could run it.

"I am so very touched you are interested in being 'updated' on my 'project.'" He scratches the air with talons so filthy he might well have spent the previous night in a thunderstorm on the heath. "But if you had shown the slightest support a few months ago, the administration might have granted my request that classes be canceled so the students could attend my teach-in."

As director of an institute that brings in no revenue, whether from government grants, patents, or plastic surgery, Maxine wouldn't be able to persuade the administration to pay for another round of mold abatement, let alone a day off from classes so Carleton Marius might tutor the undergraduates on the need to turn off their cell phones, go somewhere out of range of government surveillance, and do something they wouldn't ordinarily do if they were being watched. She looks around the drab, windowless conference room, whose cracked, stained walls she and Rosa have tried to enliven by posting portraits of the most far-sighted scientific pioneers, including as many women, African Americans, immigrants, foreigners, gays, and Jews as they could think of, which has the effect of making Maxine feel she is hiding them from the Gestapo and will soon, when their funding runs out, be forced to turn them in.

"Carleton," she says, "I'm sorry we can't help you with your efforts to cancel classes. But you have the institute's full support to publicize your Awareness Day."

Knowing she has left Carleton despising her for her wishy-washiness, she steers the conversation toward the fund-raising event that Mick, with Rosa's assistance, has been planning for the past six months. What they need is something that will impress the country's most innovative thinkers and generous financiers into donating to their institution. Unfortunately, the best Mick and Rosa have come up with is a banquet at the natural history museum, with a showing of *From the Big Bang to Inflation* in the planetarium and a chance to be chased through the gloomy halls by a herd of Velociraptors created by the special-effects team from *Jurassic Park*.

"Are you shitting me?" Alphred asks. "Maybe if you reconstitute a few actual T. rexes, then throw in a Neanderthal, that might begin to impress those guys."

"You know what?" says Wally Klein, one of Alphred's compatriots in the AI racket. "Bring in Ray Kurzweil. Tell them if they donate a few million, when the Singularity comes, old Ray will beam them up into the Great Supercomputer in the sky and they'll live forever."

Maxine has to laugh. She came up with the idea of studying immortality long before Ray Kurzweil. But Kurzweil has done a far better job marketing the idea than she has. He even prophesied a date when the so-called Singularity will arrive: within the next fifty or sixty years, advances in genetics, medicine, nanotechnology, and computer science will synergistically accelerate such that human beings, in conjunction with machines, might achieve incalculably long lifetimes. When she first read

Kurzweil's work, Maxine nearly drove herself mad trying to figure out how she could stay alive until she reached the Singularity. How terrible to belong to the last generation of humans who would be denied the opportunity to live forever! But the more she read, the more she dismissed Kurzweil's predictions as optimistic. If the Singularity could be achieved, it wouldn't happen in her lifetime, or even Zach's. She is lucky she wasn't born in any of the millennia in which women died in childbirth or Zach would have perished from the diseases against which he had been vaccinated when he was born. Besides, with Sam dead and Zach missing, she isn't sure she wants to hang around for another year, let alone endure an eternity of grief and lassitude.

"Listen, Maxine." Alphred fingers his druidic beard. "You can try to impress the donors with your Jurassic petting zoo. But you know what will really get them wetting their pajamas? Let us set up a Turing Test. We'll put Wally in one booth, and me in another, and our prototype in a third. The money boys can pull out their checkbooks and pay to take the test." Alphred lowers his glasses. "You do know what a Turing Test is, don't you, Maxine?"

She resists splashing orange juice in his face. *Yes, Alphred. A Turing Test is when someone like me tries to tell the difference between a human-seeming computer and an inhuman prick like you.* Her friends in Women's Studies commiserate with her for needing to supervise a bunch of older white males like John Mickelthwaite and Carleton Marius. But the youngest members of the department are the ones who treat women, especially older women like her, with barely concealed contempt. Once, Alphred had been a timid freshman in a seminar Maxine taught called Nerds and Geeks: How Video Games Changed America. He stayed after class and confided the torment he had endured growing up as an overweight genius in a fundamentalist Scandinavian sect in western Michigan. Within months of taking her class, he had slimmed down, acquired a girlfriend, and founded the university's hacker collective, KRAKEN. In his senior year, he begged Maxine to supervise his honors thesis. Her letter of support helped him gain acceptance to Cal Tech, where he studied with the leading expert in Emergent Systems and Phenomena. Having recruited Alphred to return to his alma mater, Maxine overheard him dismiss her as "well-intentioned but a little soft in the head." Most of the young men Maxine mentored acted as if they were embarrassed to admit they had sprung from her professorial womb. Never mind that she had been punching cards on an IBM mainframe thirty years before any of the AI guys were born. She had been too busy teaching, serving on committees, and raising a son to keep up with the latest advances in computer vision and voice-recognition software. Never mind that she had created the perfect environment in which young male geniuses like Alphred and Wally could thrive. They treated her with the condescension they might employ while showing their grandmothers how to set up an account on Facebook.

Admittedly, she did need Alphred's help in setting up her blog, www.professorofimmortality.com. What had he called her—a "technopeasant"? Alphred predicted that, like most bloggers, Maxine would soon grow tired of writing entries. To spite him, she had struggled to come up with new material, meditating on the effects of immortality on human culture. But after a few months, she had given up. So what if maintaining a presence on social media might raise her institute's profile and attract more donors? Wasn't there already a whiff of something, well, *grandmotherly* about the very word "blog"?

The true heart of the AI guys' animosity derived from her unwillingness to believe a computer could be intelligent. The question seemed nonsensical. If intelligence meant an awareness of one's self, how could a machine become aware? Of what? That it had no self to be aware of? If a person couldn't tell she was conversing with a computer, what you had was a machine capable of fooling a human into thinking she was carrying on a conversation with another human. That didn't make the computer a human being, any more than a whistle that attracted a duck could be considered a duck. A computer might come up with a plan to replicate itself. But it would never be conscious of creating what it created. Only beings with bodies could experience the hunger, the pain, the yearning for a mate that ignited the desire to communicate with another being. And only with language could a creature become aware of its desire *as* desire, its self as a being separate from the other beings from whom it was begging food or protection for a child. Believing a bunch of digital switches might, by achieving a certain level of complexity, make a synergistic leap to consciousness struck Maxine as ridiculous. One day, everyone would look back on such a belief and laugh, as we now laughed at the idea that a mouse might spontaneously arise from a dusty rag or a rotted cheese.

Still, running a Turing Test for their donors is a brainstorm. Humbled, she begs Alphred to add his expertise to Rosa's and Mick's. Maybe the fundraiser will be a success after all. Or avoid looking like an abject failure.

That leaves only a request from Jackson Sparrow, the institute's resident poet, who asks that he be allowed to read a poem. Rakish enough in his youth that he earned the nickname "Pirate," Jackson is now more likely to bring to mind the nervous little bird the other reading of his name implies. He grew up in Detroit, then paid his way through Wayne State by working in an automobile factory; he hasn't performed manual labor since the 1960s, but the experience still serves as the subject for his poetry. Having read Alphred Kisbye's essay "Establishing Guidelines for the Post-Human Era," Jackson had come up to Maxine and demanded a literal place at the literal table where such guidelines were being made. How could anyone so casually accept that the future would be "post-human"? What did "post-human" even mean? If there is anything about the future Jackson Sparrow doesn't oppose, Maxine doesn't know what it is. He refuses to buy a cell phone. He types his poems on a manual Royal typewriter, then publishes them on a hand-cranked press he and his late wife purchased at a junk shop. Even though he doesn't hesitate to fly to Paris or Beijing to accept prizes for his poems, he makes a point of walking or biking elsewhere.

That said, Jackson is a gentle, thoughtful widower who, a few months earlier, invited Maxine to see the printing press in the basement of his house, which is down the street from hers. There, as she cranked the crank and printed a broadside of one of Keats's poems, Jackson leaned in and kissed her. The kiss hadn't been unromantic. But his skin felt dusty and dry, his chest so frail she was afraid he would crumble like a mummy.

"I'm sorry," she said, "I can't." Then she climbed the stairs and ran out with her copy of "Ode on a Grecian Urn" still drying in her hand.

Now, at the meeting, Jackson asks permission to read a poem he composed that morning by stitching together outtakes from the bomber's manifesto. Before anyone can object, he unfolds a sheet of yellow legal paper from the pocket of his denim shirt. "The Madman Is Sometimes Not Mad," the poet intones. Five minutes later, he reaches the concluding stanza:

"Pain is no longer pain. Pain is the failure of pharmaceuticals. Work is no longer suffering. Work is no longer work." Everyone starts to argue. Even if Jackson agrees with the bomber's cracked ideology, does he truly believe those ends justify the blood-soaked means? Maxine doesn't join the discussion. She needs to prepare to teach her next class. Will these men never stop their speechifying? She suddenly feels so desperate to get to her office and read the manifesto she can't breathe. Why does she think it is up to her to protect the bomber's next victim? Worse, why does she believe the victim might be someone she knows and loves? Or maybe the bomber is the one she knows?

The fluorescent lights flicker as if an inmate at the other end of the basement is being electrocuted.

No, it's only Rosa snapping the light switch on and off. "Mick, you have five minutes before Bill Moyers is calling you for an interview."

Mick leaps from his chair. "Rosa, my dear, whatever would I do without you!" For a moment, Maxine thinks he might kiss Rosa on the mouth.

Everyone except Jackson files out. This is the first time he and Maxine have been alone since their encounter in his basement.

"Any chance I can persuade you to join me for lunch?" Jackson asks. "That last time . . . I apologize if I moved too quickly."

Too quickly? As lonely as she is, she would tear off Jackson's clothes right here if only . . . If only what? If he didn't insist on writing his poetry with a fountain pen? If he weren't limping toward seventy and likely to die before she did?.

"I'm sorry," she says. "I can't. I'm teaching a class at one." Although what she really can't do is survive another husband's death.

. . . Reads a Manifesto

H er office is as drab and poorly lit as the conference room. The plaster and paint buckle and crack to reveal the moisture and mold beneath. The only furnishings consist of two gray metal chairs, a metal desk, and metal bookshelves crammed with books. The chemical tang from the industrial, metal-gray carpet no doubt adds carcinogens to the air. If only the sun in the poster on the wall were real. Or the bright blue photograph of planet Earth where a window would have been if her office had windows. Or the image of the Milky Way, viewed head on, like a pinwheel. When she is feeling overwhelmed by bureaucratic details, these posters provide perspective. Even if she spends her remaining years sitting in this dreary underground warren, responding to memos, applying for grants, editing jargon-ridden reports on tenure and promotion, she is helping her fellow humans see beyond the next meal they cook, the next diaper they change, the next meeting or corporate retreat they survive, into the next millennium.

Her first priority should be to read her email. But logging in is as appealing as opening a can of bees. She hasn't checked since the day before. Swatting away the sixty or seventy bellicose insects that come swarming out would take hours, if not the entire day. Her students message her with requests no student in Maxine's day would have considered making. "Hey!" they start. Or: "Dear Miss Sayers, " as if she is their second-grade teacher (Sam's students addressed him as "Professor," or "Doctor," unless they called him "Sam"). They send her messages at three a.m., demanding extensions on papers due that day. They email to ask what font they should use to print those papers. She even receives messages from her students' parents, complaining about their children's grades.

So why not stop using email? Because typing a few lines and hitting "send" requires less effort than finding an envelope, buying a stamp, filling out an address, walking to the corner mailbox, then waiting days, if not weeks, for a reply. Because email allows her to send a message to the dean without the anxiety of a face-to-face appointment. Human beings aren't stupid enough to mindlessly accept innovations that destroy their humanity.

Well, maybe they are. But she can resist answering her email for just one morning. She pulls the newspaper from her pack. Already the pages have the brittle, faded feel of a historical document.

As Tobin hinted, the bomber has prefaced his screed with an epigraph from a novel Maxine has taught for years, *The Secret Agent* by Joseph Conrad. "The sacrosanct fetish of today is science," the quotation reads. Conrad was ahead of his time in predicting society's dependence on—and revulsion toward—mechanization and surveillance. Yet she sympathizes with her students, who complain that the novel's characters creep them out. There is corpulent Mr. Verloc, the owner of a Victorian porn shop, who pretends to be a revolutionary while snitching on his comrades to the London police; the Professor, who stalks the streets with a chemical apparatus snaked up his sleeve such that, if anyone attempts his capture, he can blow them all up; and various officers of the law who try to keep the anarchists in line, unless they are manipulating those same anarchists for their own ends. But the novel remains on Maxine's reading list because its author envisioned a time when people might rebel against the very progress that was bringing them prosperity and longer lives.

That a terrorist has the same taste in literature as she does makes Maxine so queasy she can barely move on to the first paragraph of the manifesto:

> The Industrial Revolution and its consequences have been a disaster for the human race. They have greatly increased the life expectancy of those who live in "advanced" countries, but they have made those same lives unfulfilling and inflicted severe damage on the natural world.

She finds little to object to in that paragraph. Or in the pages that follow. How can she disagree that industrialization has cut us off from nature, fettered us with far too many forms to fill out, appointments to keep, an addiction to the new technologies? Governments monitor our every move. The medical-entertainment complex has convinced us that if only we consume the right medicines, eat the right foods, and undergo the prescribed medical procedures we might retain our beauty and fitness ad infinitum. To reap such benefits, all we need do is conform to the system. From a young age, children are "buttonholed" into slots ("buttonholed" being the terrorist's word), forced to spend hours studying for exams, only to be labeled hyperactive if they can't conform to such inhuman demands, drugged, pressured to follow ever-lengthier regimes of training to equip them for employment. If any adult becomes too anxious or depressed to keep up, they need to be medicated and/or confined.

The Technobomber scoffs at the fear that machines might take us over by force. Rather, human beings will become ever more dependent on complex digital systems as fewer and fewer technocrats understand how such programs work. Unlike primitive man, who was able to see and fight his predators, modern man lives with a floating dread he might be exterminated by an atomic blast, the malfunction of a worldwide computer system, or decisions made by businessmen and politicians whose judgment has been corrupted by greed and self-interest.

Humankind, the bomber writes, "finds itself at the crossings road." A core of dedicated revolutionaries needs to lead their fellow citizens in destroying their computers, disabling nuclear and coal-fired power plants, dismantling the industrial farms that supply our obesity-inducing food, blowing up the nerve centers of government surveillance and high-tech laboratories. The bomber calls on everyone to tear themselves away from pornography and violent video games (this from a man who mailed bombs to sixteen victims!) and force themselves to go outdoors. Everyone needs to throw away the drugs that mask an unhappiness generated by a society whose insanities no longer will be tolerated. With each of us engaged in the very real goals of growing our own food, hunting, educating our children, and creating shelter for our families, we won't need artificial ways to consume our time or create false meaning in our lives.

Such a revolution will, "in one felt swoop," return humankind to its natural state. Better to die now than live under the government's watchful eye, hemmed in by rules, cut off from the essence of our humanity. The gains of a revolution will far outweigh the dangers. "Mankind cannot be eating his cake and having it, too," the bomber writes. This is why, if he doesn't see signs his demands are being met, he will continue to mail his packages.

Something about the writer's voice causes the hairs on the back of Maxine's neck to stand up. "Buttonholed," he has written. "In one felt swoop." "Eating his cake and having it, too." Hasn't she circled these same misused phrases on her students' essays? Unless she is only imagining she knows the author. In her many decades teaching, she has come upon dozens of such warped locutions. *For all intense and porpoises. Toad the line. I am appealing to common cents. The reader should bare her mind.* The ideas the writer of the manifesto discusses are obvious. Stop anyone in Ann Arbor and you might hear these same complaints. For that matter, you could have heard them when Maxine and her husband and son sat arguing over breakfast.

Rosa sticks her head in the door. Maxine isn't sure why but she feels the urge to hide the manifesto.

"So, how did that pizza date go last night?" Rosa asks.

Maxine sighs. "You should have seen the skid marks."

Rosa snaps her heavily ringed, green-nailed fingers. "You think men don't want to go out with a woman scientist. But I know a poet who is very sweet on you."

Maxine hasn't told Rosa about the kiss in Jackson's basement—Rosa would scold her for spurning his advances. "Did you come in to give me a hard time about my love life? If you did, we're going to have a very short conversation."

"No," Rosa says. "I came to find out what am I supposed to do when I am projecting our expenses beyond the point at which we have money to pay them."

"I have that meeting first thing tomorrow with the new

provost," she reminds Rosa. "I'll ask her to tide us over until after the fundraiser."

Rosa curls her lips to indicate they both know the provost was hired with the sole purpose of whipping the university into better financial shape by making it run like a corporation. The accounting metrics Rosa has been required to learn almost drove her from the job. "While you are down on your knees, perhaps you could beg Provost Bell to pay for the Velociraptors and, what is it called, this Turing Test?"

"Here's what you do," she tells Rosa. "Drain everything from the director's emergency fund."

"The whole account? What if we have an emergency?"

Just as Maxine's mother can't comprehend she is really dying, Rosa seems not to understand that unless this long shot pays off, they won't need to worry about emergencies.

Rosa points to the manifesto. "Is that going to be as much trouble as I think?"

Again, Maxine feels accused. "The commotion should die down soon," she tells Rosa. "Just let Mick handle the reporters."

Rosa hands Maxine a leftover sesame bagel slathered with the honey-walnut cream cheese Maxine loves. "Just be careful," Rosa says. "It is easier than you think to be swept up in a revolution."

For a moment, Maxine can't figure out what revolution Rosa means. Then she remembers Rosa was caught up with SDS in the 1960s, or maybe it was the Panthers. "I am not starting a revolution," Maxine promises. "Or even joining one."

Rosa waggles her head, as if Maxine might yet find herself at the barricades, breast bared, holding a tyrant's bloody head.

Maxine thanks Rosa for the bagel—she won't have time

for lunch. But Rosa hovers as if she, too, expects the manifesto might blow up in Maxine's hands. When Maxine asks her to shut the door on her way out, Rosa fixes her with a glare so stern Maxine wonders what Rosa suspects she intends to do in the privacy of her office.

Never mind. She picks up the manifesto and finds where she left off. "Within a few decades," the bomber writes, "with the increased use of robots, 3-D printers, manufactured housing, and an abundance of super-calorific foods, most people will be freed from want." This might be fun, for a while, he says. But pleasure will give way to boredom. Whereas early humans needed to expend their energy to assure survival, those who live in the future will occupy their time with hobbies, video games, ultrareal pornography, a feigned interest in "literature" or "art," and the frenzied acquisition of whatever possessions the advertising-entertainment complex convinces them to acquire. Already we need to invent reasons to move our bodies, "running" and "cycling" on tracks that accomplish nothing and get us nowhere.

The artificial nature of most jobs can be demonstrated by the fact that few people would work if guaranteed the necessities. How many of us are born with a desire to study calculus? Scientists don't pursue their experiments for the good of humankind. If they did, they wouldn't devote their lives to perfecting weapons, or products whose manufacture spews carcinogens in the air, or pharmaceuticals that have more side effects than benefits.

Nor can technological advances, once unleashed, be dismantled. Take the transportation system. In the old days, if a man wanted to get from here to there, he walked. The method was slow. But he didn't need to work long hours at a job he loathed to buy a car. Everyone has been brainwashed into believing capitalism is a superior way of life. ("Holy robots! The world might fly off its orbit if the Japanese sell more cars than we do!") Most scientists are egomaniacs, the bomber charges. They believe they can solve whatever problems their inventions create, even as they keep creating newer and deadlier problems.

Maxine can't help but feel accused. Plenty of scientists are egomaniacs. But not everyone needs to be coerced into studying physics or math, the way the bomber apparently was forced to do. Would Sam have sacrificed his life to conquer malaria if his altruism weren't real? The world the bomber is trying to reconstruct sounds like one of those reality shows in which the contestants are left to survive a winter in Plimoth Village. Wouldn't it be better to figure out how to use all that free time productively rather than force everyone to return to a miserably short existence in which they need to gather wood, draw water, hoe weeds, and fight off predators?

She isn't surprised to find herself arguing with the manifesto. That's how academics spend their days. But she has the feeling she inscribed these same arguments in the margins of some student's paper. She remembers shaking her head at the corniness of "Holy robots!" Unless that's an expression every hacker uses? In her old office at the Residential College—an office she rarely visits—she has a stack of essays her students never bothered picking up. Maybe those essays can jog her memory. But she needs to teach her class, after which she needs to rush home, get her car, and drive to the nursing home to feed her mother.

Then again, if the bomber is threatening to send another bomb, isn't it her duty to find the time?

The landline rings. Why does she think it's the bomber calling?

"Hello?" Maxine hears labored breathing. "Mom? Is that you?"

"Something terrible," her mother croaks, "has happened."

Even before the Parkinson's slowed her voice, her mother spoke with the put-upon whine of a woman who believes she has been singled out for more than her fair share of punishment. The tone bothers Maxine, especially when she hears it creeping into her own voice when she complains to Rosa.

"It's okay, Mom. I'll be there for dinner. Nothing terrible is going to happen between now and five o'clock."

"The letter!" her mother says. "I put it in my drawer. And it isn't there!"

For decades, her mother has been carrying on a lawsuit against Maxine's father's former business associates. Not that her mother doesn't have grounds to sue. Maxine's father built his business from nothing, then died just as the rewards were coming in. His own father had peddled trinkets to the tourists at Saratoga Springs, so disheveled and inept that Maxine's father had sneaked away and joined the army to escape the humiliation of being his son. Trained as a radar specialist, her father had returned from the war to discover his father trying to interest the housewives of upstate New York in frozen vegetables to stock the freezers just coming into vogue. After a few days helping schlep soggy bags of melting green beans door to door, her father decided the real money lay in selling the freezers and leaving the vegetables to A&P. He found a vacant store in a town north of Saratoga and used his GI loan to stock it with the latest refrigerators, washing machines, radios, toasters, and television sets. When these appliances began to break down, he added a repair shop. As his customers complained of the lousy reception they were getting on their new Motorolas, GEs, and RCAs, he borrowed several thousand dollars from a war buddy named Spider Macalvoy, whom he had hired to work in the appliance store and charm his customers, along with Drs. Simon and Vincent across the street. He used the borrowed funds to build towers on the mountains around town. Then he strung cables to his customers' houses, charging them a monthly fee for the three major channels, plus a few they hadn't been able to pick up before.

At the time, Maxine had been too young to appreciate her father's entrepreneurial genius. Inventing cable television made less of an impression than her father's talent in repairing any machine a customer brought in to have fixed. She had been twelve when he died. How could she have known to caution her mother, addled by grief and her fear of poverty, that she shouldn't accept the offer from her late husband's partners to buy out his share for fifty-thousand dollars, an offer that seemed generous unless you knew that Leonard Sayers had been in the midst of negotiations to sell his cable television company to a conglomerate that eventually became Time Warner.

By the time her mother figured out that her late husband's so-called friends had swindled her, they had taken their millions and retired to Florida and Arizona. Enraged, Maxine's mother harassed her husband's cousin Joel, a bespectacled lawyer who worked for the Department of Taxation in Albany, into suing. Over the years, Cousin Joel had become even more obsessed with obtaining a settlement than Maxine's mother. Of the three original defendants, Dr. Simon and Dr. Vincent had passed away. Maxine is sure her father's war buddy, Spider Macalvoy, is only waiting for her mother—and Cousin Joel—to kick off so he can enjoy his ill-gotten gains in peace.

"I'll be there at five," Maxine says. "I'll look for the letter then."

Her mother sighs the sigh Maxine has been hearing all her life. "Remember to bring those tweezers. The ones with the pointed tips. And the *tissues*. The ones with the lotion in them." She coughs so violently Maxine is afraid her mother will choke to death while she sits there listening. "My hair appointment is ten tomorrow morning. But the time zone in the basement is an hour earlier. If you're not here by eight forty-five, don't bother coming."

That a woman as rational as her mother can think time varies according to which floor of a building you are on proves no mind is independent of the body it inhabits. If her mother is so wacked out because the dopamine in her brain is a little off, imagine how much more wacked out she would be if the AI guys uploaded her consciousness into a computer. "Don't worry," Maxine says. "I'll get there in time. I promise."

"Never mind that!" her mother says. "I keep forgetting. It's about *Zach*."

"What about him?" Given how unlikely it is that her mother knows Zach's whereabouts, Maxine's terror makes little sense.

"I saw him. On the news."

"What are you talking about?"

"Stop yelling! I didn't see Zach. I saw the *other* one. The one he used to play with. The one who blows people up."

Maxine should be relieved. Her mother must have seen a report on TV and conflated the terrorist in the news with Zach's childhood friend, Norm Fishburn, who often got Zach in trouble. "I'll see you at five," she says, then hangs up before her mother can reveal anything that makes her think the comment about Zach being friends with the bomber is any more than a hallucination.

. . . *Teaches a Class*

Maybe because she is nagged by the suspicion a former student wrote the manifesto she just read, Maxine enters her Intro to Future Studies class thinking it isn't always easy to tell which of her students merely are experiencing the turmoil of adolescence and which are so troubled they might do harm to themselves or others. For that matter, it isn't always easy to guess much about her students just by looking.

Take Yvonne Switalski. Face willfully blank, body swelling from a dress she might have sewn in the 4-H Club in her tiny town in Michigan's so-called Thumb (Maxine's colleagues make fun of the kids who hold up their palms to demonstrate where in the state they come from, but Maxine loves when her students do this), Yvonne speaks only when called on. But if Maxine does require Yvonne's opinion, Yvonne mumbles the answer Maxine has been holding in reserve so she can startle the class with her own superior professorial insight.

Or Patti Querk. Chinless, pale, she is treated as invisible by the sorority girls who come to class in tight black pants and slouchy sheepskin boots so hideous only women as confident as these could carry them off. And yet, the papers Patti hands in are so imaginative Maxine urged her to apply to graduate school, a suggestion Patti met with a suspicious glare, that's how rarely anyone had praised her.

Then there's Obayo Stevens, who huddles in the back of the room, Tigers cap pulled so low Maxine wouldn't recognize him outside class except by his whispery mustache and the giant cross that depends from his stovepipe neck. Everyone assumes Obayo must be at Michigan to play football. But he is pursuing an engineering degree. The papers he turns in leave something to be desired in terms of spelling (he writes "aks" instead of "ask"). But their content shows an intimidating boldness of mind, as well as a *Wikipedia* breadth of knowledge, material he must have picked up on his own, given that the library at the high school he attended in Detroit is bare of books.

Maxine's specialty is encouraging students like Patti and Obayo. But she is equally proud of the way she handles disgruntled white male geniuses like Russell Charnow. At the beginning of term, Russell took a seat in the first row, grimacing and groaning at whatever Maxine said. And yet, she welcomes young men like Russell. A few weeks into term, she invites them to visit during office hours. In they shuffle, expecting her to harangue them, the way their mothers always do. *Sit up straight. Stop playing those awful video games and go outside. Ask that nice Miller girl to the prom.* She doesn't criticize their behavior. Instead, she tells them she is sorry they are bored in her class. *Is there anything I can do to make the semester more challenging? Come talk to me anytime. I'm interested in what you're thinking.* Dazed by all this good will, the young men become her fiercest defenders. At the very least, they stop confronting her with so much belligerence.

"Miz Sayers?"

The hand in the third row, if she follows the length of the

arm to which it is attached, belongs to Luther van Dyke, whose father is a state rep from a conservative district to the west. Luther wears a large rubber ring inside each earlobe. One lanky arm is tattooed with a raven; along the other arm runs FOREV-ERMORE. Maxine has given up trying to deduce what political statement the rubber rings and tattoos convey. Or what arguments must transpire between father and son over Thanksgiving dinner.

"Miz Sayers? You know that manifesto thing in today's newspaper? My dad asked me to ask you, are you on the same side as that nut job?" Luther blushes. "Those are my father's words, not mine. He called and told me I had to ask."

"I'm glad you brought that up." Even though she isn't. "The problems the Technobomber describes do need discussing. But you can assure your father I would never allow anyone to distort what I teach into an ideology that advocates violence."

Luther lets down his tattooed arm. Few other students seem to have read the manifesto. But Luther's question awakens whatever objections have been slumbering in his classmates' consciousness all term. Or they sense an opportunity to stall the group reports they are due to present that day.

"I'm premed," announces pouty Narissa Hymes. "And my anatomy professor told me it's ridiculous to think anyone will live forever."

The trick is never to let your students sense your fear. "Your professor is probably right," Maxine says. "But the human lifetime is going to be significantly extended." Here, she cites the research of a biologist who proved that altering a single gene in a roundworm's chromosomes will double its lifespan. And the findings of her institute's own Gavin Reinhardt, who works on preventing the telomeres at the ends of chromosomes from unraveling. (With his hollowed cheeks and sunken eyes, Gavin could pose for the prophet Ezekiel crossing the Valley of Dry Bones, shouting about the evils of fat and calories and promising a deathless life to anyone who follows the dietary commandments his god laid down. The one time Gavin and Maxine went out for dinner, he consumed nothing but a few celery sticks and pomegranate tea. He confided he was into Tantric sex. But who wanted to spend thousands of years being brought nearly to orgasm but never climaxing?)

Maybe scientists will never be able to replace every organ with its lab-grown equivalent, Maxine tells her class. But biophysicists will add decades to our lives by perfecting artificial livers, lungs, kidneys, hearts, eyes, and exoskeletons. Even if we only end up living an extra two or three hundred years, we will need to radically rethink our culture. "Besides," she says, "contemplating our responses to immortality is a good philosophical exercise."

"For what?" Narissa asks.

"For examining why we value what we value. Thinking about what life is for." Maxine laughs one of those professorial laughs she hopes won't sound stagy. "I want you to think critically about all these new technologies and not accept them blindly."

"Don't worry," someone says. "Whatever it is, I'm already sick of it."

"Oh my God," another student moans. "If I can't find my phone for, like, five seconds, I feel like I'm going to die. And all these stupid games! Yesterday I missed my psych lab because I couldn't stop popping bubbles so Snoopy could rescue Woodstock."

"Yeah. Can somebody please decree that Facebook is

already dead? We all know it's going to be over eventually. Can't someone just end the pain?"

Another student snaps his fingers—apparently, this is a new method of signaling agreement. "No matter whether you wear it on your glasses, or implant it in your eyeball, whatever new thing Google comes up with is just going to turn you into a jerk. And that telepathy thing we were talking about the other day? Why would anyone want texts coming at them *inside their brains?*"

Maxine feels her faith in the human race affirmed. Young people might be ignorant. Moody. Self-centered. Prone to drinking and getting high. But they aren't as easily duped as the Technobomber seems to believe.

"Okay," she says. "Enough time-wasting. First group up: Marcos, Amina, Seth."

To lead the discussion about the effects of immortality on religion, Maxine has selected a Catholic, a Muslim, and a Jew. Or maybe she has crafted the setup for a joke. The three students shamble to the front of the room. Then sloe-eyed Marcos Costello puts forth the theory that if the human race does achieve immortality, any religion that depends on heaven or resurrection will be in trouble.

Luther raises his hand. "So you're saying, like, Christianity might be obsolete?"

She reminds herself she has tenure and can't be dismissed even if the students complain their professor taught them that Christianity is on its way out.

"I don't know about the whole religion," Marcos says. "But yeah, the part about making you be afraid you might burn in hell, that part won't work."

"But Judaism was never that big on hell in the first place,"

Seth chimes in. "What I like most is where you say a prayer to appreciate the small, good things in life. Like eating bread. Or drinking wine." He imitates chugging a glass; his classmates titter appreciatively. "Or, you know, seeing a rainbow."

"Except, dude," Marcos says, "would you really keep appreciating all those rainbows if you had been seeing them for a million years?"

Amina elbows her way between Marcos and Seth. "I think Buddhism might still be useful. No one would care about getting reincarnated. But everyone would still need to learn to live with suffering and desire. Because even if you have all the food you can eat, and a nice house, you'll still suffer about *something*."

Maxine thanks the religion group. Then she summons the students assigned to the effects of immortality on art. With his chiseled cheekbones and black hair drawn up in a contemporary version of a Samurai topknot, Hideyo Suzuki looks the part of the Hollywood filmmaker he hopes to be. Hideyo kicks off his group's presentation with a quote from Woody Allen to the effect that he doesn't want to achieve immortality through his work, he wants to achieve it through not dying. Maxine guesses few students know who Woody Allen is, other than some creepy old man who married his girlfriend's adopted daughter.

"What the Woodman is saying," Hideyo explains, "is if people make art only to be remembered, and you can be remembered by not dying, will anyone bother to keep making art?"

"Sure they will," says another member of Hideyo's group. "With so much time on everyone's hands, the demand for art is going to explode through the roof."

"Nah," says a kid at the back of the room. "People are just going to keep putting everything off. Worse. Because in the future, they'll have forever."

"Yeah," says another boy. "I took philosophy freshman year. I was blown away by the stuff we read. But do I want to sit around reading philosophy books? I could be seven hundred years old, and I'll still be looking at those philosophy books and thinking, 'Someday I'll get around to rereading that shit.'"

This provides a natural segue to the group assigned to discuss the effects of immortality on education. If people live hundreds of years, will they go to school only for the first two decades? Will they work only one job their entire life? Will there be any work left for them to do?

Which leads to the marriage group debating how long people will screw around before they settle down. If science can rejuvenate any organ, might a woman give birth at any age? And if you do stay married to one person for hundreds of years, imagine how devastated you will be if they get run over by a car. Or if your kid dies young and you and your spouse spend centuries mourning him or her.

But wait. Will people even be having kids? If so few people die, will the planet have room for more? And if people have kids when they're young, and then they have grandkids, and great-grandkids, and great-great-great-grandkids, will the old people remember their grandkids' birthdays? Will any of the grandkids feel special, the way grandkids feel today?

Maxine checks the clock. As long as she stands here listening to these young people contemplate a world in which no one dies, she can postpone visiting the nursing home where she will need to spoon soup into the mouth of her own bitter, dying mother. Wearily, she summons Yvonne Switalski and Patti Querk, along with Tommy Bruce, a baseball player who otherwise might never spend a minute contemplating the status of women's rights in the coming centuries, or even this one.

"So," Tommy says. "Our group was assigned women. And how it might affect, you know, sexism. We—I mean, Yvonne here, and, um, um, *Patti*—we were talking about this last night, when we met at Starbucks. Whether women could keep having babies even when they get really, really old. But that already got talked about by the other group, so I don't know what else to say."

Patti steps forward and in a voice double her normal volume says, "What Yvonne and I came up with is women might have time to raise their kids, then get back in the workforce and spend hundreds of years catching up, so they might reach a point where they aren't being penalized for getting pregnant. Maybe women will finally end up earning as much as men who do the same job."

"Except, if the guys start out earning more," Yvonne says, "maybe the gap will grow even bigger?"

"Are you kidding me?" groans Gothed-out Margo Korck. "In whatever century we're talking about, women are still going to be getting paid less than men?"

"You know what else?" says Narissa Hymes. "Women are going to need to spend that many more centuries staying in shape and not letting their faces and tits go saggy."

The last panel of the day, on racism, takes the same direction. While Mindy Gasparian puts forth the idea that increased longevity might allow black people to overcome the effects of poverty and inferior schools, Obayo Stevens, from beneath the rim of his cap, blows a noise that signals his disagreement. "White people live hundreds of years, just going to give them more time to get farther ahead. They'll leave the rest of us in the dust. When they do die, they'll leave all that much more money to their kids."

"So things are going to get *worse*?" Mindy asks. "I thought if no one died we'd end up living in, what did you call it, Mrs. Sayers, a utopia?"

"I think about dying *all the time*," Patti blurts. "I am so scared of dying I can't breathe. But dying makes me think everything I do with my life is important. Would I care so much if I knew I had forever to make something of myself?"

"Yeah," says Tommy Bruce. "My mom died when I was, like, seven? And I don't ever want to make my kids feel as sad as I felt then. Or as sad as I still feel, whenever I think about my mom." He puts his wrist to his eye, but he can't keep from crying.

Class ends. Not a student moves. Patti lays a palm on Tommy's shoulder and whispers something in his ear. He nods. Yes, thank you, he's okay.

The spell breaks. They all pull out their phones (Hideyo's is shaped like a cartoon cat). Maxine can't blame them for not wanting to be alone with their thoughts. Given the choice, wouldn't she pull out her own phone and talk to her husband, or her son?

Only Russell Charnow lingers. Russell's group presented its findings last week, although Russell disdained adding his comments to his groupmates'. Maybe he wants to share those insights now?

"Russell?" she says. "Is there something I can do for you?"

"No," he says flatly. "Teachers like you, you always think there's something you can do. And there sure as shit is not."

He turns and hurries out. On another day, Maxine might have hurried after him, or she might have called the campus police, or the dean of students, or a psychologist at the counseling service. But with everything weighing her down, she can't find the energy. Besides, didn't Russell just say there's nothing she can do to help? She has been fooling herself to think she has made any difference in the lives of the angry young white men she has mentored. Maybe she saved a few. Most likely, she failed them all.

. . . Foils a Break-In

Walking home, she manages to shake off her apprehension. It's only mid-April, but she doesn't need to put on her jacket. Sometimes she thinks Midwesterners are secretly in favor of global warming. Winters will be less severe. The Great Lakes will provide water to withstand a drought. New Yorkers and Californians will get their comeuppance for thinking they are superior. Who cares if all those blacks, Jews, Mexicans, and homosexuals get washed to sea? Even Maxine catches herself welcoming the unseasonal warmth. It's like receiving a tax refund you know is the result of a computer glitch; you will need to return the money, but how can you not enjoy spending it in the meantime?

In front of a rental along Packard Avenue a dozen students celebrate the sunny weather by tossing a beanbag through a hole in a board. If a player misses, he or she must take a drink. One of the young men—tall, with a narrow waist—reminds her of her son. Not that Zach would waste his time drinking and playing cornhole.

She stops behind the elementary school. The children in aftercare play on the ceramic turtles and plastic slides that have taken the place of the metal climbing structures that populated the schoolyard when she and Sam moved to Ann Arbor. In first grade, Zach lost his grip and plummeted from the monkey bars, breaking his wrist. Still, Maxine was dismayed when the new principal replaced the jungle gym with a wooden pirate ship whose only intriguing feature was the rope ladder by which a child could ascend the prow. The principal, Mrs. Greer, prohibited the children from playing any game that involved a ball, the theory being this would protect children who weren't adept at sports from bullying. Rather than banning Field Day, she decreed none of the activities could involve keeping score. Not long after—Zach must have been eleven—someone set fire to the pirate ship, a crime whose details Maxine learned from Zach's friend, Norm Fishburn, while Norm was eating dinner at their house.

"We heard the fire engines," Norm said, bits of vegetarian meatloaf flying from his mouth. "You could see the flames from my bedroom. All that was left was this pile of soggy black crud. And the fake cannon. Except the fire melted the cannon into this really crazy shape."

Sam asked if the boys knew who set fire to the ship. She was surprised he suspected arson. Her own hunch was teenagers must have been smoking dope and gotten careless.

"I don't know," Zach said. "But whoever burned it did us a big favor. Why did Mrs. Greer have to name it the SS *Friendship*? Why take a vote if you're not going to do what the vote tells you to do?" When Mrs. Greer asked the students to suggest names, everyone thought hard and put some really good names in the suggestion box. "We knew she wasn't going to let us call it anything with Death in the title. Or Killer. Or Destroyer. But we figured she would let us use the *Jolly Roger*. Or even the SS

Recess. One of the girls thought that one up, and it would have been better than SS *Friendship*." He spit out the name *Friendship* as if he had discovered a piece of gristle in the fake meatloaf he was chewing. "How dweeby is that? You can't *make* people be friends. Nobody is going to be sad somebody splashed stuff on the boat and burned it down."

Sam shot Maxine a meaningful glance. "And how do you know someone splashed gasoline on the boat?"

Norm darted his eyes toward Zach.

Zach sat straight up, as if he had nothing to be ashamed of. "I've seen you try to light the grill, Dad. Even charcoal won't catch fire unless you squirt that stuff from the can." .

"Zach," Sam said, "if you and Norm know who set fire to that ship, you'd better tell us. Someone might have gotten hurt. The whole school could have caught fire."

Zach moved his jaw and scowled, arguing in his head. "It was the middle of the night," he said finally. "And the school is made of bricks. Bricks are even harder to set on fire than wood."

Clearly, Zach knew more than he was telling. But did Sam honestly think their son set fire to that ship? His bedroom was on the second floor; she would have heard if he tried to sneak down the creaky stairs in the middle of the night. Across the dinner table, she could see Sam decide if he should press Zach to reveal the name of whoever set the fire. When he let the question drop, she was so relieved she asked if anyone wanted to walk to Dairy Queen for dessert.

The case of the SS *Friendship* was never solved. Within a week, workmen had put up a plastic version of the ship, much smaller, minus the cannon and ladder. The entire play area was cushioned with rubber pads. The kids playing on the playground now will never know children once climbed to the very top of a metal structure, hooked their knees, and dangled far above the macadam. The only ball in sight is tethered to a pole, as if it otherwise might escape.

When the woman supervising the children begins walking toward Maxine, she forces herself to move on. Really, how can she object to making a playground safe? She passes a vine-shrouded Tudor she has always coveted. A weathered but elegant three-story Victorian. A blue-shuttered Cape Cod. Sure, the parents in Burns Park wish they had a few more hours each day to hang out with their families. To read a book. To take a hike in the Arboretum. They have too many passwords to remember. Too many soccer games and ballet classes to get the children to on time. But who would trade the rigors of a middle-class life for subsistence farming?

Then again, if the children of Burns Park are so blessed, why did they set fire to the SS *Friendship*? Why are they so obsessed with zombies, vampires, werewolves, and other narratives of mass destruction? If zombies ate your parents, sure, you would be upset. But you wouldn't need to keep answering their texts about how you had done on your biology exam or whether you had practiced your violin. What frightens these children more—that a nuclear war might wipe out this paradise in which they were lucky enough to be born? Or that they might grow up to become their parents and end up living here?

She turns down the street to her house. Garbage cans stand lined up along the driveways. She dragged out her own can that morning. But she didn't bother to take out the recycling bin. The truth is, she has been tossing the bottles and cans in the trash. If only Sam would return from the dead and scold her.

Her backyard is enclosed by a fence. Not until she unlatches the gate does she notice a ladder leaning against the rear wall of her house and a man in a hoodie climbing to Zach's old bedroom.

"Excuse me?" she shouts up at the thief.

The man turns and looks down. He is young, with a bushy Afro and a wild brown beard. A wasp buzzes, and he swats it in childish panic that brings to mind Zach and Norm horsing around at the Dairy Queen, their Blizzards attracting bees.

"Norm?" she says.

"Uh, hi, Professor Sayers."

"What are you doing up there?" Like her own son, Norm stands six foot three inches tall, so thin that when he and Zach used to hug each other you couldn't help but wish they would meld to form one normal-weight boy. As kids, Norm and Zach bonded over their love of computer games. But when Zach moved on to other passions, Norm remained reluctant to commit to becoming an adult. He enlisted Zach's help in inventing ridiculously complex board games. After the SS *Friendship* burned, Norm began designing fantastical playgrounds where children could climb a tower, jump off, and coast to the ground on gliders. Or burrow through hills of clay. Or roll like marbles through gigantic Rube Goldberg contraptions. In high school, Norm had drawn up plans for a playground to be constructed in a nearby park using nothing but tree stumps, boulders, and a stream already on the site. When the city refused, Norm and Zach constructed the playground on their own, although the city undid their efforts.

Even though Norm has an off-the-charts IQ, he refused to apply to college. It was as if, from his great height, he had looked around and foreseen that the usual career paths wouldn't appeal to him. Instead, he took the occasional carpentry class at the community college and supported himself caring for a disabled child.

Maxine hasn't run into him in months. At least, she doesn't think she has. Maybe the hair and beard have kept her from recognizing him.

"Um, sorry, Professor Sayers." Norm backs down the ladder, which, Maxine realizes, came from her own garage. "I guess you could say I was breaking into Zach's old bedroom."

"In broad daylight?" How can he not realize a black man in a hoodie climbing a ladder to break into a white person's house runs the risk of being shot?

"Zach asked me to do it."

"You heard from Zach?" She grabs his hoodie and pulls him down the last few rungs. "You weren't going to tell me?"

"He made me swear not to. But, um, I wanted you to know. I guess that's why I waited until you might be coming home."

Even on the ground, he towers above her. She can smell his sweat, so like her son's she wants to wrap herself in the hoodie with him. "Is he all right? Please, Norm! I've been worried sick!"

"He called me," Norm says. "But it didn't say his name on the caller ID. I thought it might be a spam thing."

"Do you remember the area code?" Zach is alive. He is healthy and sane enough to find a phone and call his friend.

"He said somebody came to see him in California, and he went away with that person, and he can't be in contact by email or phone, not with anyone, even by regular mail. But he needs money. He has all these savings bonds socked away from his bar mitzvah. They're behind that panel in the wall next to his bed. I'm supposed to go in and find them, then wait until he tells me where to send them."

She knows the hiding place. She once needed to call the plumber to fix the shower. The pipes were accessible only through the panel behind Zach's bed. When the plumber pried it off, a bag of marijuana fell out, along with a bong fashioned from a Diet Coke can. Zach refused to affirm or deny the pot was his. But Sam said, "It's Norm's, isn't it. You were hiding it for Norm?" And Zach hadn't denied he was. Sam had grabbed the baggie. "You tell your friend to hide his drugs at his own house." He took the bag and scattered the contents behind the garage. Maxine steals a glance at that weedy patch, half expecting to see a secret garden of marijuana.

"It wouldn't be like I was stealing from you," Norm says. "Zach said the savings bonds are made out to him."

"Norm," she says, "if Zach wants his money, he can have it. But the only people who can cash those savings bonds are Zach and me. When Zach gets back in touch, I'll give you the proceeds. And I won't ask any questions. As long as you promise to tell Zach I've been really, really worried. If he's in trouble, he can come to me for help. Tell him I won't yell at him. Or judge him in any way." She hopes Norm won't see her crying. Then she thinks: *Let him see.* Maybe he will tell Zach he made his mother cry. "Are you sure you don't know anything else and you're just not telling me?"

Norm shakes his head. "Zach said if he told me anything else, you'd get it out of me." He pats her on the shoulder. "I've done a lot of stupid stuff to worry my parents. But I never did anything as bad as the shit Zach pulled on you." He hooks the ladder across his arm. "The window to Zach's room never did close all the way."

"No," she says. "It never did."

After he leaves, she tries to make sense of what Norm just told her. Her son is alive. He isn't in jail. But why does he need his bar mitzvah money? Who is this person who came to see him? Why did whoever it was demand Zach quit his job, give away his belongings, and drop out of sight?

She grabs a snack, then heads to the garage to get the car. *Please,* she prays. *Don't let my mother ask if I heard from Zach. Don't let her say she saw her grandson on the news and Zach has some connection to that crazy bomber.*

. . . Feeds Her Mother

As a girl, Maxine looked down on her mother for devoting her life to cleaning their house, cooking, fussing about her appearance, and pestering her daughter to do the same. She vowed to become anything but a housewife. Whenever a dispute arose, she sided with her father.

Now, she wonders how she could have missed that her mother was the victim of a system that denied her an education or any sense of worth except what she could acquire by snaring a talented, ambitious husband. Maxine's father joined the army and received training in radar and electronics. What assets did her mother have except her straight blonde hair, her chiseled nose, her fair complexion, and her belief she was entitled to more than might be expected for the daughter of an illiterate Jewish poultry farmer in upstate New York? Her mother's father died when Maxine's mother was in high school, leaving nothing except an evil-smelling chicken house. She took a job at the one emporium for women's clothes in Fenstead, where she zipped her former classmates' zippers and knelt with pins in her mouth to tack up their hems. How could she not develop an obsession with her appearance? Her only hope of rising from her knees was attracting a better class of husband.

The first time Maxine's mother and father met, Lennie Sayers was traveling door-to-door, carrying frozen foods. But a year later, when her mother ventured into his appliance store to replace the icebox, she was more favorably impressed with the store's proprietor. Stunned by her beauty, Maxine's father offered her a special price on a Frigidaire. After they married, he built his wife a split-level ranch equipped with the most up-to-date conveniences. When his widowed mother-in-law showed signs of what in those days was called "senility," he invited her to move in upstairs.

Maxine is pained to remember how dismissive she was of everything her mother valued. But how could makeup tips or schemes to redecorate the living room compete with her father's eagerness to enlist her in his campaign to bring about the Age of the Messiah? Not that her father believed in God. For Leonard Sayers, the Age of the Messiah would come about when human beings brought it. "Our end of the bargain," he used to say—and by "our" he meant scientists and engineers—was to come up with new methods of agriculture to keep people from starving, robots to prevent workers from wasting their days in drudgery, medical treatments to stave off illness and death. The Messiah might cajole the remaining tyrants into abdicating their thrones and consigning their arsenals to the sea. But the Kingdom of Heaven would be attained only by dreamers and doers who used their brains and hands to harness the mysterious yet tamable forces of magnetism, gravity, and electricity.

Maxine reified her father's memory. When anyone asked how she had come up with the idea of studying the future, she described riding on her father's shoulders as he skipped them from exhibit to exhibit at the 1964 World's Fair in Flushing. "Mark my words," her father said. "In your very own lifetime, Maxie, human beings will be living on the moon. Maybe even in *my* lifetime," he added wistfully, not knowing he wouldn't live to see his daughter graduate from junior high.

Even then, the word "lifetime" had given Maxine pause. Contemplating the length of a person's life was like arriving at the fair in the morning, wide-eyed and full of energy, and thinking how tired she would be at the end of the day, trudging back through the parking lot to the car. She would walk and walk, trusting that when she no longer could take another step, her father would whisk her in his arms and carry her.

If Leonard Sayers ever placed his faith in his father's god, his harrowing encounters with death during World War II had replaced any lingering religiosity with a faith in science. When Maxine watched her father dig a grave for the family cat, he told her if she were to return with a shovel later, she would find nothing but bones and claws. But she couldn't accept that the universe would go to all the trouble of creating a cat, let alone a child, and adults would go to even more trouble teaching a child everything she needed to learn to become a grown-up, if, after a number of years even Maxine could understand wasn't very long, she would be buried and stop existing.

One day, she would discover a way to stave off death. Hadn't she heard her father's salesman, Spider Macalvoy, extoll the powers of their new casket-sized freezers? Once, Spider had gathered some frogs from behind his house, then popped them in an Amana. He took these frogsicles out and set them on a towel. Maxine sat spellbound, watching the crystalline eyes defrost, the rubbery legs unfold, and the throats resume their pulsing, until the frogs looked blandly at their new surroundings, hopped off the display counter, and set Maxine hopping after them. A human being wasn't a frog. But if all went well, before she was scheduled to die of old age, she could ask to be frozen, with a request that she be chipped out and defrosted a century later, allowed to look around and see what wonderful new inventions had been invented, whether life on other planets had been detected, and what those civilizations might be like.

Because that was her other obsession: whether humans would make contact with intelligent beings in the universe. Once, at a sleepover party, she made the mistake of asking her friends if they believed there was life in outer space. The voices from the other sleeping bags rose to such a crescendo of scorn—"Aliens!" "Outer space!"—she might as well have been an alien herself. Only her father enjoyed discussing such possibilities. She loved the hours she spent at his shop, sitting on a high stool surrounded by television sets in various stages of disrepair, oscilloscopes, tube testers, pliers, screwdrivers, soldering irons, capacitors, resistors, fuses, and knobs, learning the difference between an RCA Victor CTC, a Zenith 25CC50, and a Motorola Quasar 2. She can still smell the dust from inside the cases. The scorch of the burnt-out tubes. The Windex her father sprayed on each screen before he fitted it back inside its box. She can hear her father's Brooklyn twang urging her to examine the appliances and diagnose what was ailing them.

"Don't jump right in, Maxie," he would say. "*Look*, sweetheart. *Think*. Visualize what connects to what. You can't make even the smallest repair without understanding how the entire apparatus works." He trained her to see from an inventor's point of view. "How did Alexander Graham Bell get a voice to travel along a wire? What is sound made of? What might be used to record a human voice?" She loved when her father demonstrated the latest product some manufacturer's representative had brought to the store. "Maxie," he said, "someday, in your very own lifetime, you will be sitting in your living room, and the characters on your favorite television show will act out their parts, not on the TV screen, but right in front of you!"

His dream was that she would enroll at nearby Rensselaer Polytechnic Institute—he couldn't bear to let his Maxie live where he couldn't drop by to see her. Once she had acquired the education he hadn't had the finances to attain, who knew what they might accomplish.

She might have carried out this plan if her father hadn't died of a faulty heart valve one rainy day in May when Maxine was twelve. She had stopped by after school. Spider asked her to mind the shop while he returned a damaged clock radio to the post office. She passed the time popping the bubble wrap from a shipment of cassette recorders. She had just popped a particularly satisfying bubble when she heard a thump from the back of the store. Somehow, she sensed what she might find if she went to investigate. As long as she stayed out front, her father would remain alive in back.

A customer came in—Mr. West, whose son Bobby was a year ahead of Maxine at school. Had Bobby's stereo been repaired? She sent Mr. West to ask her father, continuing to pop bubbles even as Mr. West hurried back out and slipped behind the register to use the phone. Spider hadn't returned from the post office, so no one thought to keep Maxine from watching the volunteer firemen carry her father to the ambulance. According to the coroner's report, he had been dead when he hit the ground. But something about popping that bubble at the exact moment her father's heart burst led Maxine to think of a human life as nothing but a bubble of air kept intact by a fragile membrane.

She cried. Of course she cried. But not nearly as much as her anguish warranted. Not until a few months later, as she sat watching Neil Armstrong bounce around on the moon, did she begin sobbing so violently she couldn't breathe. "Oh, Mom. Can't you almost see him?" And her mother agreed that she, too, had been thinking of Maxine's father. *Didn't I predict this? Didn't I tell you to mark my words?*

When the time came, Maxine applied to RPI. But SUNY Binghamton turned out to be less expensive. She considered premed. But the human heart seemed less an organ, a muscle, than a machine to be repaired or replaced by a more lasting and effective model. In the end she chose engineering, a field for which she seemed uniquely prepared by all the years she had spent acquiring skills even her male lab partners envied.

The problem was, she had loved tinkering at her father's bench because she had loved tinkering beside her father. The smell of soldered lead caused her eyes to tear up from a longing to feel her father's arms around her as he guided her hands on the red-hot iron. Without him, she hadn't a clue what gadget to invent. She considered changing majors. But what would she change her major to?

And then, toward the end of her senior year in college, Maxine's mother demanded Maxine come home to sort through her father's possessions—her mother was moving to an apartment and couldn't bear to throw out his things. With a heavy heart, Maxine climbed to her parents' attic. Each cardboard box stood labeled with Magic Marker—"Leonard's War Memorabilia," "Taxes," "Maxine's Art Projects"—the flaps interlocking in the way Maxine remembered her mother teaching her. She opened the first box and found her father's bulky Model B View-Master, which he brought back from the war. As she inserted the first disc, she heard him discourse on the importance of Navy gunners being able to distinguish our aircraft from the enemy's. *Imagine, Maxie, shooting down one of your own planes, then living with the knowledge you killed a pilot from your own side!* She remembered him explaining how much easier it was to distinguish an airplane in three dimensions than in two, how many lives had been saved by the stereographic View-Master she was holding.

As she lifted the Model B to the attic's window, she could hear her father muse on the horrors he had witnessed in the Japanese theater of operations. *Oh, Maxie, you have no idea what war really is. That burning ship! Those poor boys leaping overboard! And believe me, no matter what you might hear to the contrary, neither side has a monopoly on goodness.* Hearing that phrase, "theater of operations," she had pictured soldiers fighting on a stage while bystanders watched from bleachers like the ones the janitors set up in the auditorium at her elementary school. Or the bystanders looking on while the injured soldiers got operated on, the way Maxine and her friends huddled around the cardboard man whose organs they so carefully removed when playing Operation. How could a ship, which was surrounded by water, burn? If Monopoly was a game, what did it mean that neither player was any good? Only later did she realize those young men must have been leaping from their ships because they preferred a watery death to frying in the oily flames. How miraculous, that her father's words could lie dormant in her brain, only to be released by the sight and feel of this heavy black View-Master, with the added gift that she could finally flesh out his words with the knowledge she had since acquired.

She took so long in the attic her mother came up to see if anything was amiss. Maxine tried to explain the memories the

View-Master had unleashed. And her mother, who so rarely took an interest in Maxine's observations, surprised her by saying, "That's why I couldn't bring myself to throw any of this away."

A few days later, Maxine had given up on her idea of becoming an engineer and applied to MIT's new Program in Science, Technology, and Society. For her doctorate, she designed and carried out a series of extensive interviews and psychological tests in which she attempted to quantify just how much of our emotional lives actually does reside in objects. In a way, she owes her career as much to her mother as to her father. The trouble is, she genuinely loved her father, while she often needs to convince herself that she loves her mother. She pays for her mother's care in Ann Arbor's best nursing home. But she often catches herself wishing her father might be the parent upon whom she is lavishing so much care in his twilight years.

She stops at CVS to pick up the tweezers and tissues her mother requested, then crosses the Huron River and continues up the winding road to Sunrise Hills. ("Sunset Hills would be more like it," her mother had remarked upon being driven there on her tour.) At the gated entrance, Maxine brakes for an elderly man bent at ninety degrees over the handles of his walker, moving as slowly as the Galapagos tortoise he so resembles. She parks in a spot for visitors. At the front desk, a security guard in a red blazer makes sure she signs the logbook. Maxine specifies she has arrived to visit Henrietta Sayers in Room 553 and is entering at 4:30 p.m. If she takes her mother from her room, she will need to sign another log at the nurses' station. Then she will need to sign her mother back in when she returns her.

"Ma'am! Ma'am!"

Maxine looks back.

"You made a mistake." The guard points to the clock. "It's 4:37."

Maxine studies the clock. "Yes," she agrees. "It is."

The guard jabs her finger at the book. "Then why did you write 4:30?"

She picks up the pen, which is attached to the desk by a chain of tiny silver spheres, each like a crystallized second, and changes the "0" to an "8." As she heads to the elevator, she can feel the guard watching her, as if she might yet pocket a few loose minutes from a resident who can barely spare them.

The elevator is located across from the gym. Seven women and two men lift weights no bigger than a turkey leg, curling them to their chests, raising them overhead, like an army training for an invasion by a superior force they are determined to withstand. The elevator takes forever to come. Maxine pictures residents wheeling themselves in and trying to remember which button to push. The doors open and a middle-aged man rushes out, so eager to regain his freedom the guard needs to shout after him, "Sir! Sir!" to remind him to sign the logbook.

She pushes the button for the fifth floor. After an interminable series of comings and goings, the doors open on a cluster of withered residents. Rocking. Clawing at their faces. Moaning. Her childhood terror of death rises in her throat.

"Help me!" a woman shrieks.

She looks up so imploringly Maxine asks, "What is it? What do you need?" But her question agitates the woman more. She snatches at Maxine's purse.

"Help me!"

Maxine clings to her purse. The woman snatches the CVS bag. Maxine snatches it back. She hurries along the corridor.

"Please!" the woman pleads. "Help me! Help me! Help me!" Maxine needs to summon her deepest powers of indifference to keep from turning.

Beside the nurses' station, a boiled old man sits cradling a stuffed lion. Did someone give him the toy to calm him? She read about a nursing home in Japan where each resident is provided with a robot baby seal. The old people can enjoy the companionship of a pet without needing to take it outside or clean a litter box. The same home is experimenting with robot caretakers that roll from bed to bed, making sure the patients take their medications. The robots bring the old people meals, sing songs, challenge their memories with riddles, and monitor the corridors to make sure no one gets lost.

Here, in America, a few aides loiter behind their desk, chatting and filling out forms. Most genuinely care about their charges. But a few seem to resent ministering to residents who snarl at them, curse, and hurl racial invectives that make Maxine want to beg forgiveness for the entire white race. Forget robots. Wouldn't it be easier to pay the human aides higher salaries?

She finds her mother lying fully clothed on her bed—to lie beneath the covers during the day would be an admission of defeat. Maxine pulls up the one chair in the room and lifts her mother's veiny hand—even in her sleep, the Parkinson's causes it to twitch like a fish. Her mother wears a blouse printed with a Paris street scene and polyester pants with an elastic waistband her mother hates, but how could she manage zippers?

Maxine shifts to the end of the mattress, takes one of her mother's gnarled feet, and massages it. The toes straighten. The stiff sole relaxes. Her mother smiles in her sleep. Until recently, the two of them rarely touched. That they are touching now, with her mother so near death, brings tears to Maxine's eyes.

She remembers how Sam used to sit on the sofa massaging her own feet as they watched the evening news. He began with the soles. Then moved up to her ankles. Worked his way higher to her thighs.

Her heart overflows with belated sympathy. If Maxine is so bereft here in Ann Arbor, where she has so many colleagues and friends, how much more isolated must her mother have been in their tiny upstate town? How furious she must have been at Spider Macalvoy, the army buddy her husband raised from nothing to become a partner in the company he built from the ground up. Or Dr. Vincent, who delivered Maxine and must have been aware his friend was working on a deal to sell their company. Not until Sam died did Maxine understand what it was like to lose the man you had slept with for so many years. The father of your only child. A child who would now be grieving in ways that made your own heart tear open even wider.

Her mother had adored Sam, who reminded her of her own brilliant and inventive husband. And Sam had been wonderfully attentive to Maxine's mother. Courtly. Demonstrating the manners he had been tutored in as a child. "He is such a *gentleman*," her mother used to say, the highest praise she knew how to give. She had been devastated when Sam died. True, she couldn't help but make her son-in-law's death yet another of the tragedies she was fated to endure. But she idolized her only grandson. She lavished so much affection on Zach, he couldn't help but lavish it back.

"Why does Grandmom have to live in that awful retirement home?" Zach had asked. Maxine explained she had offered to sell their house and buy one that wouldn't require his grandmother to climb stairs. But at the outset her mother had preferred to live among people her own age, with whom she might develop a regular bridge game or attend a concert. And then, as the Parkinson's had progressed, she had grown too infirm to be cared for in Maxine's home. The sight of all those elderly people rocking in their wheelchairs clearly bothered Zach. But he usually was the one to suggest they visit. During the week, he would ride there on his bike. Later, when he was visiting from MIT, he would borrow his father's old VW bug and stop at Stucchi's so he could bring his grandmother the Grasshopper Pie ice cream she adored.

Now, sitting beside her mother, Maxine's eyes wander to the photos crowding the nightstand: Zach toddling after a duck in Fenstead; Zach standing stiffly beside his prize-winning science-fair project on the workings of the photovoltaic cell; Zach in a thrift-store tuxedo, with his much shorter, frailer prom-date folded against his side. What was the prom date's name? Angelica? Angelina?

The autumn of Zach's senior year in high school, Maxine had been working in her office when she was seized by a craving to be outdoors. She blew off a meeting and drove to the Arboretum. When she reached the rapids, where a local eccentric had arranged the rocks in the shape of a giant heart, she noticed a couple wading toward the opposite shore, hand in hand, the foliage orange and red behind them. Then the couple turned, and she realized the young man was her son.

She managed to slip into the woods just before Zach and his girlfriend could see her. But as she bushwhacked to her car, it occurred to her there had been something wounded about the girl. The way one arm turned out from the wrist. The way she leaned against Zach, as if using him to steady her balance. She had been pretty enough, with hair so shiny, dark, and long it might have been its own tributary of the Huron River. But Maxine suspected the girl had some neurological disability. Which might have been why her kind-hearted son had fallen in love with her.

That night, she had hinted to Zach that if he ever were to, well, *like* a girl, she hoped he would feel free to bring her home. Maxine would make a nice meal. She would try not to embarrass him.

Zach said, "Okay, Mom. Someone tipped you off I'm seeing Angelina. If you promise not to cook anything Mexican, I'll bring her to dinner this Friday night."

And Angelina had been a very sweet guest. She brought Maxine flowers in a milk-bottle vase she had painted herself. But Zach had been the one to carry the gift from the car—he had driven to Ypsilanti to pick her up—because Angelina would have had trouble carrying the vase while maneuvering up the walk with a brace on each arm. All of which gave Maxine the impression the girl was literally using her son to lean on.

Up close, Angelina was even more attractive than Maxine thought. Her words seemed thick in her mouth, but she was a charming, loquacious talker. She and Zach had met in study hall, she said. She wasn't that good at math, but Zach was wonderful at explaining algebra. Her father ran a landscaping business. She loved taking Zach to the Arboretum because she knew the names of all the bushes and trees and he didn't know anything except maple and daisy. After they graduated, she was going to work for her father and save up enough money so she could open a nursery of her own.

Maxine brought out the strawberry-rhubarb pie she had baked for the occasion. Angelina stood, put on her braces, and attempted to clear the plates. Unsettled by the sight of her son's disabled Mexican-American girlfriend stacking the family's dirty dishes, Maxine said: "Go, go. I'll clean up. You two go out and have a good time." Later, after Zach came home from the movie, Maxine managed to recite his girlfriend's positive qualities. But then she found herself saying—as mothers often do—exactly what she knew she shouldn't. "Zach, it's fine if you fall in love with someone who has, well, limitations. But you need to make sure you aren't falling in love *because* of those limitations. I mean, because you pity her." As soon as the words were out of her mouth, she was horrified. "Oh, God, Zach. I am so, so sorry. Angelina is a lovely person. I don't even know what I meant by that. I won't say another word. I promise."

Zach lifted his hands. "Mom! You don't get it! Angie is the one who's taking pity on *me*!"

Over and over, Maxine apologized. But Zach had never again brought Angelina home. Maxine hadn't even realized he was taking her to the prom until he showed up in that tuxedo. The photo by his grandmother's bed had been taken at Sunrise Hills, with the same Nikon that Maxine's father had used to take pictures of Maxine on her prom night. Not that she'd had a date. Her father had insisted she "gussy herself up" in one of her mother's cocktail dresses and escorted her to a showing of *That's Entertainment* in Saratoga.

Her mother's eyes flutter open. Her arm flies up and she fusses at her matted hair. "Tomorrow morning," she reminds Maxine. "My appointment is for ten. But time is *different* in the basement."

"Sure," Maxine says. "I'll be here by nine." She reaches into the CVS bag and pulls out the tissues.

"Do those have the lotion already in them?"

"Yes, Mom." She puts the box on the bedside table.

"These flat boxes take up too much space."

"Sorry. I'll get the smaller box next time." Maxine takes out the tweezers. The only thing she hates worse than plucking hairs from her mother's chin is knowing Zach will one day need to do the same for her. "Hold still." She leans so close she inhales her mother's fusty scent, like an overripe peach. She grasps a spiky bristle.

"Ow!" Her mother flinches. Maxine struggles to get a grip on a silky filament. After several aborted tries, she yanks. Three more hairs and Maxine is finished. "Yes," her mother says. Not *thanks*.

Maxine hopes this will be the end of ministering to her mother's vanity. But her mother has requested Maxine buy the exact shade of mascara she has been using for forty years, and Maxine needs to explain—yet again—that the company discontinued making it. Instead, she shows her mother the slightly lighter shade she bought at CVS. With her mother's hands jerking so violently, how is she going to apply mascara anyway? To divert her, Maxine suggests she allow her to wheel her to the dining room for dinner. But her mother protests that Maxine promised to look for the envelope from Cousin Joel. "I put it somewhere. Now I can't find it. Maybe it's in that drawer."

Twice in the past week Maxine has searched her mother's bureau, which holds only a few panties, brassieres, and nightgowns, and the drawer beneath the nightstand, in which her mother keeps an emery board and a tube of ChapStick. But she goes through the motions. She shuffles through the book of crossword puzzles, which, until recently, her mother worked to keep her mind sharp. The week's menus from the dining room. The calendar of activities at Sunrise Hills. The tattered manila envelope in which her mother has stowed the birthday cards and letters Zach used to send when he went traveling.

"Sorry, Mom. There's nothing from Cousin Joel."

Her mother screws up her face to signify that even though she never attended college, she has been blessed with more common sense than her daughter. "I'm not doing this for myself. I'm doing it for your son. That boy could accomplish great things. If only he had the resources. And Sam's mother won't leave a *cent*."

Maxine understands her mother's concern with money. She grew up poor. Her share of Sayers Appliances ran out while Maxine was in high school. Aside from a pittance from Social Security, her mother has nothing. And she isn't wrong that Zach won't be getting an inheritance from Sam's mother. Sam's alcoholic father lost what little remained of the Pardue family shipbuilding fortune. The proceeds from Sam's insurance went to pay Zach's tuition at MIT. All of which adds to her reasons for not telling her mother Norm has heard from Zach. If her mother finds out her grandson really does need money, she will drive herself even crazier about the lawsuit.

"It's all right, Mom. Let's get you ready for dinner." She slides her arms beneath her mother's back so she can lift her to her wheelchair.

"Stop!" her mother shouts. "You're hurting me!"

Sick at heart, Maxine keeps maneuvering her mother's rigid torso.

"Stop! You always hurt me!"

In all honesty, Maxine doesn't have a clue what she is doing. Yesterday, when she tried to help her mother pull on a sweater, her mother's arms got caught in the sleeves and she sat writhing like an animal in a trap. If only her mother would allow herself to be transferred to the floor for residents who need around-the-clock nursing. But that would mean admitting she is dying.

Maxine braces herself, then swings her mother from the bed. She wheels her to the bathroom, lifts her from the chair, and settles her on the toilet. She turns her back and waits. Have any of the geniuses who are trying to keep humans alive forever actually cared for an aged parent? Presumably, what they are promising is immortal life without the need for some kind soul to wipe your genitals.

With difficulty, she settles her mother back in her chair and wheels her to the dining hall. Eleven years earlier, when her mother moved to Sunrise Hills, she struggled to ingratiate herself with the best-dressed and most attractive female residents. But that was when she resided four floors down, in Independent Living. Here on the fifth floor, the staff arranges the seating based on who is cogent enough to carry on a conversation.

"Hello, Elizabeth!" her mother shouts to the stout, white-haired lady to her right. "Such a beautiful sweater you are wearing!" The Parkinson's causes her mother's eyes to squeeze shut. Her mouth contorts. Her arms flutter around her head. And yet, she incorporates these distortions into her usual gestures, like a housewife who hopes no one will notice a mess because it blends with the pattern on the rug. The effect for Maxine is to make her mother seem a grotesque caricature of her younger self.

The other women dip their spoons into their mushroom barley soup. Maxine's mother, knowing if she attempts to spoon soup to her mouth she will dribble it on her lap, hasn't circled "soup" on that day's menu. She looks longingly at the roll on her bread plate, which some sadist has sealed in plastic. Maxine unwraps the roll. Without acknowledging the help, her mother tears off a piece. Hands jerking, she conveys it to her mouth.

"You must be Henrietta's daughter," says the well-preserved

redhead to Maxine's left.

"Yes," Maxine says, bracing for what will follow.

"Do you work at the university?" When Maxine answers yes, the woman asks if she knows her daughter, Megan Kavornick, who teaches in the political science department. Yes, Maxine says, she knows Megan slightly. The woman asks what subject Maxine teaches.

"She studies the *future*," her mother says dismissively. "She is trying to figure out how we can live forever."

"Ha!" another woman barks. "No thank you very much!"

The redhead finishes her soup. She looks up happily. "Oh," she says. "You must be Henrietta's daughter. Do you know my daughter, Megan Kavornick? She teaches at the university. She's a professor in the department of political science."

"Just ignore her," her mother orders.

"I'm sorry, no," Maxine says. "I don't know your daughter."

"That's a shame. What do you do at the university? What subject do you teach?"

Luckily, one of the staff, an older black woman who has as much trouble walking as the residents, brings the main course. Because Maxine's mother can't swallow solid food, her dinner consists of three scoops of mush, one beige, one green, one yellow. Her mother jabs her fork in the yellowish mound, which might be pureed chicken. Her arm jerks, and a dab of mush lands on her blouse, between the Eiffel Tower and the Folies Bergère. Her mother refuses to wear a bib; if Maxine offers to feed her, she snarls and says she doesn't need any help. She finishes her roll, then sits shaking and grimacing while her tablemates pursue their only slightly more successful attempts to feed themselves.

The waitress brings ice cream. Her mother allows Maxine

to pry off the lid, then uses the flat wood spoon to convey the ice cream to her mouth. Maxine is dying for coffee. Not wanting to trouble the waitress, she crosses the room to a station where a glass pot squats on a Bunn-O-Matic. And whom does she see but Arnold Schlechter, using his maimed hand to spoon ice cream into the mouth of an elderly man who must be his father. With his flyaway white hair and the patch on one eye, the younger Schlechter doesn't seem far removed from a nursing home himself.

"Pop," he says, "come on, you've got to keep up your strength." He swabs a dash of vanilla from the old man's lip. "Remember when you used to walk me to Coney Island to get a treat? And I asked if they named the island after the ice cream cones?" His father nods happily. Sensing a presence behind him, the younger Schlechter looks up. "Oh," he says dully. "Marlene, isn't it? Your husband directs that global technology group."

Maxine doesn't bother to correct him. "I didn't know your father was here. My mother is over there."

Schlechter doesn't even pretend to search the room. "My wife and I moved Pop here from Brooklyn last month. But it's taken longer than we anticipated for the jackass workmen to install a ramp on our house and add an accessible bathroom." He turns back to the old man. "We'll get you out of here day after tomorrow, Pop. I promise."

She wants to explain that her mother refused to come live with her, that she preferred the independence of Sunrise Hills. "It must have been hard for you today," she says.

"Hard? No. That son of a bitch gave me the chance to go on national television and take a logical knife to his idiotic ravings. Because of him, the ideas he detests have become far more widely promulgated than otherwise would have been the case."

Despite his vehemence, Maxine suspects that if you had

asked Arnold Schlechter whether he preferred to let someone shoot out his right eye and blow three fingers off his right hand in return for a national forum for his ideas, he wouldn't have accepted the proposition. Oddly, Schlechter and the bomber don't disagree that computers threaten to destroy humanity. The major difference is that Schlechter believes the ugliest effects can be warded off, while the bomber maintains a revolution will be required. Maybe that's enough to warrant the bomber's hatred. But she is nagged by the suspicion that the bomber has met Arnold Schlechter and taken a personal dislike to the man. Or he is channeling Maxine's own repugnance.

"I'm sure you've thought of this before, but is there any chance the bomber was one of your students?"

Schlechter puts down the wooden spoon with which he has been feeding his father—she can't avoid staring at his stumps. "First of all, I long ago turned over my student rosters to the FBI. If they found a match, they would have notified me. Second, I am not going to waste my time trying to understand what drove this cretin to commit such heinous acts. I don't care if he grew up 'oppressed,' or 'abused.' Despite what you liberals think, evil exists. And I am singularly ill equipped to comprehend it. I refuse to allow an act of terrorism to alter who I am, or what I might believe, or how I might behave."

"Yes," she says. "I can see that. I'm sorry I brought this up."

"I did think I might find a little peace and quiet here, of all places. I thought I might be able to share a pleasant dinner with my father. Right, Pop?" He takes the old man's withered hand and presses it to his cheek, beneath the eye patch.

"I'm sorry," she says again. At the coffee station, she pours a cup of room-temperature sludge but spatters the liquid on her pantyhose. Avoiding the Schlechters, she takes the long way to her mother. She brushes the crumbs from her mother's lap, then tries to wipe the stains from her blouse.

Her mother flails to make her stop. "Take me to my room," she orders.

Maxine backs her mother's chair from the table. "Good night, Mrs. Dean. Good night, Mrs. Cooper. Mrs. Kavornick, if I see your daughter, I'll tell her you said hello."

"Oh?" Mrs. Kavornick says. "You know my Megan? Do you work with her at the university?"

Maxine wheels her mother to her room. Her mother wants to watch the news, so Maxine switches on the television. And there he is, Arnold Schlechter, standing against a painted backdrop of the university's iconic bell tower, spraying saliva as he says he doesn't care to discuss the terrorist's so-called motives because we need to recognize evil when it blows up in our faces. The déjà vu feels uncanny.

The anchor displays the sketch of the bomber everyone has seen a million times. It shows a man wearing aviator sunglasses and a hoodie. He reminds Maxine of no one she has ever known.

"That's the one," her mother says. "That's the young man who played with Zach."

"Norm?" she says. Except for the hoodie, the man in the sketch looks nothing like her son's friend. They aren't even the same race.

"No! Norm was only a silly boy. I mean the one who played with him after school. You never were careful whom you allowed . . ." She gasps for breath. "To associate with. My grandson."

Instantly, Maxine knows who her mother means. She knows, because she has spent the entire day pretending she didn't know. "Thaddy?"

"I don't remember the name. But yes. He was always telling

Zach to turn off his computer. Throw it away. *Smash* it. He wanted Zach to go outdoors. Which I approved of." She gags on her own saliva. "But something about that young man put me *off*."

Maxine is glad she hasn't eaten dinner—she feels like vomiting. "How do you know all that? Did Zach talk to you about Thaddy?"

"Zach liked this Thaddy. But what the young man told Zach worried him. It worried *me*. Even before I met him."

"You met Thaddy?" As Maxine remembers, Thaddy refused to drive a car.

"They bicycled here to visit me. But I could tell something was off. Your son always was too kind. You could have left him in the care of an axe murderer . . ." She struggles to breathe. "And Zach would have said the man was *nice*. So as not to hurt his feelings." Her mother screws up her face. "You were the same way, as a child." She uses her left hand to capture the right and imprison it in her lap. "You still are."

"Why didn't you tell me?"

"I brought up my concerns." Her mother coughs. "I told you he might be . . . *after* Zach."

"After him?"

"You let them go camping!" Her mother licks her lips. The gesture seems salacious, even though Maxine knows her mother licks her lips because talking requires such effort. "Maybe this young man wasn't *homosexual*. But something bothered me. About his eyes."

Maxine needs to steady herself. Years ago, she asked Thaddy to keep her son company a few afternoons a week, after school. Zach was thirteen. Maybe fourteen. Thaddy hadn't minded. He liked Zach. It wasn't as if she hired him as a babysitter. But she allowed Thaddy to take Zach on a sleepover in the Arboretum.

Thaddy wasn't gay. But if he was as lonely as she remembers him. If the women his own age kept turning him down.

No. That isn't what she is afraid of.

"Oh, Mom!" she says. "What if Zach . . . What if I tell the authorities about Thaddy, and Zach ends up having something to do with . . ." She can't bring herself to say "the bombings." But what if Zach remained in contact with Thaddy even after Thaddy left Ann Arbor? What if that's why Zach quit his job and went into hiding? She braces herself for her mother's diatribe condemning Maxine for neglecting Zach in favor of her research. For allowing him to spend time with a graduate student she didn't know very well. For not hiring a detective when Zach went missing.

Instead, what her mother says is: "If you think for one minute my darling *grandson* . . ." Her features cloud. "Unless this student of yours might have hurt Zach? Might be involved in his disappearance?"

"God, I have to figure this out. Are you going to be okay? Should I help you get back in bed?"

"Go." Her mother jerks her hand. "But don't forget my appointment. The time in the basement is an hour *earlier*."

Maxine forgives her mother for thinking about her appearance at a time like this. After all, she believes her grandson to be incapable of anything hurtful or illegal. Maxine also believes her son is innocent. But she can't help thinking that somewhere in America, the mother of the young man who actually is responsible for all these maimings and deaths believes her son to be incapable of such evil, too.

. . . *Regrets Something She Failed to Do*

So many months have passed since she visited her old office in the Residential College that Maxine feels like a ghost here. Or an emissary from these students' future. They laugh and high-five each other, skittering through the shadowy passages on their way to rehearse some artsy production of *The Tempest* or the Cuban drumming concert for which posters line the corridor, unaware that one day they, too, will be mourning a spouse, missing a child, or caring for an elderly parent.

Or maybe they won't be. By the time these undergraduates are in their fifties, the medical profession might have conquered aging. When the withered crones rocking in her mother's nursing home were born, penicillin hadn't been discovered. Scientists didn't have a clue as to the existence of DNA.

Her office door is taped with yellowing cartoons of every variation of a fish evolving into an amphibian who crawls onto dry land and evolves into a small, lumpy mammal, who evolves into a stooped, hairy primate, who evolves into an upright man, who evolves into the punchline of the gag: a bearded hippie protesting with a sign that reads THE END IS NEAR; a fat, balding hacker slouched over a video game; or, Maxine's favorite, a woman waiting to ask, "What took you so long to get here?"

She flicks on the light, sets her backpack beside the desk, which, unlike the metal desk in her office at the IFS, is made of wood, as are the bookshelves, the filing cabinet, and the chair in which she sits. On a ledge above the radiator sits the stuffed beaver Sam gave her the year they met—the beaver being the mascot of MIT.

That year, the year they met, Maxine had been twenty-one and Sam four years her senior. He had just started work for an affable if demanding Iranian engineer who had been commissioned by the United Nations to come up with low-cost methods of manufacturing building materials in developing countries. Whenever Sam got frustrated, he would go out and pace the Harvard Bridge. This was Maxine's first year studying for a degree in a field the university called Science, Technology, and Society and her classmates in engineering called Good Luck Finding a Job. She would be sitting in her cubicle at the library when her anxiety would build to such a pitch she jumped from her seat, abandoned her notebooks and pens, even her precious new TI-30 calculator, and jogged to the Longfellow Bridge, past its salt-and-pepper-shaker towers, along the Boston side of the Charles, past the sailing club and the bandshell, then back across the Harvard Bridge to the library, where, panting now, calmer, she felt able to confront whatever problem she had been trying to get a grip on, as if her mind had been working all along, the way the pickerel, eels, and alewives had been carrying on their lives beneath the shadowy surface of the Charles River even as she jogged past them.

Sadly, she knew as much about proper running technique as those pickerel and eels knew. The day she met Sam, she took too big a leap and landed awkwardly. She winced, then hop-skip-hopped across the bridge, trying not to put too much weight on the damaged ankle. When a reedy, bearded stranger asked if she needed help, her impulse was to tell him no. She had just spent four years surrounded by men who gazed at her across a laboratory, hoping she might ask their assistance connecting a circuit or debugging a program. Even if she had been crawling across that bridge with four shattered limbs and a machete protruding from her back, she would have insisted she was fine.

But she couldn't tell this stranger no. He was like some dog that had been trained its whole life to assist a human in need. Although Sam told her later the opposite was the case. He was determined to avoid the trap the world sets for the children of alcoholics. Namely, turning them into world-class rescuers. What attracted him was Maxine's obvious determination *not* to be rescued. Plus, he liked the way she had piled her hair atop her head, so he could see the sweat bubbling on her neck. He would have an excellent excuse to settle her on a bench, unlace her shoe, hold her swelling foot and ask, "Does this hurt? Does that?"

Maxine didn't yet know that this man had a penchant for women's feet. Any more than she knew they would marry and have a son and live together for twenty-four mostly harmonious years before he expired from a particularly virulent strain of West Nile virus he picked up while trying to make a new ultrafine mosquito netting available to every family in Nigeria. Lacking such clairvoyance, she had looped her arm around his back and they staggered across the bridge as if competing in some slow-motion three-legged sack race. Until then, her experience had been that men expected you to match your rhythm to theirs. Girls were taught to walk smoothly—her home ec teacher ticked off marks in a book as each female member of their seventh-grade class crossed the room with a yardstick balanced atop her head—while boys were left to develop whatever swagger or slink or gallop allowed them to cross a room without damaging the furniture or themselves. She had no idea what gay men did, who matched his gait to whose. But heterosexual men assumed their female partners would swagger or slink or gallop in tandem with them. With the few men she dated before Sam, they tripped each other up, elbows and hips colliding. So she was astonished when Sam matched his gait to hers. She worried he might be put off by her funk. But Sam loved a woman's funk. Having been raised by WASPs who equated strong scents with the lower classes, he longed for the reek of body odor, onions, garlic, curry. On his trips abroad, he told Maxine later, he enjoyed nothing more than wandering an outdoor market. A woman would pass, and the oils in her hair, mingled with the smoke clinging to her robes, turned him on so much he needed to fight the urge to run after her.

Still, like most engineers, especially those who attended all-boy high schools, he hardly was adept at pickups. He asked Maxine if she knew the bridge they were crossing was under-strength for the load it was carrying. "Whenever I'm on this bridge and I see a bus and truck cross at the same time, I consider the very real possibility I'll end up going for a swim."

The bridge vibrated ominously beneath their feet.

"Do you know about the smoots?" He pointed to the markings along the walkway, and Maxine didn't have the heart to say she knew all about Oliver Smoot and the way, one drunken night, he had been laid end-to-end by his fraternity-mates so they could inscribe his measurements on the bridge, with the nearly mystical result that its length in smoots equaled the number of days in a year. (The length of the Harvard Bridge turned out to be 364.4 smoots, "plus or minus an ear," as some wag had painted on the macadam nearest MIT.) And yet, Maxine lied and told Sam no. This admission of false ignorance surprised her. Back then, she was more likely to pretend to know something she didn't than feign ignorance of something she did. She wasn't a braggart. But the men at MIT assumed she knew nothing at all.

"I shouldn't admit this," Sam said, "but I have a soft spot for the guy. My middle name is Oliver." Which was something of a tease because he hadn't revealed his first or last names. "And we both stand five feet, seven inches tall." Which made Maxine an inch shy of a smoot herself. "What I admire is the way he allowed himself to be picked up and carried along. He let a prank define his fate. The guy trained to be a lawyer. But do you know what he actually did become?"

This time, her ignorance was sincere.

"The president of the International Organization of Standardization. The man could have lived his life as a short, round lawyer with a funny name. Instead, he became the worldwide King of Measurements. He made the name 'Oliver Smoot' immortal."

They passed the final smoot mark. Sam ushered her to a bench. Prince Charming in reverse, he knelt and unlaced her cheap red Ked. She considered jerking away her leg. But she derived a weird pleasure from the sight of this man caressing her bare foot. If her rescuer turned out to be a fetishist, would that make her his fetishee?

Sam must have thought better of the whole sordid affair. He dropped her foot and ran to fetch his car. She felt foolish driving off with a man she had just met. But cell phones hadn't been invented. Besides, she was so new to Cambridge she hadn't made any friends. When Sam pulled up in his wimpy blue VW bug, what could she do but allow him to transport her back across the bridge to the emergency room at Mass General? The doctor applied a cast. Sam drove her home and helped her up the three flights to her apartment. He ran out and bought her groceries, along with the latest issue of *Scientific American*. In the weeks that followed, he drove her back and forth to school, brought her sandwiches from the deli across the street and ice cream from Emack & Bolio. She was desperate to be kissed. But the WASP code of conduct apparently forbade a man from taking advantage of a lady's injured ankle. He waited until the cast had been sawn off. Then, standing at the bottom of her stairs, knowing he would never again have an excuse to help her up them, he asked if she wanted to go see *Superman*.

"Sure," she said. They drove to Copley Square, then sat paralyzed by desire through a movie they would go on to quote for the entirety of their married lives. *Who am I?* one of the two might ask. And the other would respond: *Your name is Kal-El. You are the only survivor of the planet Krypton. Even though you have been raised as a human, you are not one of them. You have great powers, only some of which you have as yet discovered.*

After Christopher Reeve had saved the planet by revving it backwards in time, Sam drove her home. She led him upstairs, limping from habit.

"Don't worry," he said, laying her across the bed. "I promise I won't hurt you."

"I believe you," she said. Because even then she knew he couldn't inflict the slightest pain on her without suffering the same pain, reflected doubly, on himself. What she couldn't have predicted was he would leave in such a way that he wasn't around to feel the pain he caused by leaving.

Neither of the two men Maxine had slept with before Sam

approached her with such determination. It was as if he were
trying to persuade an important piece of apparatus to light up
and buzz. And, before Sam, she hadn't felt nearly so eager to
light up or buzz. Neither of them considered themselves to be
people who could achieve the erotic bliss they saw movie stars
achieve—or simulate achieving—on the screen. But here they
were, entwining in a superintuitive, synergistic collaboration
that left each feeling more human, more real, than either had
felt before.

They married. They moved to Ann Arbor. True, Sam's
appointment was much more prestigious than her own. The
Residential College had seen its glory days in the sixties and now
served as a repository for any oddball spousal hire the university
didn't know what to do with. But Maxine couldn't have been
more content. The students at the RC seemed more receptive
to her classes on the effects of technology on human behavior
and psychology than would have been the case elsewhere at
the university. She and Sam would spend the week teaching,
conducting their research, grading papers. Then, on weekends,
they would loll in bed past noon, satisfying their desire, rise, and
spend the remainder of the day canoeing the Huron River, sniff-
ing vegetables at the farmer's market, or drifting from painting
to painting at the museum in Detroit. Come Monday, she and
Sam would shower in the same stall, then dress and walk to
school, kissing on the Diag before heading to their respective
offices. Who wouldn't love waking to a life like that?

After Zach was born, she grew happier yet. She would nod
off in the middle of a feeding, only to wake and find her son
snuggled between her breasts, fragrant and warm as a loaf of
newly baked bread. When he grew old enough to escape his
crib, she would discover Zach's face at the edge of her mattress,

willing her to open her eyes and pull him up, where she tickled him through the soft cotton of his pajamas, printed with cars or airplanes. She packed him off to daycare, then set to work on her first book, so she wouldn't be disgraced when she came up for tenure. In later years, she rose each morning eager to meet the challenges of directing the institute she had come to see as the fulfillment of her childhood dreams.

Then Sam died, and whatever neurochemical fizz kept her excited to be alive got zapped out in the storm. Friends tried to fix her up. But she couldn't summon the energy to meet someone new. Just as Oliver Smoot became the unit by which the world measured the Harvard Bridge, Maxine's dead husband assumed the measure of what a man was meant to be.

Occasionally, she still teaches a course in the Residential College or meets a student here for a tutorial. But she avoids spending time in this office as much as possible. She doesn't want to be reminded of all the afternoons she and Sam made love on the grimy wood floor, her husband grinding into her as she prayed the janitor wouldn't choose that moment to unlock the door and empty the trash. Once, as Sam was extricating himself from her arms so he could hurry back to meet with a Global Initiatives donor, she had said, "Why do you get to direct an institute and I don't?"

He admitted she had a point. "No one is going to say: 'Now, there goes a woman who deserves to direct an institute!' But if you come up with an idea and ask the university to help you start it —"

Oh, come on, she had said. The only reason the university hired her in the first place was she was a bargaining chip to get him to accept his offer.

"Sure," Sam said. "But then you surprised them. You pub-

lished a book. You earned tenure. If a female faculty member pro-
poses an institute, and they look around and see that every other
institute at the university is directed by a man, they'll be embarrassed to turn you down."

She realized he was serious.

"How do you think any other program got started? Someone had the balls to propose a plan."

She had waved toward her nether regions and joked that
the last time she looked, she didn't have any balls to speak of.
But Sam had refused to laugh. "No," he said. "But the last time
I looked, you had a highly intelligent vagina." Then he issued an
assignment: She was to spend the day dreaming up an institute
she wanted to direct. At bedtime, she would present her idea to
him.

Naked as she was, she began describing her idea right then.
She wanted to bring together the best minds of their generation, or the best minds she could find on campus, and set them
figuring out the effect of all these new technologies on the
human soul. With Sam egging her on, she drew up a proposal
and approached the provost—not the provost who occupies the
office now, but kind, scholarly Terrence Stanford. She wrote
grants. She wooed the trustees of big foundations. She cajoled
her colleagues into joining her. She developed an entirely new
field, the study of immortality. Sam had lived long enough to see
the Institute for Future Studies become reality. But six months
after it opened, he was felled by that West Nile virus.

The floorboards where she and Sam used to make love
glow so luridly the outline of her husband's body might have
been drawn in chalk. The filing cabinet where she keeps notes
from the classes she used to teach is tacked with Zach's school
portraits from the first to seventh grades. Zach made most of

the frames himself—from Popsicle sticks, acorns, buttons. His face narrows from year to year, skin coarsening, hair growing longer, then shorter, then longer, a boy evolving to a man, like the cartoon series on her door.

Most afternoons when Zach was in elementary school she picked him up and brought him here so he could play games on her computer while she met with students or attended whatever meetings she needed to attend before they could leave for the day. Later, when Zach was in junior high, he walked here on his own. She liked to think he had been as happy spending time with her as she had been to putter around her father's repair shop. Sometimes she and Zach left early and visited the dinosaurs at the museum. A juggler might be practicing on the Diag, or a group of students protesting some injustice.

Still, there had been plenty of afternoons when neither she nor Sam could look after their son. Her mother nagged her to hire a nanny. But Sam didn't want Zach to be coddled the way he had been coddled as a child. By seventh grade, Zach had refused to be minded by a sitter anyway. With Sam traveling so often, she had allowed Zach to spend too many hours playing video games. That was why she asked Thaddy to hang around with him after school. She ought to have been warier. But she hoped the two lonely young men, despite the differences in their ages, would be good for each other. At least they would keep each other company.

She takes out a blue cardboard file labeled "Ethics of the New Technologies, Fall 2002." Along with the usual texts on the sociological implications of robots displacing workers and the effects of social media on our attention spans, she required her students to read Herman Melville's brilliant but depressing "Bartleby, the Scrivener," along with equally bleak works by Kafka, Huxley,

Wells, Pynchon, Dostoevsky, and yes—she feels a chill—at the bottom of the list, *The Secret Agent* by Joseph Conrad.

Hands shaking, she leafs through her lecture notes. Beneath these, she discovers the essays three of her students handed in but didn't pick up. That used to hurt her feelings. Didn't they care what she had to say? These days, she comments on her students' papers digitally. (On the rare occasions she writes by hand, she finds herself driven mad by how slowly her fingers move and the failure of the page to correct her typos.) This arrangement is more convenient, but it means her students will have no physical copies of their papers. Years from now, they will come across no yellowing essays or blue books prompting them to marvel how much smarter they were in college, how devoted to reading a difficult text and pondering what it meant. They won't have mementoes of their professors, as Maxine treasures her own professors' handwritten notes.

Thaddy had typed his final paper. But he penciled his name across the top, the printing spiky and cramped, as if he were writing Hebrew. On the back page he had written this note: "You are the only actual human being on this campus. Merry Christmas. Or happy Hanuka (sp?). I will stop by later to pick this up. Thaddy R."

Everything comes rushing back. The way, eleven years ago this past September, she had stopped by the mailroom to pick up the roster for her seminar. The way she noticed, toward the end of the list, the name "Thaddeus Rapaczynski," which she looked forward to pronouncing correctly because the shop teacher in her hometown used to pound a hammer on a nail to drive home the proper pronunciation of his name: Mr. *Rap-rap-rap*-a-chin-ski. The way, when the class gathered around the seminar table that first afternoon, Thaddy signaled by his expression how little he wanted to be there. How much smarter he was than his fellow students. How much more deeply he had considered the topics they would be discussing. When she handed out the syllabus, Thaddy snorted. When they discussed the reasons for the recent Y2K panic, he sat shaking his head, no doubt because Maxine's knowledge of the technical shortcuts that might have led to a crisis was so limited.

At the end of the second class, she had asked Thaddeus if he would drop by to see her. He didn't seem surprised, as if he guessed she wanted to lecture him on his failure to be agreeable. A few days later, he shuffled into her office—this one, at the Residential College—and stood by the door, having fulfilled his end of the bargain by showing up.

"So," she had started. "Can I ask why you signed up for my class if you are not interested in the material? Or don't you think I'm qualified to teach the course?"

He seemed taken aback by her honesty. Flustered, he crumpled to the one extra chair in her office and clasped his big, knuckly hands between his knees. He was a graduate student in mathematics, Thaddy said. The university had this idiotic rule that everyone, no matter his department, was required to take a class outside his area of expertise. At one time, Thaddy might have welcomed the chance to explore his other interests. But he already had accomplished enough research to earn his doctorate, having published two seminal papers in a field called Boundary Functions, which, he told Maxine, she couldn't possibly understand. All he wanted was to finish his degree and leave. He had chosen her seminar because it was the only class that appealed to the questions he had been considering on his own. But then he had seen the reading list. Why had she assigned fiction? Novels and short stories were based on nothing but emotion. An author could spout any sort of speculative nonsense without subjecting his statements to rigorous logic or empirical evidence.

Maxine allowed Thaddy to express his views. She humored him—to a point. He was correct in assuming literature couldn't be proved. But if one's object was to study the effects of technology on human society, then the emotions of the humans who were being influenced by that technology might be worthy of analysis. Maybe, if Thaddy examined his reactions to her seminar, he would find that his disappointment had little to do with the material but rather with the class being taught by a female professor. Sexism wasn't logical. But even the most rational mind might be blighted by such a flaw.

Thaddy's face—square jawed, a cleft in the chin—seemed locked tight as a safe to which even the owner couldn't remember the combination.

Then he emitted a strangled sound and the safe flew open. What it was holding inside was pain. Why didn't women ever like him? What was he doing wrong? The undergraduates in his classes hated him. He was a good teacher. Really! He prepared hours for every class! He was shy, that was all. He wasn't a performer. He didn't like making jokes. When he did make a joke, the students just sat there. They wrote mean comments on his evaluations. Was it his fault they preferred a clown, an entertainer, to someone who wanted to convey the beauties of the mathematics they were supposed to learn?

He looked so baffled, so hurt, Maxine wanted to assure him a woman would fall in love with him. There was something wounded about him, sure. He was too intense. But he was a surprisingly handsome man. He was like the quiet, brainy guy you got assigned to in your electronics lab. You hadn't really noticed him. But when you were huddled over the same hunk of circuits, trying to make sense of the wiring, you realized how good-looking he was. How determined to make you like him.

Still, she was his professor, not his therapist. She said that trying to be entertaining while teaching math must be frustrating. After that, she simply listened. Which, she suspected, his fellow mathematicians rarely did.

What he said was that he had grown up in an immigrant neighborhood in west Chicago. His parents had sacrificed everything to escape Communist Poland. His mother had been a homemaker. His father worked at a sausage factory. But they were the only residents on their block who weren't mired in the backward views of the Catholic Church. They spoke grammatically correct English—Thaddy's own accent betrayed only the high-pitched vowels of the winds blowing off the lake in his native city. They didn't oppose integration in the schools; they welcomed it. They took Thaddy and his younger brother to museums, ball games, concerts. When Thaddy demonstrated a precocious ability in mathematics, they insisted he be skipped not one grade, but two.

"I felt like a freak," Thaddy said. "I felt like a smart little mouse that got sent into a cage every day for the cats to play with."

She couldn't recall which details Thaddy told her that first afternoon and which he revealed on his later visits. But she knew he had been hectored by his parents not only to earn high grades but to prove himself socially popular. A real American teenage boy. To please his parents, Thaddy joined the Boy Scouts. But he hated the uniforms and thought the adult leaders creepy and dumb. He signed up for the chess club and the math club. He took up trombone and joined the band. But there wasn't a single girl in either club, and he felt too shy to approach his female bandmates. His father was a distant, demanding man—not the sort of father who might give advice on what to say to a girl. Besides, when would Thaddy have found the time to hang around with normal kids? How, when his parents pushed him so hard to make them proud of their little genius?

The only time he hadn't been bullied was when he was adopted as a mascot by the older boys in his chemistry class. They allowed him to pal around because he did their homework. But he hated those guys. Once, they doused a cat with alcohol, then set the poor animal on fire. They tried the same experiment on a drunk they found passed out in the baseball dugout behind the school. Panicked, Thaddy ran off. He didn't think the man died. But he vowed he would never hang out with those boys again, no matter how often his parents asked why he was sitting alone on a Friday night rather than going out with the nice new friends he had made at school.

Finally, the boys pressured Thaddy into using his knowledge to set off an explosion in their chemistry class. "I didn't want to," Thaddy said. "But they were bigger and older. How could I tell them no?" They wanted Thaddy to destroy enough equipment so they wouldn't have to do any more experiments that year. But he engineered a bomb that would just make a loud noise and a lot of smoke. The teacher figured out who was to blame. What other student was smart enough to build a bomb? Thaddy knew better than to rat out his classmates, so he was the only student to be suspended.

"Too bad the suspension didn't go on my record," Thaddy said. His high school had never gotten a student into a really good college, so the principal made sure the incident didn't ruin Thaddy's chances to be admitted to Harvard. "I wish I had been thrown in jail," Thaddy told Maxine. "I wish, instead of going to Harvard, I went to the community college down the block."

At sixteen, Thaddy had been the youngest in his freshman class. Also, the only student whose father worked at a sausage-making factory. He was treated even more cruelly by the preppies at Harvard than he had been by the jocks in high school. (Maxine flinched: Sam had been a preppy at Harvard, too.) The girls were two years older and far more polished. Thaddy hoped the anti-intellectualism he suffered in high school would be replaced by a dedication to the life of the mind. But the students in Cambridge seemed even more superficial and dedicated to getting drunk.

Sophomore year, Thaddy signed up for a class in behavioral psychology. The professor talked about how neurobiologists would soon be able to hook electrodes to your head and shape your memories. Such knowledge might be used to cure tendencies toward violence or pedophilia. But Thaddy was afraid the government would use these new techniques to make people like him conform to some placid, easy-to-manipulate standard of behavior. How would Big Business resist brainwashing the population into buying whatever useless crap they might be selling?

The professor asked if anyone wanted to participate in an experiment. Thaddy, who was desperately poor, signed up. Not only did he need the cash, he wanted to prove his professor's theories wrong.

Instead, what happened was that the professor's team of graduate students locked Thaddy in a room and forced him to answer question after question designed to elicit his reaction to every possible social situation. Over the following year, they used a series of punishments and rewards to reprogram his responses. When Maxine pressed him for an example, Thaddy said, "I can't. It was too humiliating. I felt like a puppy who took a shit on the floor and got his nose rubbed in his own excrement." What was worse, the system worked. After two semesters of being subjected to their experiments, Thaddy found himself responding in ways the graduate students trained him to respond.

Maxine had no way of verifying what Thaddy said. But neither did she disbelieve him. He might have been an angry, eccentric young man. But he didn't seem delusional. He would have dropped out of society a long time ago, he told her. But even a bare-bones existence required enough money to purchase a few isolated acres, build a cabin, and buy whatever necessities he couldn't grow or make himself. That was why he was studying for his PhD. He hoped to find a job that would allow him to save enough money so he could give up his position and live for himself rather than to please his parents or feed the maw of the corporate-military-industrial complex.

In the meantime, he said, his life wasn't so terrible. The other mathematicians were as nerdy as he was. No one taunted him. What drove him crazy was that even the other nerds succeeded in attracting girlfriends. The one time he persuaded a young Korean statistics major to join him for coffee, the afternoon ended in disaster. When Thaddy walked her to her bus, he tried to kiss her. She pushed him off and told him even though he was a "nice boy" and "highly intelligent," she was interested in no more than friendship. Upset, he tried to board the bus so he could apologize. But he didn't have his wallet or student ID, so he needed to race back to his room, find the card, and take a later bus. Getting off at the development where the woman lived, he wandered around asking if anyone knew the smart Korean mathematician with the long black hair. When he happened to run into her, she got very upset and told him he was "stalking" her. Later, she complained to his adviser she was "uncomfortable" having an office on the same hall as Thaddy, and he was moved to a different floor.

"What did she think I was going to do, corner her in her office and attack her?" Sure, he hoped she might kiss him back. But if she didn't, he at least wanted to know someone might care for him, as a friend.

Maxine took this as a hint. The more he stopped by to talk, the more she came to think he saw her as the mother he wished he'd had. A mother who didn't care about his grades. Who didn't criticize him for his tendency to stammer and slouch and crack his knuckles. So many young men were desperate to escape their mothers, Maxine thought. But they were desperate to be loved and approved of by those same mothers. They ran away as soon as they were old enough to escape. But they craved a woman's touch. They tried to attract a girlfriend. If they couldn't, their rage at all women—mothers, girlfriends, bosses—amplified to ominous proportions.

So yes, she had wanted to be Thaddy's mother. Or, like most teachers, she had given in to the temptation to save a student no one else seemed willing or able to save.

To delay reading Thaddy's long final paper, she refreshes her memory of Conrad's novel. She has reread it every semester she has taught the course. But never with an eye toward determining whether it might have inspired a terrorist to send explosives to a dozen victims. She reads again about Mr. Verloc, who pretends to be an anarchist while serving as the agent of a foreign power. Called in by his handler, Verloc is ordered to blow up the Greenwich Observatory, which might cause the British government to crack down on his fellow anarchists. If a terrorist blows up a church, the public might see the perpetrator as hating religion. If he blows up a palace, the terrorist might be expressing his resentment of the rich. If he assassinates an official, he might be protesting a specific party. But to strike at science itself? Whoever aims a bomb at science must be determined to sweep away the most rational basis of society.

As Maxine recalls, Thaddy also had been attracted to a character named Karl Yundt, who ranted about the need for a band of men to free themselves of compassion and enlist death in the service of all humanity. The students in Maxine's class debated whether such a band of revolutionaries might be justified in destroying fossil-fuel plants if this meant preventing millions of human deaths and animal extinctions from global warming. Thaddy supported one side of the argument. The rest of Maxine's class argued for the other.

"How can you not see I'm right?" Thaddy had demanded. "How can you not justify a few deaths now to ward off a massive disaster later?"

Thaddy had grown so vehement Maxine prohibited him from mentioning Yundt's band of destroyers or writing about them further. In response, Thaddy shifted the topic of his fascination—and his long final paper—to Conrad's creepiest creation, "the Professor." Unattractive, lacking in social graces, the Professor had turned his intellectual gifts toward designing the perfect detonator for a bomb. To avoid capture, he rigged up a device such that, if he were threatened with arrest, he could press a rubber bulb in his pocket and blow himself up, along with anyone in his vicinity. Shabby and insignificant, the Professor nonetheless exerted a fearsome power stemming from his disdain for conventional morality and his willingness to blow himself up to attain his aims.

Maxine remembers being shocked by Thaddy's admiration for such a character. At the time, she told herself he was only playing the devil's advocate. But Thaddy maintained that Conrad, whether intentionally or against his will, had created a man who embodied an unassailable position. If technology was destroying the planet, then violence in the service of destroying that technology must be acceptable. After all, if a despot like Hitler threatened to destroy millions of innocent citizens, wouldn't assassination prove the moral course? Any compassion a revolutionary might feel toward his victim needed to be replaced by logically based ideals.

Maxine disagreed. Violence was rarely, if ever, justified. The Professor had invented his ideology as an excuse to take revenge on a society that scorned him because he was ugly and short. Surely there was someone Thaddy loved? Someone whose suffering evoked compassion he couldn't dismiss as the result of childhood brainwashing?

No. He felt nothing toward anyone.

Not even his parents?

Thaddy had shaken his head. Then his expression softened. "My brother. He promised he would run away with me. There was this nice piece of land I found. We were going to give up the stupid, soul-killing lives we managed to get stuck in. Build a cabin. Live on the land."

Maxine asked Thaddy what had happened. Why hadn't he and his brother run away?

His expression turned to scorn. "He met some woman. She convinced him to go back for a degree in social work. Social work! Now he's just another henpecked husband, rattling on about the ratio of phosphorus and nitrogen in the fertilizer on his lawn and how he's never going to afford his kids' tuition. His wife won't let him go on a camping trip, let alone drop off the grid and live with me."

Again, it seemed Thaddy hated his brother less because

the younger man had sold out than because he had managed
to attract a wife. Like the Professor, Thaddy manufactured an
ideology that would justify his revenge on a world that didn't
recognize his superiority. A world that left him lonely and in so
much pain.

Finally, she feels ready to read Thaddy's paper. After she finishes, she returns to the manifesto. Then back to Thaddy's paper.
By midnight, she can't remember where she has read which
phrases. "Can't be eating your cake and having it too." "Rule
of thumbs." "One felt swoop." "Out of the sky blue clear." She
expects Thaddy to step through the door and laugh in that creaky,
startled way. *Good for you. You're cleverer than I gave you credit for.
I was wondering how long you would need to figure this out.*

But he is never coming back. She did something to humil-
iate him. Or he felt humiliated by something he confessed to.
Something he was embarrassed to have her know. It happened
in mid-December, the days so short that when Thaddy showed
up at her office, Maxine was already dreading the walk home in
the windy dark. Even paler than usual, Thaddy stepped inside
and shut the door.

He couldn't stand it, he said. It did weird things to a person, being so alone. Never being touched. It made you physically
sick. The graduate students who shared the room on the other
side of his wall kept having sex. He could hear them. Moaning.
Calling each other's names. He couldn't take it anymore. If he
didn't feel a woman's arms around him, soon, he was going to
kill himself.

So he had made an appointment with a psychiatrist. He was
going to lie and tell the doctor he wanted to change his sex. You
could do that these days, he told Maxine. You could lie and say
you were a woman who had been born inside a man's body, and

if you convinced the doctors you were unhappy enough, they would give you a bunch of hormones and perform some operation, and, eventually, you became a woman. Then he could be held in a woman's arms. His own arms. But those arms would be a woman's. He no longer would be a man, so maybe he would feel less pain. Maybe, as a woman, he wouldn't feel the same torture. Maybe he would be more attractive. Maybe he would be desired by a man. Or by another woman. He could pretend to be a lesbian. Then again, he wouldn't be pretending. He would be a woman who wanted to be made love to by another woman.

He told Maxine he had waited in the psychiatrist's office for an hour. But when the receptionist called his name, he apologized and ran out. Afraid of what he might do in his apartment, listening to his housemates make love, he had hurried to find Maxine, hoping she would be there.

She wasn't sure what to say. Even then she knew Thaddy wasn't really a transsexual. He wasn't a woman trapped inside a man's body. He was going to lie and pretend to be one so he could fool the doctors into transforming him into a woman. How could anyone be so starved for a woman's touch he would think of changing his gender—taking hormones, allowing himself to be medically castrated—so he could feel a woman's arms around him? His *own* arms. She pictured Thaddy in his room. The same square-jawed, masculine face. But with long hair and a woman's breasts. Crossing his now-feminine arms across his chest. That afternoon, in her office, he had been wearing his usual button-down shirt and khakis trousers, his skin whiter and smoother than actual flesh. The sweat stood out on his forehead like water on a plastic shower curtain.

"Oh, Thaddy," she had said. "A woman—a real, actual woman—will fall in love with you. You just need to be patient.

You have so much to offer."

"Yeah?" he said. "Like what."

"Well," she said, "you clearly are going to be very successful in your field. A lot of women will find that compelling. And—I don't mean to be inappropriate—you're a very good-looking man. Someday, you will meet a woman . . ." She didn't know how to put it. A woman who would be as awkward and inexperienced as he was? A woman who would love to be loved as much as Thaddy? "A woman who will appreciate you for who you are."

"Right. Just like I had girls falling all over me because I was the star of the math club in high school. I *am* smart. And I do care. But none of that matters. No woman could ever love me. No one!"

He was hunched over, crying in his hands. He was only ten or twelve years older than her son. Her arms physically ached to hold him.

But professors weren't supposed to hug their students. Especially not graduate students as good-looking as Thaddy. She told herself she would be hugging him not as his professor but as his mother. But she wasn't Thaddy's mother. She had always sensed some degree of sexual tension between them. He had been, what, twenty-three to her forty-four. But back then, she could have passed for her early thirties. What if Thaddy took her embrace the wrong way? Every rule in the book forbade physical contact between a student and a professor. Especially in an office with the door shut and the blinds drawn. After a conversation so heavily freighted with sexual content.

She had sat there so long he grew embarrassed. She wanted to suggest he check himself into the hospital. But she couldn't bear to think of him confined to a locked ward with a bunch of psychotic inmates. Instead, she urged him to make an appointment at student services. How could she have been so stupid? Thaddy would never have consented to being counseled by a female social worker barely older than he was.

He mumbled that he wasn't serious. Fooling the doctors into making him a woman was only a passing idea that scared him. He never would have gone through with such a crazy plan.

He left. He didn't show up for their final seminar. He handed in his portfolio by slipping it beneath her door. She sent him emails begging him to stop by to talk. Clearly, he had been mortified that his professor had seen him at his weakest. Or maybe he was angry she had failed to provide what any decent human being would have given him. Maybe, if she had taken Thaddy in her arms, she would have prevented his later violence. Unless that was only another form of her messiah complex.

No, she didn't see herself as a messiah. She saw herself as Mother Mary, holding the suffering, broken Christ in her arms. Given how lonely and confused Thaddy must have been to consider what he was considering, what could she have done to assuage his misery? Maybe she was at fault for assigning all those depressing books. For adding fuel to Thaddy's worries about technology. Feeding him with statistics. But half the students she taught had parents worse than Thaddy's. Parents who pressured them to earn good grades, to justify the sacrifices the parents had made as immigrants. A significant number were as lonely and starved for love. They were as anguished about the damage to the environment, the negative effects of industrialization and technology. But they hadn't reacted by becoming terrorists.

And Thaddy hadn't gone directly from her office to building bombs. He had remained on campus for another year, at least, finishing his degree. From what she could tell—she pulled out her laptop and googled Thaddy—he had been hired as an assistant professor at Berkeley. He taught there two years, then resigned. A year after that, someone left a package in the parking lot outside the Berkeley engineering school, with the return address of a professor in that department. A diligent employee returned it to the supposed sender; when the man's secretary opened the box, a pipe bomb ripped off her arm.

Maxine barely remembers that first incident. But she does recall the second, which nearly took down a plane. And the third, which targeted Arnold Schlechter. And the fifth bombing, after which the FBI released that sketch. The man in the aviator sunglasses and hooded sweatshirt looked nothing like Thaddy. Never in a million years would it have occurred to Maxine to suspect her student. Until that morning, she would have had no more reason to associate the bomber's manifesto with Thaddeus Rapaczynski than with a host of students and colleagues who entertained similar dissatisfactions. If not for the quote from Conrad. If not for the phrases that reverberated in her mind as Thaddy's.

She goes back online and studies the list of computer experts, airline executives, oil company CEOs, and manufacturers of pharmaceuticals who have been the bomber's targets. Slowly, he had progressed from sending simple pipe-bombs to devices with increasingly effective detonators, until he sent his first lethal package to a professor at Harvard who believed he could brainwash people into good behavior. Had this been the professor who used Thaddy as a guinea pig? She assumes it was. And yet nothing could justify the man receiving a bomb that blew off his hand and severely injured his wife and two young daughters.

Afraid she might pass out, she puts her head to her knees, then slumps to the bare wood floor where she and her husband made love. How did she allow her son to hang around with Thaddy? To *continue* hanging around with him, even after Thaddy revealed his plan to change his gender? Thaddy hadn't gone through with his crazy scheme. But what he confided to Maxine that day proved how unbalanced he really was.

Her mother's suspicion that Thaddy had sexual designs on Zach can't be true. Can it? What Thaddy craved was a woman's touch. Okay, if he was so desperate for sex he considered changing himself to a woman, he might have been willing to overlook her young son's gender. Zach had never been effeminate. But he had been so gentle. So thin. So ethereally beautiful, as only an adolescent boy can be.

No. That never had been the danger. The two young men met right here in her office. Zach had been playing video games on her computer when Thaddy stopped by to discuss whatever text Maxine had assigned that week. Zach was, what, thirteen? He had given up hanging out with his childhood friends—he wouldn't tell her why, just that he preferred playing on his computer, although she later found out the other boys had taken to using drugs, pressuring Zach to hide their stashes. The only boy he remained friends with was Norm, who was so far behind Zach in his emotional development they couldn't talk about much except World of Warcraft. At thirteen, Zach considered himself too old for a babysitter, but he was too young to be left on his own for extended periods. She and Sam had been trying to figure out a solution, but Sam had flown off to Zimbabwe, and as usual, Maxine had been stressed by her obligations at work. Thaddy must have seen himself in her son. Or he saw Zach as a younger brother to replace the brother who had deserted him by getting married. Whatever his reasons, Thaddy offered to take Zach to the Arboretum.

"Come on, champ," Thaddy said. "Let's do something more fun than sitting in front of a computer." Zach looked to his mother for permission. She shrugged and said why not, as long as Thaddy had Zach home for dinner. She saw no reason to be suspicious. Not then. This had been months before Thaddy confessed about wanting to change his gender. The Arb was walking distance from her office. So even though Thaddy and Zach hadn't made it home until six-fifteen, she hadn't been too upset. On the contrary, she invited Thaddy inside to join them. But he hung back. He might not have known Sam was out of town. Or he did know, and he figured he would feel out of place sitting at the table with Maxine and Zach, as if they were a mockery of a family. Or maybe he just felt shy.

At dinner, Zach prattled on about how Thaddy had shown him which plants were safe to eat and which were poisonous. How Thaddy talked to him about the reasons you were wasting your life if you spent your time playing make-believe games in a computer world. How, in most cultures, a boy, in order to become a man, needed to survive in nature. Maxine had never seen her son with such a healthy glow in his cheeks. Never had he gone up to bed without needing to be hectored into it.

She ought to be have been warier. But Zach begged her to let him camp out with Thaddy. This was the last warm week in October. Reluctantly, she agreed. Sam, who had returned from his trip, was all in favor of Zach spending more time outdoors. He pooh-poohed her concern that the city didn't allow camping in the park. But the next morning, when Zach straggled home on his bike, he seemed filthy and ravenous. When Maxine demanded to know why, he blurted that Thaddy hadn't brought a tent. Not only that, he tried to prevent Zach from eating the peanut butter sandwich and banana he brought from home, insisting they get by on the roots they foraged and the fish they snagged from the Huron River. Zach had the good sense to eat the sandwich and the banana. But when Maxine said she didn't think Zach should hang out with Thaddy anymore, Zach had seemed incredulous. "Are you kidding? That would hurt Thaddy's feelings! Thaddy and I are friends! He's right about not wasting your life playing stupid video games. He already taught me an amazing amount of important stuff." On and on, until Maxine promised they could keep hanging out after school.

Her mother was right. She ought to have been suspicious that a young man in his twenties would want to befriend a boy of thirteen. Now that she thinks about it, that was around the same time Zach began to argue with Sam, to protest that his father was bringing all the bad stuff from America to poorer countries that would be better off without factories that polluted their rivers and ruined their forests and isolated people from their families and homes. He must have picked that up from Thaddy.

Then Sam died, and her memory got even blurrier. Crippled by her own grief, she neglected her son's. Had Zach still been hanging around with Thaddy? After Thaddy left for Berkeley, had he and Zach remained in touch? By the time Zach graduated from MIT and moved to Oakland, Thaddy hadn't taught at Berkeley for, what, five or six years? Then again, Thaddy might still have been living in the Bay Area. Maybe he had shown up in Silicon Valley and gotten in touch with Zach. Maybe he persuaded Zach to quit his job and run away with him.

Unless they had been in touch the entire time. Which could

mean Zach knew about the bombings.

No. That couldn't be true. Thaddy had kidnapped Zach. Or blackmailed him into leaving. Maybe Thaddy had shown up and begged Zach for money, and Zach wasn't willing to tell him no.

The room spins, the two young men blending with each other. Then they blend with a third young man, a character from Conrad's novel, Winnie Verloc's weak-minded younger brother, Stevie. So good-hearted, so idealistic, he couldn't bear to see horses beaten, or hear about criminals being branded with an iron, or capitalists "nourishing their greed on the quivering flesh and the warm blood of the people." She thinks about Zach refusing to eat because children in Malawi were starving. Zach walking around Mexico City on a family vacation, picking up trash and crying because there was nowhere to put it. She remembers how Thaddy taught Zach to make a baking-soda rocket. How thrilled Zach was when the rocket cleared the house. Did Thaddy use the same ingenuity to teach Zach to make explosives? Did he pressure Zach to help him manufacture bombs, the way the older kids pressured Thaddy into setting off an explosion in their chemistry class, or the way Mr. Verloc manipulated young Stevie into carrying the Professor's bomb to the Greenwich Observatory, where Stevie tripped on a root and blew himself up? Is it her fault if Thaddy and Zach took her ideas more seriously than she took them herself? Should she have been more freaked out by her son's extreme compassion? Should she have taken him to a psychiatrist?

Maybe she and Sam had pressured Zach in the same unreasonable way Thaddy's parents pressured him. Not only to succeed in school, but to demonstrate his empathy for those less fortunate than himself. Every morning, along with those decadent breakfasts, Sam had served up the day's injustices. How many times had he recounted the Story of the Exploding Stove? After college, Sam had gone backpacking around the world. In Tanzania, he had become intimate with a family whose son had been grotesquely burned when their improvised stove blew up. Watching the boy writhe in agony, Sam realized that if God didn't exist, and Sam was sure He didn't, the child's suffering didn't matter. Of course it mattered to the boy and his parents. But in the context of infinite time and space, nothing that happened on this puny speck could be said to matter. The thought was so horrifying Sam had sunk to his knees and vowed that if the boy's suffering didn't matter to anyone but the boy and his family, it damn well better matter to him. He swore to spend his life finding ways to bring safe, low-cost technology— affordable, fuel-efficient stoves that wouldn't explode—to people like this grieving family in Tanzania.

That her husband told this story once or twice made sense. But Sam couldn't help repeating it to their son. Over and over. Compassion was fine. But they rubbed Zach's tender heart raw. They opened him to infection by every passing stranger's pain. To whatever Thaddy taught him.

She needs to alert the FBI. Whoever wrote that manifesto has sworn he will keep killing new victims until the revolution starts. What if Thaddy kills someone while she is dithering about what to do? But how can she turn him in if it means implicating her son? Even if Zach isn't with Thaddy now, the FBI will want to find Zach and question him.

Oh, God. What if Zach is holed up somewhere with Thaddy, whether of his own free will or as a captive, and the agents go barging in, shooting, the way they did at Ruby Ridge and Waco? What if, in the course of a manhunt, Zach's photo gets plastered across the news as an accessory to all those crimes? What if Thaddy is innocent and she ruins not only his life, but Zach's? What if she gets one or both of these young men killed? The story she has been spinning might be nothing but a product of the human tendency to believe we have some relationship to whatever tragedy is playing out on the news. How can it be that of everyone in the world, only *she* has the power to stop the bomb ticking in the corner of the TV screen—the image of a metal sphere with a sputtering fuse on Channel 7, or the phallic stick of dynamite on Channel 2?

She gathers everything related to the seminar—Thaddy's papers, the syllabus, the roster of students, her copy of *The Secret Agent*—and stuffs them in her backpack. She turns out the lights and locks the door. She finds her way through the ghostly corridors and, after a few confused circuits around the block, remembers where she parked the car. But she can't go home. Like Thaddy, she might go mad if she can't be comforted. If she can't be held in another person's arms.

She drives to Ypsilanti, turns down a modest cul-de-sac, and stops in front of Rosa Romanczuk's one-story brick cottage. She switches off the ignition and sits watching her breath fog the windshield. Only then does she notice, parked across the street and a few houses down in a not-very-effective attempt to camouflage that its owner is spending the night at Rosa's, a handcrafted yellow sports car with a vanity license plate that reads THWAITE.

. . . Opens a Package She Knows She Shouldn't

The car grows cold. Ever since she inherited her mother's Buick, the clock on the dash has refused to work. Still, she can sense the minutes pass.

How can Rosa, whose nose twitches at a whiff of insincerity, have become intimate with a man who, before he leaves his house, douses himself in Eau de Pretension? How can a scientist who prides himself on his advice to the nation's presidents tolerate the beliefs of a woman who is convinced she can divine the powers that influence a person's life by studying a pack of cards?

Then again, how moved Rosa must be, seeing a distinguished scientist like John Sebastian Mickelthwaite shorn of his defenses. Crying after an orgasm. Professing his gratitude in her arms. And Mick, relieved of the need to keep up all that pretense. Able to admit his disappointments. Heartbreaks. Failures.

Mick is in his seventies. Doesn't Rosa worry she will be widowed a second time? Technically, Rosa and Mick ought to have let Maxine know about their romance. Probably, they were embarrassed. Or they wanted to spare her envying their companionship. If so, their assumption makes her feel even lonelier.

She ought to drive home. But her bones seem to be dissolving. She stretches sideways and closes her eyes. Time passes. The cold and damp wake her. Her legs and hips are cramped. The stopped clock—it reads 4:35—is close to being right. The yellow sports car is gone. Waking Rosa seems unthinkable.

Maxine walks up the sidewalk and rings the bell. A minute passes. Maybe she should leave. But the light comes on and Rosa opens the door. She doesn't seem to have been asleep. Did Mick just leave? At work, Rosa wears voluminous skirts, embroidered vests, and beaded shawls, so when she comes to the door in a flimsy white nightgown that reveals a faded dove tattooed above her left breast, Maxine thinks her friend has been keeping this a secret, too—that she is a small, aging widow who is raising two sons alone.

"Maxine? You look like you got run over by a bus. Is it Zach? Come in."

For all the times Rosa has been to Maxine's house—in the weeks after Sam's death, and to set up for departmental parties—Maxine has driven to Rosa's house only once, when Rosa's car was in the shop. The cottage, unassuming on the outside, reminds Maxine of Jeannie's home inside the magic bottle on the television show she and her father used to laugh at (or rather, Maxine laughed while her father ogled Jeannie). She follows Rosa through the red-flocked foyer, then down the hall past Rosa's sons' bedrooms. Both boys are studying at Michigan State. They want to follow in their father's footsteps, Dwayne in the music-producing business, Jamal as an entrepreneur who, like his father, wants to revitalize black-owned businesses in Detroit. Rosa must worry even more for their safety than Maxine worries for Zach's. In marrying a man of a different race, Rosa had been trying to create a future that wouldn't be defined by history. But her husband was killed by the blindness of that same history. Even with degrees from MSU, the prospects for two dark-skinned young men living in Detroit are grim.

Rosa fills the kettle. Her broad Slavic face radiates the same hope as the sunflowers on the tablecloth. She settles beside Maxine and rubs her back until Maxine is crying in her arms. That's all anyone wants, isn't it? To be held? Isn't that the best Terror Management System any of us has devised?

Rosa offers Maxine a paper towel to wipe her eyes. "You can't be this upset because you found out I'm fucking that jackass we both know no feminist in her right mind could fall in love with."

Maxine takes deep breaths to stop her shaking. Then she tells Rosa everything she can think to tell her. Rosa makes all the right noises. Expresses amazement, then concern, then shock that Maxine might hold herself responsible for her student's violence. Or think Zach might be mixed up in this madness.

"You don't know my son," Maxine says. "Everything you've ever heard about Zach has come from me. I've been deluding myself for years." Once, she says, she got a call from the principal at Zach's elementary school. Her son tried to set another child on fire. Zach? Maxine had said. My son tried to set another child on fire? How could that be? For goodness' sake, the boy was in kindergarten. What kind of kindergartener would set another child on fire?

The principal ushered her into his office with the gravity of a man about to tell a mother that her child, for the good of society, ought to be kept under lock and key. Zach had lit a match, held it out to another boy, and told him if he took another step, Zach would burn him.

Naturally, Maxine had been appalled. Her son did what?

He threatened to burn another little boy? Where were the adults? Did this happen in a classroom? Where did Zach get the matches?

No, the principal said. The incident had taken place on the playground. Zach's teacher hadn't been present. But Zach didn't deny his victim's claims. Zach refused to divulge where he got the matches. But he admitted he had practiced lighting them in the boys' lavatory, which, on its own, warranted his expulsion.

Maxine asked if Zach offered an explanation for what he did, and the principal glared and said, "Do you really think there is any possible justification for one child threatening to set another child on fire?" He suspended Zach and refused to allow him back unless Maxine took him to a psychologist.

Maxine had found a quivering Zach on the bench outside the principal's office. She knew she should be horrified by what he'd done. And yes, she should make an appointment to have him evaluated by a child psychiatrist.

She had knelt and shaken him by his shoulders. Zach, she said, it is never, ever, okay to hurt another child. You know that! You're not allowed to hit anyone. So how could you think it was all right to set someone on fire? To burn him? You know what you did is very, very wrong. Don't you?

Zach stared stonily ahead and refused to speak.

She told him she knew he wouldn't have threatened to hurt another kid if he hadn't thought he had a good reason. So what was going on? Why did he threaten to set that other child on fire? Even saying the words had made her sick. How could she imply he had a reason?

"They were hurting us!" Zach burst out. "Every day, the bigger boys make us be afraid. They won't let us do *anything*. And they hurt the girls. I mean, they really hurt them! And they hit some of the smaller boys. Especially Norm. I'm not as big or strong as they are. There was nothing I could do."

She asked why he hadn't told the teacher.

But he *had* told the teacher. And Mrs. Barnard said they needed to figure out how to get along. She told the bigger boys to be nice to the younger children. But the older boys got even madder at Zach for tattling. So Zach called a meeting and said the younger kids needed a weapon. So they could protect themselves. Norm made slingshots, but those didn't work. So Zach got the idea one of them should take matches from their house. He knew they weren't allowed to light matches. But they could *say* they would light the matches. They could use the matches to scare the bigger boys. Zach wouldn't really have set Benny on fire, he told his mother. He didn't even know how to light a match! He practiced in the boys' room, and he couldn't get the match to work. All that happened was he got a little smoke out of one match, and he made sure there wasn't any paper in the can before he threw it in. In the end, Zach held out an unlit match and told Benny he would burn him. Benny started to cry, and he ran to tell Mrs. Barnard. "I wouldn't really have burned him!" Zach had sobbed. "But no one was protecting us!"

Maybe she had been wrong, but she told Zach that even though what he had done was very wrong, she understood he had been trying to protect the other kids. When they got home, she confined him to his room. But she ended up bringing him dinner in bed, so it seemed more like a picnic than a punishment. The next morning, she went back to see the principal. Of course, she said, Zach had been wrong to steal those matches, let alone practice lighting them in the restroom. And he certainly had been wrong to hold out a match and threaten to burn another boy. But he hadn't intended to carry through his threat.

And why hadn't the teacher done more to protect the smaller, weaker children from the bigger bullies?

The principal threw her out. "You're fooling yourself," he had warned. In all his years as an administrator, he had never heard of a kindergartener coming up with such a disturbing plan. "Your son has very serious problems! If you cannot recognize that he needs psychological help, then you have problems, too!"

She might have been shamed into taking Zach to a psychiatrist. But Sam wouldn't hear of it. How dare the principal fault their son for standing up to bullies! Were they raising a child who was afraid to protect the weaker members of his community? Zach was six. How could he be expected to understand the true consequences of setting another child on fire? The threat was like saying, "I'm so angry I want to kill you!"

Sam had gone in to talk to the principal. But Sam ended up angering him even more. The other boy's parents threatened to sue the school if Zach wasn't suspended. Which the principal was only too glad to do.

Maxine waits to see which side Rosa will take. Will she say, "They blamed Zach? They threatened to put a six-year-old in jail?" Or will she hint Sam and Maxine were blind that their son was headed down a dangerous path, albeit in the name of righting the world's inequities?

"Listen," Rosa says. "I never met this Thaddy Rapawhosit. I have no way of knowing if he's the lunatic who wrote that gobbledygook in the newspaper, or if you are making too much of some garbled clichés anyone might spout. But I do know your son. I watched him grow up. I do not need special powers to know he has a good heart. And I do not mean a heart so good it tips over into blowing people up. You are his mother! How can you not have as much faith in your son as I do?"

Maxine feels nauseated she even suspected her son of being in cahoots with the crazy bomber. What if Zach finds out his own mother believes him capable of committing such terrible crimes?

The kettle shrieks, which makes Maxine jump up from her chair.

"You have to relax," Rosa tells her. "There's nothing you can do, at least not this early in the morning." She fixes Maxine a cup of tea and slices her some homemade oat-and-walnut bread. "Come on," she urges. "I know you're dying to ask how long Mick and I have been carrying on."

Maxine knows Rosa is only trying to divert her from worrying about Zach. And it does feel good to stop, if only for a minute. "You must hate me for saying all the horrible things I've said about Mick. He's actually a very good man."

Rosa laughs. "When he isn't being a pompous old fool." She crosses her arms across her breasts, as if she only now realizes her tattoo is exposed. "We were going to tell you. Mick doesn't directly supervise me, so I doubted the administration would object. But I hate everyone thinking I'm just some secretary trying to get ahead by sucking a professor's dick."

Maxine is afraid the image of Rosa putting John Sebastian Mickelthwaite's penis in her mouth might make her ill. But the idea of her two friends lying in bed pleasuring each other pleases her, too.

"We haven't been together very long," Rosa says. The relationship started when Mick began asking Rosa for advice about his granddaughter. The girl had been living with his dead daughter's lover. But the man was arrested for selling heroin, so Mick will be adopting the girl and caring for her on his own.

"I couldn't help it," Rosa says. "I saw a side of him none of us has ever seen. And—stop me if this is too much information—one thing led to another. I saw *parts* of him none of us had ever seen." Rosa puts her hand to her mouth. "I'm going to be a grandmother!" The child's name is Risa, which means "laughter" in Spanish. "Don't you just love it? 'Rosa, meet Risa. Risa, meet your new *abuela*, Rosa.' How can I pass that up?"

That her friend has found companionship fills Maxine with joy. But her happiness for her friend fails to calm her panic for her son. "If I don't go to the police right away," she tells Rosa, "Thaddy might kill another victim. But if I do go, how can I keep Zach from getting mixed up in this mess?"

"Listen to me," Rosa says. "You do not know this student is the bomber, let alone that your kind, sweet, beautiful son has heard from the guy since he was, what, fourteen? It would be irresponsible of you to go to the FBI with nothing but your suspicions. You need to go straight home and hire a lawyer. Well, *first* you need to take a shower. After that, you need to find a lawyer."

A lawyer! Maxine doesn't know any lawyers. Except the one who helped her settle Sam's estate. "I guess I could use the university's legal department. If I'm right about Thaddy, they're going to end up getting involved anyway."

"No," Rosa says. "If it comes down to the university covering their ass, their lawyers won't hesitate to throw you to the wolves."

Maxine doesn't care about herself. Even if Thaddy is the bomber, she can't be sent to prison for having taught him. But she doesn't want to hire a lawyer who won't put her son's best interests first. She can just see Zach hobbling down a prison corridor in an orange jumpsuit. As tall as he is, Zach has always walked with a hunch, as if he feels guilty for taking up too much space. Guilty for growing up white, male, straight, middle-class. Maybe prison is where he has always wanted to be. Hobbled. Restrained. Her son will find a way to be useful to the other prisoners. Helping them fight their legal battles. Teaching them to read and write. But he will stand up to the guards. If not on his own behalf then someone else's. Even if he gets out in one piece, the remainder of his life will be in tatters.

"Don't worry," Rosa says "Mick plays golf with the attorney general. He'll find you the best criminal lawyer in Michigan."

"Really?" Maxine says. "He would do that for me?"

"Of course he would!" Rosa says. "There's nothing Mick loves more than doing favors that prove he still has connections to people in high places." Rosa glances at the clock—it's after six, and Maxine knows Rosa needs to get ready for work. Maxine herself has a seven-thirty appointment to meet the provost. And she needs to show up at the nursing home by eight-forty-five to take her mother to get her hair done.

She uses Rosa's bathroom to clean up. Hugs Rosa. Thanks her. Then gets back in her car and drives to campus, where she steers her mother's giant old Buick into the garage behind the institute. Up and up she drives, maneuvering the LeSabre along each narrow ramp. This is why she usually walks or bikes to work. There are never enough spaces. Employees like Rosa who live too far to walk or bike need to waste hours searching for a parking space or waiting for the bus. Why is she studying immortality? The quality of most people's lives is determined by their ability to get to work on time, with a minimum of frustration.

She emerges from the dark, dank garage into a Michigan morning so humid she might as well be living inside one of

Zach's terrariums. Since when does April in Michigan feel so tropical?

When she pushes through the frosted doors to the institute, the first thing she notices is the stack of packages. Ordinarily, Deidre, the receptionist, would have sorted the previous day's deliveries. But Deidre is still on maternity leave, and Rosa left early to price venues for the fundraiser. (Pairing Rosa and Mick on the fundraising team had been Maxine's idea, hadn't it? Mick would provide the contacts, Rosa the know-how. Unless they came up with the idea themselves?) Even before she notices her name on the top package, she recognizes Zach's name in the upper-left-hand corner, followed by his address in Oakland. The wrapping is fashioned from a grocery bag, the way Sam taught Zach to cover his schoolbooks. They even used grocery bags to wrap presents, except for the year Zach's class sold wrapping paper to raise money to replace the pirate ship.

She touches the box, lightly, with her fingertips. Was it only the day before that Mick warned her not to open any suspicious packages? She lowers her palm, pressing it to the address. How can she not open a package from her son?

Then again, if Zach wanted to send a package, why wouldn't he send it to their house? Why a package and not a call? Maybe the contents are so valuable he doesn't want the gift to sit on their porch. But how can he afford to buy a gift if he asked Norm to steal those savings bonds?

The package—the size of a cigar box—lies sandwiched between her hands. She shakes it—carefully. If a box this small explodes, how badly might she be hurt?

She carries it to her office. She should call the police. But this package is from her son. According to the return address, he is back in Oakland. Maybe he mailed her a gift to make up for all the worry he has put her through.

She slits the wrapping. The grocery bag came from a Trader Joe's. But which Trader Joe's? When she visited Zach, was there a Trader Joe's in his neighborhood?

The box, which has been crafted from a lightweight wood, like balsa, is fastened with a clasp. As she nudges the hook, she knows she will find nothing inside but a gift from Zach. Even as she knows the contents will blow up in her face.

She falls back, hands flailing at her eyes. Her head radiates pain where she cracked it against the coat rack. Her face stings. But when she puts her hands to her cheeks, she doesn't feel anything raw or wet. In the windowless room, powder hovers in the air. Anthrax? She stops breathing. Then again, if it is anthrax, she already is good as dead.

Sprawled there, entangled in the coat rack, she pats herself for injuries. The gray carpet seems unstained by anything except the orangey smudge where, weeks ago, she dropped a meatball sandwich. Beneath the desk lies one of the objects that must have exploded in her face. She fishes it out—a spring, narrower than a soup can, which someone meticulously stitched inside a gray felt cover. That same person must have compressed the spring, then set it in the box and closed the hasp. Maxine discovers two other snakes beside the bookcase. The white dust sifts to her desk, coating her stapler, her papers, the collection of wind-up robots her students have given her. She sniffs more deeply—if she isn't already poisoned, she will be now—and is transported to her mother's bedroom in Fenstead, where, as a little girl, Maxine loved to inhale the Jean Naté talcum powder her mother dusted beneath her arms to keep from sweating. Who would have gone to such elaborate lengths to pull a prank? She might have been blinded by a spring. Even as she forms these thoughts, she can hear Sam shouting these same questions to their son. A package had arrived at Sam's office; when he opened it, snakes sprang from the box, frightening him half to death. When Zach came home, Sam was waiting for him in their living room.

"We didn't mean to hurt you!" Zach had cried.

"'We'?" Sam echoed. "Who is this 'we'? Don't go blaming Norm. Norm might have the smarts to rig up a contraption like this, but he would never say boo unless you put him up to it."

Maxine remembers a change coming over Zach's face, so subtle only a mother would have noticed it. "Yeah. Sorry. I shouldn't try to blame Norm. It was only me." Even then, Maxine suspected Thaddy had prodded Zach into carrying out the plot. What boy wouldn't think it great fun to play a prank on his father? No one would get hurt—they would cover the springs to make sure they didn't poke out his father's eye. The "smoke" would be nothing but baking soda, harmless as the fuel Zach and Thaddy had used for the rockets they set off behind the house. Why hadn't Maxine shared her suspicions with Sam? Because even then she knew Thaddy hated her husband. Hated him because he was bringing technology to people who would be better off in their primitive, authentic state. Hated him because he was married to a woman Thaddy fantasized about being married to himself. In sending that earlier package, Thaddy had been letting her know he could have found a way to kill her husband. He was sparing Sam, for her sake.

And now, what kind of message is Thaddy sending? Is he saying she mustn't divulge what she knows or the next package won't be so harmless? *Please*, she thinks. *Let Thaddy have typed Zach's name and return address because he knew I wouldn't be able to resist opening any package with my son's name and address in the upper-left-hand corner. Please let it mean Thaddy has no idea Zach has moved.*

She leaves everything where it is. Finding no one in the corridor, she hurries to the ladies' bathroom. Her face is pale, not only from shock but from the powder. She looks like a high-school thespian made up to play an elderly woman by the seventh-grader in charge of makeup.

She sneaks back to her office, gathers the three felt-covered bedsprings, the paper bag with the Trader Joe's logo on one side and her name and address and her son's name and address on the other side, then jams these inside her backpack, along with Thaddy's portfolio, the Conrad novel, and her copy of the manifesto. She sets the cigar box atop her bookcase. She almost wishes it had contained a real bomb because the explosion would have destroyed the evidence. Even then, the bomber's true identity might have been revealed by some telltale clue. In Conrad's novel, Verloc's wife sews their address into her brother Stevie's coat so if he ever gets lost, the police will know where to bring him. Then Stevie blows himself up, and the police find the label among the shreds of flesh and bits of bone that remain of him.

The muggy day feels even more surreal than it did before. The temperature must be in the seventies. She crosses the street and takes the elevator up to the provost's office.

"Provost Bell is finishing another meeting," the receptionist tells her. "If you would please take a seat?"

Maxine settles into one of the maize-and-blue Lucite chairs and stows her backpack beneath the maize-and-blue Lucite table. Mindlessly, she pages through a brochure that showcases the university's most generous donors, nearly all of whom have given money to build the new center for entrepreneurial research or to renovate the sports facilities. Useless to think any of them might donate to her institute. Maybe if she could promise their grandchildren would never die. But a donation to the medical school would be more likely to achieve that aim.

Three men in suits emerge from the provost's office. Maxine picks up her pack and swats a powder stain from her skirt.

"Maxine!" Provost Bell rises from her desk, upon which stands a large wooden statue of a wolverine. "So good to see you again!" She looks Maxine up and down. Her nostrils dilate as she sniffs the flowery scent. She motions Maxine to take a seat. "Have you given any more thought to the topic we discussed the last time we spoke?"

From where Maxine sits, she can see the screensaver on Perpetua's computer—the Bell family in front of their cottage up north, five girls and two boys, plus Perpetua's healthily tanned husband, his arms draped around his wife and children's shoulders.

"Yes, Perpetua," she says, "I have. And I have serious reservations about making our services available to outside industries. How can we remain objective if we know we can make more money by saying what the company funding our research wants us to say?"

The provost has the startled look of a woman who isn't accustomed to being disagreed with. "Oh, no, no, no. The university would never put you in a position where you would be pressured to do anything unethical. Look at the medical school. The pharmaceutical sector does provide funding for basic research. But the faculty would never allow such funding to affect their findings."

"I'm sorry," Maxine says. "I can't go against the wishes of my faculty." Although for all she knows, her faculty would readily accept a contract from whoever puts up the cash. She thinks of placating the provost with an overly optimistic report on the institute's fundraiser. Maybe she should pitch her new focus on Immortality Studies. Then again, feeling the way she feels, she can't imagine why anyone would want to spend a day longer than necessary on this planet.

Loneliness. That's what they ought to be studying. The loneliness of a widow who has lost a beloved spouse. A parent who has lost a child. A child who has lost a parent. The loneliness of the adolescent white male who can't measure up to his parents' expectations, whose classmates bully him and beat him up, who is seething with desire but whose every encounter with the opposite sex is greeted by humiliation. All those geniuses in Silicon Valley keep inventing gadgets to distract themselves from their pain. They don bionic exoskeletons to show off their superhuman powers when what they really want is to avoid opening the clasp on their hearts and confronting whatever emotional snakes and shrapnel come bursting out.

That's when she starts to shake. She might have been blown up. By her son. Or by the crazy terrorist to whom she introduced him.

Perpetua notices how distraught she is. "I'm sorry, Maxine. Ever since Sam's death . . . I know you haven't had the same energy. Maybe it would be better to disband the institute. You would still have your appointment at the Residential College. Everyone on your faculty would have his or her home department to return to."

Even in her nauseated state, it occurs to her this isn't true. "Not Mick. Mick doesn't have any other appointments."

Perpetua looks abashed. "But Professor Mickelthwaite just celebrated his seventieth-third birthday. I'm sure he wouldn't mind accepting the very generous retirement package we would offer him. And I'm equally certain no one on your faculty would mind losing an office in that smelly old basement. We haven't released the plans for the new Thomas and Betsy Winkelmann Center for Entrepreneurial Research, but we would be happy to set aside a floor for your institute, if only you reconsider changing your focus to the more entrepreneurial aspects of Future Studies."

So that has been their strategy. If the university dragged its feet in getting rid of the mold, if they starved the institute of funding, then the faculty would give in and accept corporate contracts.

The outrage registers dully. All Maxine wants is to exit the office without vomiting on the hideous maize-and-blue rug.

She makes it to the door, then stops to say she does have one request. If the institute closes, might HR find a suitable new position for her chief administrative officer, Rosa Romanczuk?

Perpetua purses her lips. "That depends on her skill set." She rattles off a list of spreadsheet formats and bookkeeping applications whose acronyms mean nothing to Maxine and will mean even less to Rosa. Maybe none of that matters. Mick must have savings socked away. He can pay the tuition for Rosa's sons. He and Rosa will be able to devote their energy to looking after Mick's granddaughter.

Maxine shakes her head. "Rosa's skill set is of entirely different order. A skill set you seem to have no idea how to value." Then she hurries past the receptionist, down the stairs, and across the Diag to the garage. She locates the Buick and tries to focus on guiding it down the ramp. As the gate swings open, she drives out without looking and nearly runs down a student. Motioning she is sorry, she drives across town and crosses the mist-shrouded Huron River to Sunrise Hills.

She signs in, then waits for the elevator. Across the hall, a troupe of elderly tai chi students move at a glacial rate, as if, by slowing their motion, they might stretch out the final few moments of their lives.

"Hello! Hello!" This from an old man sitting to one side of a potted plant. An aide in flowered scrubs waits behind him. At his feet lie matching pink suitcases. Tied to the armrest of his wheelchair is a yellow balloon printed with a giant smile. The old man—she needs a moment to place him as Arnold Schlechter's father—beams up at her as if he expects her to pat him on his head and take him home.

"You're my Arnie's friend! From the university! Maxine, isn't that your name? Today is the day! My Arnie is coming to get me! He said he wouldn't be here until nine, but I am rather eager to be sprung from this chicken coop." He looks up at the woman whose dark hands rest on his chair. "Not that I haven't received the most excellent attention. Only, as they say, there is never any other place like home. Or rather, the home I am going to be making with my son and his darling family, who have been generous enough to take me in."

"It's so nice to see you again," Maxine says, wishing the elevator would come. How can she face Arnold Schlechter, knowing the identity of the man who blinded him and refusing to divulge it to the FBI?

"Tell me," the old man says. "You and my Arnie, you see each other socially? I know he isn't an easy man to get along with. But he has always been good to me and, when she was living, to his mother." He lifts one palsied finger and uses it to push up his owlish glasses, which are slipping off his nose. "I am his father. But even a father can see his child is something of a know-it-all. 'Arnie,' I used to say, 'you know more than the other children. But just because you know more doesn't mean you need to point out the other person's ignorance.'" The elder Schlechter shakes his head. "If he has a lovely woman such as yourself as his friend, perhaps he has softened his edges? Perhaps you and your husband will join my son and his darling wife for dinner some evening?"

From the corner of her eye, she glimpses Schlechter and his wife step into the revolving door. "Of course!" she lies. "I hope to see you again—both of you—very soon!"

The elevator comes and Maxine escapes. On the fifth floor, she hurries past the residents in their wheelchairs.

"Maxine!"

She has passed her own mother without recognizing her.

"I *knew* you would be late."

"Late? It's only a few minutes past eight-thirty."

"But I *told* you! They are in a different time zone in the basement!"

"All right, Mom. But this hasn't been the best day of my life. Okay?" She signs her mother out. In the basement, she follows the arrows to the beauty salon. A tiny woman nearly as old as her mother, hair orange as a troll's, waits beside a sink.

"Ah, there's my girlfriend now!" the woman croons with an Irish lilt. She spins Maxine's mother's wheelchair so it backs up to the sink, twirls a black vinyl cape, and fastens it around her mother's stringy neck. "I know how Miz Sayers here likes to get her hair done before any of the other women, because once they start coming in we do tend to fall a bit behind, don't we, dear. And it isn't comfortable for her, waiting in that chair. And all the hairspray isn't easy on her breathing. So we have our own special arrangement. Don't we, dearie. We call it a ten o'clock appointment, but I try to get here an hour early and finish

Miz Sayers before my real ten o'clock lady comes down." She tests the temperature of the spray against her wrist. "We have our own way of measuring time down here. A lady forgets her appointment and wanders down at the wrong hour, or even on the wrong day, and Theresa finds a way to squirrel her ladies in." She squirts a thimbleful of shampoo in her palm, then rubs it across Maxine's mother's paper-thin scalp. She wets the downy hair. Works up a lather. Sprays away the soap. "There you go. That feels ever so nice, doesn't it, dearie."

Maxine's mother lies with her head tilted back at an unnatural angle, eyes closed, cheeks sunken, mouth agape. This is what she will look like as a corpse. It hits Maxine: her mother will soon be dead. After that, she won't see either of her parents, ever again. She never really cared about the future. She only wanted to bring about the Age of the Messiah because she imagined her father would be there, waiting at the Messiah's side.

The hairdresser shifts Maxine's mother so she is sitting upright. Then the tiny woman picks up a blower so big she needs to use both hands to hold it; careful not to burn the tops of Maxine's mother's ears, she blows her hair dry. Pats the fluffy white curls. Covers her mother's face with a cloth and sprays some hairspray.

"There you go!" She unfurls the cape. "Aren't you the most beautiful lady at Sunrise Hills! A teenager would be proud to have such clear, smooth skin. Did you bring your makeup, dearie?"

With difficulty, Maxine's mother retrieves a cloth bag from the side of her chair and takes out the mascara Maxine bought. She tips up her face, and the hairdresser strokes her lashes with the wand. The hairdresser uncaps a lipstick and twists the tube as Maxine's mother makes a fish face. The hairdresser inks the bottom lip, then the top, then produces a tissue so her mother can kiss and blot it. "There!" The hairdresser holds up a mirror. "At our age, we all need a little help from Mr. Makeup. You look lovely, dearie. Not a day over seventy."

And really, her mother does look much younger. Why is Maxine so stingy with her compliments? She kneels so their faces line up in the mirror—her mother's face, gaunt and fair, Maxine's own, squarer, like her father's, her hair dark and straight like his. "She's right. You do look pretty."

Her mother crooks her head as if she can only now take in her daughter. "And you look *terrible*. What's wrong? Is it Zach?"

Maxine gives the hairdresser a twenty-dollar tip, then wheels her mother to an alcove beside the laundry room. "You were right, Mom. That student? Thaddy? I should never have let Zach hang around with him. It's my fault. Everything! It's all my fault!"

"I was right?" Her mother seems stunned.

"I need to find Zach. Right away. And I haven't got the slightest idea where to look."

Her mother blinks. Her hands fly around her face. "He always did love that cabin. Sam's cabin? On the lake?"

Of course! How could she not have thought of the cabin? When Zach was young, he used to cross off the days until their vacations there. He loved planning which toys to bring. Loved packing snacks for the road and deciding whether they should take the time to visit the Call of the Wild Museum in Gaylord, or the Mystery Spot in St. Ignace, or the colonial fort in Mackinaw City. One time, Zach played a role in a reenactment of the lacrosse game in which the Ojibwas fooled the British into opening the gates, at which the Ojibwa team captured the fort and massacred the invaders.

The ride took six or seven hours, depending on how often they stopped. Zach was always the first to spot the statue of Paul Bunyan—like many lumber towns, Manistique claimed to be Bunyan's home, a boast Sam joked was mixed liberally with the excretions of Paul's giant blue ox, Babe. Zach would turn up his nose at the cabin's musty smell. Sam complained about having to unlock the shutters and turn on the pump. Maxine bitched about sweeping up all the dead flies and chasing the mice from the cabin's closets. They debated whether the animal crackers from the summer before were edible, whether the porcupines truly would eat the rubber tires on the car if Zach forgot to go out before bedtime and sprinkle pepper. But these were the chores and arguments that marked them as a family, that reminded them who they were.

At the cabin, Sam turned off his hyperactive social conscience. The one store in Manistique didn't carry *The New York Times*. The television wasn't hooked up to any channels. When they felt sated with the beach, they might take a trip to Tahquamenon Falls or hike through the Hiawatha National Forest (Maxine had been astonished to learn Hiawatha was a real person, and Gitchee Gumee was the Ojibwa name for Lake Superior). Sam took Zach fishing for walleye, which they cooked on the beach; afterward, they would sit around the fire making ghostly sounds between their thumbs to see if any of the loons on the lake would answer. Every autumn, they drove up to see the leaves. They braved more than one blizzard so they could build a fire in the fireplace and sip hot chocolate made with the fudge they picked up in Mackinaw.

Where else would Zach have spent the winter? She remembers now—he had asked if she ever planned on going back, and she said no, she couldn't bear to be up there without his father.

She hasn't received a bill from the electric company, but Zach might have switched the account to his own name and be paying it electronically. He could be using the wood stove for heat, and the kerosene lanterns for light. Still, it couldn't have been easy, getting through the long, dark winter on his own. She imagines him growing a beard. Despite everything, the image makes her smile.

She stops smiling when she realizes he probably hasn't been living there alone.

"Oh, Mom," she says. "I need to drive up to Manistique right away!" If it were summer, she might call one of the other families on the lake and ask them to check if Zach is living there. But this early in the year, the place will be deserted. And she doesn't want to alert the sheriff, not until she knows who might be hiding in that cabin.

Back on the fifth floor, she signs her mother in at the nurses' station. "Do you want me to leave you here so you can have some company?"

"No!" her mother barks. "I hate sitting here with all these *cabbages*!"

After Maxine settles her mother in her room, she asks if there is anything she needs. Maxine hopes her mother will say, "Nothing, dear," or "A glass of water." In her mind, she already is driving north.

"You could look for the envelope from Cousin Joel."

"I'm sorry," Maxine says. "I have to get up there right away. But the next time, I promise, I'll turn this place upside down."

Her mother nods. With the back of a crooked wrist, she rubs her eyes, smearing the mascara the hairdresser just applied. "Go!" her mother orders. "Neither of us could survive another tragedy."

. . . Revisits Eden

Which is how she has come to be traveling to the Upper Peninsula in the middle of a foggy Tuesday in April. Not having slept more than an hour the night before. Driving the enormous mint-green Buick she inherited from her mother. Tempted, so very tempted, to take a nap.

She cranks open the window and focuses on crossing the beautiful five-mile bridge that, in her twenty-six years of living in Michigan, she has learned to pronounce as Mackinaw rather than Mackinack. Then exhaustion sets in again. Her body keeps trying to convince her mind everything will be fine if she closes her eyes. Just for a minute. Although some other part of that same brain is fully aware that dozing off, no matter for how short a time, will result in her careening off the highway into the nearly invisible forest that lies beyond.

No one but her mother knows where she is. If she dies—by driving off the road, or by pulling off on the narrow shoulder and getting plowed into by a semi—her friends will wrack their memories as to why she might have fled in the middle of a school week to drive to this charmless expanse of what is known in their state, and largely unknown in the rest of the country, as the Upper Peninsula. Thank God she is teaching only one course this term. Tomorrow is, what, Wednesday? She doesn't need to teach again until Monday. Surely all this craziness will be settled by then.

She has another two hours' drive to her family's cabin, where she might or might not find her son. After that, she will need to drive straight back to Ann Arbor and visit the police, stinking the way she does, wearing the same sweat-stained silk blouse and wrinkled gray skirt she has been wearing since the day before, and tell them everything she knows, or thinks she knows, about the young man whose hatred of technology has resulted in so many maimings and deaths. And, if he carries through on this latest threat, will result in so many others. She will do this even if it means implicating her son in the madman's crimes. And confessing her own role in helping to shape his ideology.

Is she being too hard on herself? Or not hard enough? She should have recognized that her student's anger, his self-righteousness, might push him toward violence. She was blinded by how much she liked him. How responsible she felt for helping him channel all that rage into more productive ways of staving off the catastrophe they both agreed was menacing humankind.

But she never should have introduced such a troubled young man to her son. Zach hadn't needed an older brother. He needed *her*. And she had been too busy struggling to survive her husband's death—putting food on the table, keeping up with her teaching and research, repairing the roof—to prevent her son from getting sucked into his own maelstrom of guilt and loss. She had been so obsessed with the future she blinded herself to the present. Well, she can see everything she has been ignoring catching up in her rearview mirror.

She passes a sign for St. Ignace. She ought to pull off and

call the authorities. Not the Ann Arbor police. What do they know except how to handle drunken fraternity parties and the occasional break-in on Main Street? What she needs to do is find the number for the FBI. Although whoever picks up the phone might dismiss her as yet another crank calling because she has read the manifesto and thinks she knows who wrote it. She needs to stop by their offices in person and show them the documents that support her claim. Once she emerges from this wilderness—and by "wilderness" she means the Land That Has No Wi-Fi—she can use her phone to google the bureau's offices in Detroit. If she owned a later-model car she could pose this question to thin air and a pleasantly mechanical voice would tell her. One day, people will ask such questions of the computers implanted in their retinas. But Maxine will go to her grave arguing with her colleagues in AI and Robotics that the questions most worth asking will never be answered, in that way or any other.

Again, she fights the urge to close her eyes. If only she had a driverless car. Better yet: the ability to map her route on GPS, point and click and transport herself instantaneously from start to finish. Although if such technology had existed when Zach was young, he wouldn't have grown up enjoying the family ritual of driving north.

And what about her and Sam, driving to the cabin that first time, all the way from Boston? After thirty-six hours in Sam's trash-laden VW bug, they had stripped off their clothing and raced to the secluded beach, where they jumped in, shouting and splashing, and made love right there in the water. Sam had been insatiable in his desire. They made love on every surface that held their weight. Once, he spread her on the rickety table above the shore, as if she were a picnic. They even made love in the outhouse, Sam yanking down her shorts and kissing her as they inhaled the sweet, tangy stench of being human.

After Sam died, she couldn't bear the thought of going back. If not for Zach, she would have abandoned the cabin, left it to decay with everything they owned inside. The local teenagers would have broken in and gotten high. They would have made love on the saggy bed on which Sam had ravished her so many times. She would have deeded the property to her son. Maybe Zach would have sold it. Or spent vacations there with his family. If Zach ever had a family. But she would never again have driven up of her own volition.

She pulls off at the diner where she and Sam used to stop because Zach loved the tomato soup and grilled cheese sandwiches. "Why can't you make grilled cheese with soft white bread like this, Mom?" he used to beg. "Why do you always use that dark, hard, crusty stuff?"

In Zach's honor, Maxine orders the grilled cheese and tomato soup, with three cups of burnt black coffee. She gets back on the road and turns on the radio. For a few minutes, she loses herself in an interview with a woman who recovered from her husband's abuse by living on an isolated farm and writing poetry. But as the station fades, Maxine hears a staticky report about a professor at MIT who has been targeted by an exploding package. She twists the knob to turn up the volume. When the reporter says the victim's name—Dr. Gordon Hertz—Maxine needs a moment to jog her memory. Yes, Dr. Hertz is the professor with whom Zach had a run-in freshman year. She remembers because it had seemed so appropriate that a professor at MIT should share his name with the discoverer of electromagnetic waves. The extent of Dr. Hertz's injuries isn't clear. But he is in critical condition at the same Boston hospital to which Sam transported Maxine when she broke her ankle.

Two of the Buick's tires skid off the shoulder. Maxine opens the door and throws up in a ditch. The sandwich. The tomato soup. The bile from three cups of coffee. Ten or twenty minutes go by before she feels well enough to drive. She pulls over at a convenience store and sits shivering beside a dog run. As a freshman, Zach signed up for a computer class, then balked at turning in the project his professor assigned because it was related to Hertz's own attempt to develop more accurate systems of facial-recognition software. "I can't do it, Mom," Zach had pleaded with her on the phone. "If these guys have their way, we'll end up living in a police state straight out of Orwell. The government will be able to keep track of everywhere we travel, everyone we meet, everything we use a credit card to buy." Maxine had advised Zach to talk to his professor and ask if he couldn't get assigned to some other project. But Hertz had only grown more adamant. Facial-recognition software would be a deterrent to crime, he claimed. A face, unlike a password, couldn't be hacked. Zach had argued and argued until Hertz had demanded Zach leave his office. If Zach didn't turn in his assignment, Hertz said, he would fail the class.

Maxine offered to intervene, but Zach told her if she so much as picked up the phone he would never speak to her again. He accepted the failing grade, then went silent. Maxine had been afraid he would drop out altogether. But then, to her relief, Zach called to say he had enrolled in a course in solar engineering, and the professor—a great guy, really, one of the most innovative thinkers in the field—had invited Zach to spend the summer working at some solar research facility out West, on a reservation. Later, this professor agreed to take Zach on as his thesis student. At graduation, Zach seemed childishly excited to introduce her to this adviser, a heavyset Navajo almost as tall as Zach, with long black braids. She remembers Zach pointing to Professor Hertz and telling her that he was tempted to go over and give the man a piece of his mind, not only for continuing to work on a system that could be put to such nefarious use but for trying to bully an undergraduate into being an accomplice to his crime. Could Zach still harbor a grudge? She tries to convince herself Thaddy acted on his own, choosing his latest target based on some grievance Zach expressed to him years before. She feels sick she didn't notify the FBI the minute she suspected Thaddy. The agents wouldn't have had time to stop him. But she would have done everything in her power to prevent this bombing.

Back on the highway, she drives as fast as she dares. Spring has arrived early in Ann Arbor, but this far north the countryside is still a dull yellowish brown. Summers are so short here little can grow except potatoes. Most of the mines have closed. The landscape exerts a harsh, windswept charm. But even if you enjoy hunting, ice fishing, and riding your snowmobile, it can't be easy getting through the bleak winter nights, when there is little to do except drink and watch TV.

Then, suddenly, she is on the outskirts of Manistique. When she and Sam started coming here, the only motel was the Gray Wolf Lodge. Now she notes a Quality Inn, a Comfort Inn, an Econo Lodge. She passes the ranger station. Foodmart. Hardee's. Burger King. Pizza Hut. Do Zach and Thaddy, tired of getting by on whatever food they manage to scrounge, come to town to split a pizza? Or would that violate some code of Thaddy's? The road crosses the mouth of the Manistique River, then rounds a sharp curve. And there he is, towering above the information booth, handsome in his flannel shirt and massive boots, axe cradled across his arms—Paul Bunyan.

She turns off onto Little Harbor Road. The sun is low. Mist rises from the lake. The pine trees seem grateful to have survived the winter. With the engine off, she can hear the waves lapping the shore. Even here, the air is bizarrely tropical. The rear of the cabin is a soft, weathered gray, the roof so mossy it blends with its surroundings. She steps to the side of the house, where Sam's old VW bug—not the one he drove at MIT, but two VWs after that—has been pulled beneath the trees, as if to camouflage it from anyone who might drive past or fly over it in a helicopter. Someone has been digging a garden in the flat expanse of land above the septic system. A shovel stands jabbed in the newly turned soil.

A scream travels up from the lake. Too high-pitched to be her son's.

Too late. Neither of the people who appear between the trees is wearing clothes. She hasn't seen her son naked since he was ten. She should look away. But she finds she can't. Zach is thin to the point of emaciation. But he is as muscular as a god compared to the much frailer, shorter woman clinging to his side. She holds her wrist at an awkward angle. She walks at an ungainly pace, Zach matching his gait to hers.

As a scientist, Maxine isn't given to literary allusions. But she can't help but be reminded of the first woman and man on earth. Not yet aged or weighed down by sorrow. Still thrilled by each other's bodies. Not yet tired of repeating the act to which they were introduced by eating the forbidden fruit. A sequence of events she is able to deduce by noting this Eve is pregnant, too.

. . . *Learns about a Lie*

"Oh, shit," Zach says. "Mom! No. No. Get out of here!" By then she has turned away, holding her palm behind her. "I'm sorry! I'll wait in the car! Go, get some clothes on."

As embarrassed as she is, as soon as she is out of sight she crumples to the rutted road and offers a prayer of gratitude. Because even though her son is guilty of being caught naked with this woman, his sins don't seem to be the sins of someone who raised his hand to his fellow man. His sins are the sins of Adam, not Cain.

"Mom! You can come back now."

When she returns to the clearing, Zach is zipping his jeans. But he is still shirtless. Thin as he is, his arms seem extremely powerful. He must have spent the winter chopping wood. But that doesn't explain why he is standing so much straighter. Why he seems so much prouder and happier to be alive. He pulls on a threadbare BOYCOTT GRAPES T-shirt he must have snagged from his father's drawer and kept as a memento.

The woman—head bent, long wet hair hiding her face— pulls on an ankle-length flowered skirt that stretches to contain her belly. (A boy. That's what Maxine's mother would predict. If Angelina were carrying a girl, the bump would be lower.)

She struggles to button her swollen breasts into a blue cardigan Maxine recognizes as a Hanukah gift she bought Zach his first winter at MIT. Buttons buttoned, the girl lifts her head. How could Maxine have thought Zach was dating her only to prove he is above the prejudice most men would have against dating someone handicapped? Or because he eroticized her disability? She is a beautiful woman. Gentle. Kind. Of course he loves her.

"She's freezing, Zach." Maxine wants to put her arms around the girl and rub her. "What were you thinking, letting her go in the lake!"

Zach frowns. "Letting her? We got so hot digging the garden, we dared each other to jump in."

Angelina hobbles to the tree where she leaned her braces; like a fencer arming herself for a joust, she slips each forearm into a cuff. "It's very nice to see you again," she tells Maxine, holding out her hand, which, when Maxine takes it, turns out to be very cold, from the lake. Maxine wants to tell Angelina she is happy to see her, too. But she still is too confused to know if she is or isn't.

At the cabin's threshold, Maxine hesitates. But the one-room interior doesn't smell as musty as she expected it would smell. For one thing, the cabin hasn't been locked up all winter. The smoky scent of the stove permeates the braided wool rugs and ratty tweed sofa, with the added scent of what must be a woman's shampoo or soap. Zach puts on the kettle for tea, then brings out a tin of brownies Angelina baked.

"I'm glad they didn't burn," she tells Maxine. "I needed a month to get used to cooking on a stove that has no settings."

Maxine is so ravenous and the taste of the brownie so choc-olatey and rich she wishes she could pretend the occasion is nothing more than a mother meeting her son's girlfriend and complimenting her on her baking skills.

"It was Norm, wasn't it," Zach says.

"Norm? No. Norm said he didn't know where you were. He said . . . Are you serious? Norm knew the whole time?"

"Mom," Zach says, "guys don't rat each other out. They just don't."

Even now, she wants to demand Zach divulge the name of whoever set fire to that pirate ship. "Your grandmother figured it out."

"Grandmom?"

Maxine shrugs, unwilling to admit her mother knows her son better than she does. The water in the kettle boils. She is afraid Zach will serve her tea made from dried grass or weeds from the lake, but the tag on the bag says Lipton.

"It's just . . ." Zach says. "When Angie told me she was pregnant, I knew you wouldn't approve."

Of course. The one truly insensitive remark Maxine ever made. She had apologized and apologized. But still, how could Zach forget? "You've been seeing each other this whole time? Since high school?" It occurs to her Zach must have told Angelina what she said.

"Not the whole time," Zach says. "When I decided to move to the West Coast, we had a huge fight. Except I really missed Angie. I came home for a few days. We had, well, a nice reunion. Then I went home to California."

"I never would have made him come back," Angelina interrupts. "You have to understand. I am not the kind of woman who tries to trap a man. But when I didn't get, you know, my monthly?"

"We were really surprised," Zach says. "It's not as if . . . We're not idiots, Mom."

"I needed to tell Zach," Angelina says. "I felt it was his right to know."

"I appreciate that," Maxine says. "But couldn't you have told me, too? I'm not . . ." She wants to say "judgmental." But she did judge Angelina. Without ever really knowing her.

"If we decided not to keep the pregnancy, Angie's parents would have had a fit. And if we did keep it, there was no way they weren't going to expect us to get married. So I had the brainstorm of spending a month up here to see how well we got along and figure out what to do."

"You quit your job?" Maxine says.

"I didn't want him to," Angelina says. "Professor Sayers, this was Zach's decision. The part about quitting his job and coming here."

"I hated it." Zach's face goes rigid, the way it used to when he was arguing with his father. "I hated the whole Silicon Valley start-up thing. Everybody acting so pleased with themselves. All they're trying to do is make a killing and retire at thirty and spend the rest of their lives playing with their toys." If people really wanted to head off global warming, Zach said, we could switch to solar and wind tomorrow. Did Maxine know how much energy those tech companies soaked up with their servers? His father was right. What you really wanted to do was use the cheapest, simplest technology to make people's lives better. Basic stuff. Like clean water. Cooking fuel. Low-tech medical care. High-energy, super-efficient stoves that didn't explode.

As if to practice what he has just preached, Zach gets up and strikes a match—all these years since he threatened to set fire to that bully and he still needs three tries—and uses it to light a lamp. The scruff on his cheeks makes him seem older and more masculine than the last time she saw him, in Ann Arbor. Where she saw him overlaid by the reflections of the child he used to be.

"I guess this means . . ." Maxine glances at Angelina's belly.

Angelina smiles shyly. "When we tell *my* mother, we can lie and say she's the first to know. Otherwise, she would be very hurt."

"We haven't set a date," Zach says. "But, yeah, we're going to get married."

"Married!" She wants to tell them how happy she is. For both of them. And she *is* happy. All those years she worried Zach would end up like so many angry, politically extreme young men. Worried he would end up like Thaddy. But here he is engaged to a warm, intelligent, sensible, good-hearted woman. If only Sam were here to witness what she is witnessing. If only she could tell her father.

But she is sick at the prospect of ruining their joy with everything she has to tell them. It's all she can do not to keep the news about Thaddy to herself. To share a meal with her son and future daughter-in-law, catch a few hours of sleep on the sofa, then head back to Ann Arbor without revealing what she knows.

"Are you going to stay up here all year?" she asks. "You can't grow everything you need to eat. And you'll need health insurance. You can't have a baby and not have health insurance."

In half an hour she has gone from puking with fear that her son will get shot by government agents to nagging him about health insurance. Two years earlier, when she helped Zach load his VW for California, she numbed him with reminders to drive carefully, to make sure to change the oil and rotate the tires, to find a dentist and get his teeth checked, to sign up for the retirement package at his job and start socking away the maximum the plan allowed. Wasn't that what mothers were for? If you had a kid who went on a hunger strike, how could you help but hope he grew up to be a normally selfish adult who got a job and met a nice young woman and settled down to lead a normally selfish life? But when he did, how could you not be disappointed he was going to waste his life tending to the minutiae of middle-class existence?

Zach scowls his familiar scowl. "We only intended to stay up here until we figured out what to do. To save our money. Figure out the next step." He looks at Angelina, as if seeking permission to reveal what that next step might be. From now on, Maxine realizes, this will be the woman whose approval her son will seek.

Angelina nods, and the two of them launch into a description of a scheme in which they will find the money to buy a derelict building in Detroit. The soil has been so badly contaminated by the incinerator that has been belching soot across the city for decades they will need to gut and refit the structure with hydroponic tanks in which to grow spinach, arugula, wheatgrass, basil, and, yes, kale, to sell to local restaurants and farmers' markets. They plan to install solar panels on the roof and a geothermal heating system in the basement. If they can do so economically, they will also raise shrimp and culture mushrooms. They are hiring Norm to help them rehab the building. After that, Norm will start his own business, designing and building urban playscapes from scavenged wood and other recycled materials. Eventually, they will rent their leftover space to bakers, brewers, and makers of artisan cheese.

"We'll be like . . . urban pioneers," Zach says, as if they will be breaking sod on a virgin prairie instead of moving into a city already inhabited by hundreds of thousands of long-time residents. Is Detroit's future to be turned back to farmland? Will people who once earned their living manufacturing automobiles, airplanes, tanks, and tires settle for herding sheep and raising kale? If anyone else were relating such a plan, Maxine would dismiss it as well-intentioned foolishness. But how can she not respect her son for giving up a six-figure salary so he can move to a falling-down factory in Detroit and raise fresh produce in a city where there isn't a single decent grocery store for miles? Why should she discourage him from a plan that will ensure that he and her future grandchild live less than an hour from Ann Arbor?

She expresses as much enthusiasm as she can muster. But she can't help asking if Angelina has seen a doctor. Has she gotten her blood pressure checked? Has anyone done an ultrasound? Are they sure she is eating properly?

"Mom!" Zach says. "Do you really think I would let the mother of my baby starve?" Angelina has visited a clinic in Mackinaw City. She takes iron pills and vitamins. They eat plenty of nutritious food. Zach's savings are running low—that's why he asked Norm to send those savings bonds—but he and Angelina can last the summer, especially with eggs from the chickens they recently bought and vegetables they will be planting in their garden.

"But why the secrecy?" Maxine asks. "You're a grown man. How could I stop you from doing what you want? I never could."

"Can you really say you would have been thrilled if I quit my job and decided to have a baby? You and Dad wanted me . . . you wanted me to do so much."

"Look, Zach," she starts. "I didn't come here just to track you down. I'm glad I know where you are now. But there's been a lot going on. I need to talk to you. About something very serious. Do you remember Thaddy?"

The way he squirms and refuses to meet her gaze unsettles her so profoundly she wonders if Thaddy has, in fact, sexually abused her son. She can't bear to find out. So she keeps barreling ahead, explaining how she read the manifesto and came to suspect Thaddy wrote it. Tells him about the package that showed up in her office with Zach's name and return address on the wrapping. Mentions the time Thaddy and Zach sent a similar package to Zach's father.

Zach puts his hand to his mouth. Leans forward. Breathes harder and more erratically, rocking on the bench.

"Zach," she starts, but he cuts her off.

"Thaddy has been writing me letters. It's one reason I didn't want anyone to know where I was."

"You still keep up with Thaddy?" That can't be what he means. "You kept up contact with him, after he left Ann Arbor?"

"He's a lonely guy, Mom. I wasn't surprised he'd write me. He always used to say I was like a little brother to him." Apparently, Thaddy hoped Zach would see it as futile to reform the system from the inside. He hoped Zach would remember his promise that the two of them would drop out and live off the grid. Thaddy wrote that he quit his job and used his savings to buy a cabin in Montana. He loved spending his days outdoors, loved using his hands to achieve something tangible. Zach would love living there, too. The two of them living there together would be so much better.

"He wanted you to come live with him?" Maxine asks, even as she is sure Thaddy's request wasn't sexual. Thaddy would have preferred to live with a female lover. But if no woman would have him, then living with a younger brother he could teach to hunt, chop wood, and build a fire, someone who would listen to his philosophizing about the evils of modern life, was second best.

"He kept reminding me I promised to come out and live with him. And I did promise. But I was, like, fourteen. Plus, that whole business about how everyone would be better off if we went back to subsistence farming . . . Maybe not everything Dad did in Africa or India was for the best. But to romanticize poverty the way Thaddy does. All that backbreaking work. Not wanting people in developing countries to have any of the comforts we have here. I got tired of arguing and stopped writing back. I didn't hear from Thaddy for a few years.

"Then he showed up in Oakland." He turns to Angelina. "This was last summer? Just before you told me you were pregnant?" He turns back to Maxine. "He said the revolution was about to happen. The government was keeping surveillance on everything we did, and when people found out, they would finally rise up. Things would get ugly, he said, and he wanted me to be on the right side. The safe side. With him. Plus, he wanted me to tell him how the surveillance stuff worked. How someone could spy on you through your phone. Which they totally can, Mom. So, a lot of what he was saying made sense. But he didn't seem to be the same Thaddy. He was really thin. And he had this faraway look. You know, like that Manson guy?

"When I said I wouldn't leave with him, he got mad. He said I would be sorry if I didn't come. That wasn't the only reason I left town. I left to go get Angie and bring her here, to the cabin. But one reason I kept my location secret was I didn't want Thaddy to keep showing up and bugging me. I didn't mean to worry you so much. I just needed time alone with Angie. Time for us to figure things out. I couldn't have imagined Thaddy would send you that package. Jesus, I'm glad you're okay. You must have been scared to death. Maybe that's all he wanted to do, to scare you."

Maxine isn't sure how to put what she wants to say. "To be honest, Zach, I didn't know what to think."

"But you couldn't have . . . You didn't think I was the one who sent it? When Thaddy and I did that to Dad, I was a kid. I felt awful! That's when I stopped wanting to hang around with Thaddy. I realized he hated Dad. I thought it was about the Africa stuff. And to be honest, Mom, I kind of agreed with him. I was pretty young, and I thought maybe Dad did get off on playing the big white dude from America who showed up with all this neat technology so the natives worshipped him. But then I realized something else was going on. Thaddy hated Dad because Dad was married to you. Did they ever even meet?"

"Once," she says. She remembers crossing the Diag with Sam and running into Thaddy. Introducing the two men. Watching Sam reach out to shake Thaddy's hand and Thaddy keep his hands in his pockets, refusing to fall prey to the older man's attempt to charm him. "Thaddy was jealous of your father. Jealous that your father had a wife. Had me."

"Yeah," Zach says. "That makes sense. Thaddy started asking me all these questions about your personal life. Like, if you really loved each other? If you had sex?"

"Oh, God," Maxine says. "I never should have suggested the two of you hang out. But you were so shy. Both of you. I thought you would be good for each other."

"Of course," Angelina breaks in. She smiles and pats Maxine on the sleeve, as if she, too, knows how reticent Zach can be and, in Maxine's place, would have promoted such a friendship.

"He never . . ." Maxine doesn't want to complete her question. "Thaddy didn't touch you, did he?"

"Are you kidding? Thaddy? Mom, you know how obsessed

he was with finding a girlfriend. He didn't do anything to hurt me. And he would have dismantled anyone who tried. Don't forget how much good he did. It's because of him I didn't spend my entire adolescence hooked up to a bunch of video games." He waves to indicate the trees and lake. "He got me to appreciate the outdoors. He got me to think for myself. To be this independent. Don't you get it, Mom? Angie and I lived here all winter. We did everything for ourselves." Maxine can see Angelina nodding, looking at her son with pride. "That's why, I'm sorry, I just can't get my head around the fact that he's actually killed people. If that's the truth."

"It is the truth," Maxine insists.

"If it is, that's a side of him I never saw. I saw his anger. I saw his frustration. But I never saw anything that would indicate he could actually kill someone."

"I know this is all hitting you at once." Maxine hesitates. "But there's one more thing I have to tell you."

The bewildered look that crosses her son's face takes her back to a time when it was so much easier to protect him. When he relied on her for his survival. When the dangers seemed so much easier to fend off or control. "Zach," she says. "Your professor at MIT. Professor Hertz?"

Zach snaps his head as if he has been struck in the face. "What about him?"

"He's Thaddy's latest victim."

This revelation takes a few moments to register. "Wait. Is he alive? But why Hertz? Are you making this up?'

"I wish I were."

"Shit! Thaddy doesn't even know the guy! The only reason he would have done that would be to win me back. Maybe he thinks he's getting even with the jerk? For my sake? How could he, Mom? Hertz is okay? Tell me! Is he okay?"

"I don't know," she says. "I heard on the radio he was injured. They didn't say how badly."

Maxine moves toward her son, but Angelina is the one Zach turns to. "Oh, love, love," Angelina says, "I'm so sorry." She tries to embrace Zach, but he pulls away and paces. He regains his composure enough to ask if his mother has gone to the police.

"No," she says. "I wanted to find you first."

"I don't get it," Zach says. "Why didn't you tell them as soon as you got the package?"

She wishes she could lie. But lying would compound the betrayal.

"Wait," Zach says. "You thought Thaddy and I . . ." He puts his hands on the back of the rattan chair beside the fireplace. "Seriously? It's bad enough you didn't trust me when I said not to come looking for me. When I said I needed some time off. Some privacy to sort out my life. But you thought, what, I mailed you a bomb? I tried to kill you? That's something I would do? You and Dad . . . You suspected me of all sorts of things. Like burning down that playground? Like starving myself to death? You wanted me to care. You wanted me to change the world. You wanted me to be a revolutionary. But not *too much* of a revolutionary. I should care, but I shouldn't care too much. Well, that's not so easy. To care. To worry about all the shit you and Dad trained me to worry about. But only to worry and care a reasonable amount. You wanted me to make a revolution. But a *nice* revolution. A *gentle* revolution."

He grips the chair harder. Lifts it from the ground. For an instant, Maxine thinks he might pick it up and hurl it. But he slams it back down, hard, and walks over to Angelina.

"No," Maxine says. "I didn't think you would hurt anyone.

Not willingly. But I thought Thaddy might have . . . maybe you and Thaddy . . ." She stops trying to explain. She hadn't really thought her son capable of mailing a bomb to anyone. Had she? She has driven all this way to make sure Thaddy didn't kidnap Zach. To make sure Zach was here of his own free will. Although, to be honest, she also has been trying to prove she isn't one of those mothers who, when the police reveal her son has been stockpiling weapons, insists he couldn't be a terrorist. And in doing so, she has violated the very definition of a mother. Because even if your son does turn out to be a murderer, aren't you supposed to be the one person on earth who believes him innocent? She has betrayed her son in such a way he might never forgive her. Although, knowing Zach, he will pretend he does.

"This is all too much for me right now," Zach says. "I haven't eaten since breakfast. You must be hungry, too, Mom. And Angie needs to eat."

Zach goes to the icebox and takes out a pot of lentil stew he cooked to make sure his girlfriend receives the nutrition she needs to give birth to a healthy child. While he stands stirring it at the stove, Maxine feigns normalcy by asking Angelina if she has any siblings. Yes, Angelina says, she has an older sister, a nurse in the Marine Corps. Her mother works as an accountant for her father's nursery. Her father is disappointed Angelina didn't go to college, which was the reason he and Angelina's mother came to the United States, but he is pleased she wants to follow him into the business of growing and tending plants. Angelina's morning sickness lasted six weeks. So far, she hasn't suffered the heartburn that made Maxine so miserable when she was pregnant with Zach. They have been told the baby's gender, but if it's all right with Maxine, they will keep that a secret, for now. Angelina's words are sometimes garbled. Maxine is tempted to close her eyes so she can focus and listen harder. But she reminds herself nothing that afflicts her daughter-in-law could be passed on to her grandchild. What upsets her is that she is about to become a grandmother. At fifty-five! If she is a grandmother, there is no longer any ceiling between her and the older generation. No immortality for her. She will never live to greet the Singularity.

"What will your parents think of all this?" she asks.

"I am not sure," Angelina admits. "My parents met Zach a long time ago, when he took me to the prom. But they don't know we are still seeing each other. I am not the sort of person who enjoys lying. But they would hate him if they knew I got pregnant and he wanted me not to have the child. Or not to marry me. So I had to invent a story. I said I was going to work in the Upper Peninsula studying the trees, and it would be very hard for me to call because my cell phone wouldn't work. I have been writing letters every day so they won't be concerned. I dread when they find out the truth. But they will be happy we are getting married. My mother will jump up and down to find out she finally will be an *abuela*."

That her son's in-laws will be happy about the pregnancy highlights that Maxine isn't as thrilled as she wishes she could be. Zach has quit his job and, aside from this scheme about buying a rundown factory and converting it to a vertical farm, he and his fiancée have no way to support themselves. Maxine was two years younger than Zach when she married his father. But she and Sam waited to have Zach until they were in their thirties and had good jobs. And Sam wasn't suspected of being in league with a serial terrorist.

Angelina puts on her crutches and helps serve the dinner

Zach prepared. The stew, for all Maxine had been hoping for something more substantial than lentils, turns out to be so comforting she asks for a second helping. Thank God the cabin has no working television; otherwise, she might feel obliged to put on the news and learn whether Zach's professor has died of his injuries or Thaddy has mailed another bomb. As Zach scrapes the remains of the meal into the compost bin, she reminds him he will need to drive to Detroit the next morning to talk to the FBI. When Zach hesitates, she says this isn't the same as tattling on some kid who burned down a play structure.

"I'm not trying to protect him!" Zach says. "I just can't believe any of this is really happening." The lid on the compost bin won't close; Zach slams it with his fist. "I'm going to need time to close up this place. To make sure the chickens go to a good home."

She tries not to entertain the suspicion he will use these chores as an excuse to run off. But he is still keeping something from her. What he has told her is true, but only as far as it goes. She should insist he drive back with her, leaving Angelina to lock up the cabin. But Angelina can't drive. And Maxine already has betrayed her son by suspecting he might be implicated in Thaddy's crimes. The best she can do is get up early, drive straight to Detroit, and tell the FBI everything Zach just told her. She will assure them Zach will be coming in himself, the following morning, with whatever lawyer Rosa and Mick have found.

If only she could do what a mother is supposed to do and tell Angelina more stories about Zach as a little boy. But she can no longer keep her eyes open. She settles back on the sofa. At some point, a male presence spreads a blanket to her chin. She takes the man's hand. In her addled state, she almost presses it to her breast. Because this is Sam. Isn't it? Sam is still alive, and Zach is all grown up, working for a company in California, and Sam has come in from spreading pepper around the tires to ward off the porcupines.

She lets the hand drop, then wills herself deeper into the dream in which Sam is still alive. Hours later, she needs to pee. If she is going to force herself from the warmth of the sofa and go outdoors to use the outhouse, she might as well get up and start the long trek back to Detroit. The fire in the stove has died down, and she is looking forward to getting in the Buick and turning up the heat.

For a few moments, though, she stands at the foot of the bed and watches Zach and Angelina breathe. The quilt doesn't quite cover all of them. She bends and touches her son's filthy, callused soles. His girlfriend's much more delicate, twisted feet. How miraculous, that her son and his pregnant fiancée should be sleeping in the same bed in which his parents created him. If human beings lived forever, would the progression of generations be so compelling?

She is thrilled that her son is loved. Proud he has achieved what Thaddy couldn't. As his mother, she must have done something right. He is a compassionate human being. A man who accepts responsibility for his actions. A man of conscience. And yet, her son has been lying to her all his life. He is lying to her even now. Their troubles aren't over. Why does she suspect they are just beginning?

. . . Turns Herself In

S he has slept only a few hours in the past two nights. But exhaustion amps her into a bionic realm in which she is hyperalert to the data streaming through the Buick's windshield. Photons ricochet off a farmer's pond. A coyote slinks along the median. The breeze ripples its fur. But even as she registers all this, she is rehearsing the information she will reveal to the FBI. She will minimize her son's relationship to the terrorist. She will try to explain why she gathered evidence of the previous morning's prank and, instead of going directly to the authorities, drove to her family's cabin up north.

At noon, she catches a brief update on the radio. Professor Hertz's condition is described as "serious." The bomb wasn't as powerful as the earlier devices the suspect mailed. Maybe Thaddy is running out of cash to buy supplies. Maybe he only wanted to send a message to her son: see what I can do to get back at those assholes we know are ruining our society. Although how will she convince the government Zach isn't the most likely suspect, the professor's former student who holds a grudge?

She stops to use a restroom. Not until she sees a sign for Ann Arbor does she recognize the pain in her gut as hunger.

She is tempted to stop to eat. But if another victim is injured, she won't be able to excuse the delay. Nothing, she thinks, marks a person's dislocation from her former life as uncannily as driving past the exit for her own home.

She passes the airport. A few miles later, the giant Uniroyal tire towers beside the highway. This is the same tire that served as the Ferris wheel at the 1964 World's Fair in Flushing. Stripped now of its gondolas, it serves as an advertisement for the company that put rubber on the automobiles that made the Motor City famous. But every time Maxine sees it, she imagines the tire being rolled here by some playful giant to remind her of the fair. On one visit, her mother had declared she'd had enough of science; it was time the family did something fun. Why, only a few weeks earlier, Jacqueline Kennedy had taken Caroline and John-John on this very same ride! Against Maxine's wishes, she and her parents joined the line. Up and up they rode, until the gondola stopped to allow more passengers to climb on below. At the time, Maxine had been annoyed at her mother for caring so much about Mrs. Kennedy. Now, she realizes that in insisting they ride the Ferris wheel, her mother had made sure Maxine would have this memory to appreciate—the view from the top, the dinosaurs at the Sinclair Oil exhibit gamboling at their feet like pets, she and her parents healthy and alive, enjoying something as unremarkable as each other's company.

She reaches the outskirts of Detroit and turns off at the exit for John R, following the same route she and Sam used to take when they brought Zach to the art museum. Back then, lot after empty lot still lay mounded with the rubble of whatever building had stood there before the '67 riots. Drunks staggered down the middle of Woodward Avenue, in no danger of getting hit even in broad daylight. Steam rose from the manholes in a hellish, post-apocalyptic way. In the back seat, Zach must have taken in their conversations about how the residents made do with no electricity. How garbage piled up in the streets. How the police failed to respond to 911 calls. How rats roamed the schools and children crowded into classrooms with thirty or forty students. No wonder Zach is moving here to rehab a factory. Wouldn't Sam be proud of his son? Certainly, he wouldn't have wished for Zach to live a safer, easier life in Palo Alto.

She drives down Michigan Avenue. The meters are good only for a few hours, so she pulls into a lot where, for five dollars, she can park for the rest of the day. She grabs her backpack and—the wind has picked up—her jacket. At the guard booth, an older black man in a uniform is killing time with two companions.

"Cheer up, honey," the guard says. "Most of the folks who walk in that building, they do walk out again."

Maxine gives them a thumbs-up sign, even though she knows what he really means is that a white woman in decent (if rumpled) clothes is more likely to emerge unscathed from her encounter with the government than any of the three of them.

Beyond the lot, the street dead-ends at a set of barricades designed to fend off a truck of exploding fertilizer or a squadron of jihadis. The Federal Building rises above the windswept plaza, a Brutalist tower thirty stories tall. A helicopter buzzes her from above, as if the government already has her under surveillance. She ducks into the revolving doors. Two uniformed officers stand beside a metal detector; the wall beyond is decorated with a psychedelic mosaic, as if some bureaucrat in the 1970s wanted to convince the citizens of Detroit their Uncle Sam wasn't a forbidding old fuddy-duddy. Or maybe the mural is meant to provide something pleasant to look at while you are being searched, like the poster taped to the ceiling above her gynecologist's examination table.

The FBI has its own entrance, to the right of the main lobby, and Maxine isn't allowed to pass through the detector there until she states her business to the guard behind the glass.

"Um, hi," she starts. "I need to see an agent. Because otherwise, this man, this criminal . . ."

The guard lifts his hands, palms outward. "If you'll just show me your ID, ma'am, we can process you through and you can talk to someone on the other side."

"Oh," she says. "Sure. Here's my driver's license. And my University of Michigan ID. I teach there. I'm a professor." She knows this sounds foolish, but as an employee of a state institution, maybe she can claim a kind of camaraderie with this federal official.

The guard examines the two IDs. Hands them back. Buzzes her through. She is met by two stout guards, one of whom turns sideways so he can fit through his own detector.

"Here you go." He lays out two plastic bins. "If you would just put your bag in there. And your jacket? And your watch? And any other metal you might be wearing? And if you will allow me to take your cell phone? I will give you this ticket, and you just remember to ask me for your phone on your way back out."

She steps through the detector, surprised an alarm doesn't shriek at the guilt and fear clotting her head. So many people believe the government can read their minds. But how could anyone read her thoughts when she doesn't understand those thoughts herself? Even if the government were trying to read her brain, how could anyone decipher the complexity of her feelings for Thaddeus Rapaczynski, or her complicity in his crimes?

The guard on the other side pulls the felt-covered metal springs from her bag and regards these quizzically.

"Oh," Maxine says. "Those." Her heart races at the memory of the snakes flying in her face. "Those are part of the evidence I need to show to the FBI."

The guard rotates the springs in his hands. Stretches and compresses them. "Can't see how anyone could do much harm with these." He seems equally skeptical that these felt-covered bedsprings are going to solve a crime. He replaces them in her pack and rezips the zipper. "You have yourself a very pleasant day," he says, and Maxine finds herself touched by how welcoming these guards have been. Shocked, really. Because she grew up in the sixties? Because it's the nature of a government to be distrusted?

She walks down a short hall and enters a surprisingly stylish waiting room. A middle-aged white woman with dyed magenta hair sits on a backless sofa opposite a wizened black man in a shiny gray suit who is balancing a fedora on his knees. Maxine approaches the glassed-in office. A severe young white woman with short black hair looks up.

"Hello," Maxine says. "I'm a professor. At the University of Michigan. And I have reason to believe a former student of mine wrote the manifesto in yesterday's newspaper. Not yesterday. The day before. I see very distinct similarities. Language. Turns of phrase. Quotations from a novel we studied in my class."

The young woman leans forward so she can look Maxine up and down. Maxine hasn't washed her hair in days. She can't remember the last time she brushed her teeth.

The woman smiles suddenly, as if she, too, has remembered the importance of presenting a friendly face to the public. "An agent will be happy to meet with you and hear what you have to say." She makes a call, then directs Maxine to take a seat.

The sofa is as uncomfortable as it looks. She gets up and makes a circuit of the waiting room. There is a giant seal with DEPARTMENT OF JUSTICE FEDERAL BUREAU OF INVESTIGATION emblazoned around the rim. A video console provides a portal to any and all information a citizen might need as regards the FBI. An embossed plaque honors the only Michigan agent to have lost his life in the line of duty—in a car crash, but still. The agent was a former All-American running back. Active in his church. The father of four young children.

Maxine finds herself admiring the portrait of Barack Obama. Having spent so many decades flinching at the portraits of Nixon, Reagan, the elder Bush, then the younger, she can't believe the current president is someone she would love to meet. She sees him thanking her for bringing to justice the serial killer who eluded capture for so many years. Sees herself bowing her head as he slips a medal around her neck. Then she motions him down to whisper that Thaddeus Rapaczynski isn't the demon he is made out to be. As a student at Harvard, he was the object of a sinister, sadistic experiment. He never felt loved. By today's standards, he might be classified as autistic. The president nods, places his long, narrow hand consolingly on her arm.

She settles back on the sofa. The woman with magenta hair points at Maxine and tells her, "I have a pretty good idea where to find that bomber guy they're looking for."

"You do?" Maxine says.

"My father-in-law." She rolls her eyes. "He lives with us up in Macomb. Lost his job at the tool-and-die—this was, like, eighteen years ago? My husband bought him a trailer, parked it out back. What does the old man do? He covers the windows with cardboard. Won't let any of us inside. I offer to clean the place up. But no. He hardly bathes. When you do catch a glimpse of him, his hair is all dirty and long, and he wears one of those sweatshirts with the hood. And those aviator sunglasses? Rants about the government. Doesn't matter if it's a white guy or a black guy in charge, hates each and every one of them.

"But what he hates even more are robots. Robots took his job. Robots, and computers. When he isn't holed up in that filthy trailer, he's combing the dump. Soldering. Sawing. Running off his mouth about robots and computers and how our lives are being ruined because the government keeps track of every sneeze and fart and we'd all be better off if we went back to living in the woods and earning our feed by the sweat of our brows.

"My husband thinks I'm trying to get rid of the old man. But my father-in-law has the skills. Plus, he did something with explosives in the Korea War. I won't have it on my conscience if it's him been sending those bombs. What's the motto? You see something, you say something? Well, I seen my father-in-law, and now I'm here to say a thing or two about him."

"Yes, ma'am," the older black man pipes up from the other sofa. "You see something, you are obliged to come forward and speak what you know." He fingers the rim of the fedora in his lap. "The missus and me, we don't want to go getting anyone in trouble. Those young men renting our apartment probably not doing anyone no harm. Engineering students, they said when they signed the lease. Good boys, studying at Wayne State. Don't mean to hold anyone's country of origin or the color of his skin against him. But the missus, she sees what those boys bring into that apartment. Pieces of this machine, pieces of that machine. Wires. Batteries. Other young men stop by, they're speaking all the time in Arab. Praying, I think. I have nothing against a man getting down on his knees to pray. The missus and I, we would still be getting down on our knees if it weren't so hard getting *up*. But beards? The young men have beards. And sometimes they're wearing those flowy gowns. A man ought to be able to wear a beard. Ought to be able to wear what he wants in the comfort of his own apartment. But the missus, she point out to me, anything blowing up down there on the first floor, we're going to be going to their paradise along with them."

The woman pats the man's hat. "How could you and your wife live with yourselves? Any more than I could live with myself, knowing I'd let my father-in-law keep mailing his bombs." She faces Maxine. "And you? You see something, too?"

Maxine feels sorry for the woman, as if she is pinning her hopes on a lottery for which Maxine holds the winning ticket. "Well, there is something I think the FBI ought to be aware of. About someone who may or may not have committed a crime."

"What sort of crime?" the woman asks. But before Maxine can answer, a short, slight male agent comes into the waiting room and says, "Professor Sayers?," and the woman's expression changes, as if Maxine slipped a bribe to the woman behind the glass to be taken before her turn.

"If you will," the agent says, guiding Maxine inside. He is a scrawny, fussy man with wire-rim glasses that make him resemble the band director who tried to teach Maxine to play the clarinet in elementary school, a man who so idealized music in the abstract he couldn't believe it should be allowed to be produced by actual human children.

"Special Agent Bird Dog," the agent says, and Maxine needs a minute to figure out he is saying "Burdock." He indicates she should proceed down a corridor whose shiny modernity surprises her—she had been expecting the institutional drabness of every other government office she has ever been in. Maybe the war on terror has been good for the FBI. Especially in Detroit, with its high population of Arab residents.

"Sorry." The agent leads her past door after door. "Busy day."

She summons the courage to ask if everyone is here because of the manifesto.

"Most." He takes a seat behind the desk and motions her to sit in the other chair. "And then there's everyone who thinks he's spotted a jihadi." At that, Special Agent Burdock launches into a diatribe against citizens who don't understand that the Federal Bureau of Investigation was designed to solve interstate kidnappings, bring down organized crime, figure out who is or is not a communist. "When I started out," he says, "most of the tips were about aliens landing at the old SAC airbase up near Sault Ste. Marie. Now everybody's sure his neighbor is Al-Qaeda. Thing is, you can't dismiss the new tips out of hand the way you could the aliens." He places a legal pad and a pen before him. "Okay, professor. Before we get started, I'm just curious. What are you a professor of?"

She hesitates. If she tells him she directs something called the Institute for Future Studies, he will dump her in a mental drawer crammed with all the lunatics raving about UFOs. Nothing she says will bring back Thaddy's victims. She can't restore Arnold Schlechter's eyesight or missing fingers. Maybe, if she identifies his assailant, Schlechter will remember her name. But she doubts he will ever thank her.

"I study the way all this new technology is going to affect our lives."

He lifts an eyebrow, the way her music teacher used to do

when he suspected she hadn't practiced. "So? Whose side are you on?"

Not "which side," but "whose." The FBI no doubt favors the newest, most far-reaching technologies with which to listen, spy on, investigate. And Maxine? After all the years she has spent studying the future, does she favor progress? Innovation? Despite the detrimental cosequences Thaddy fears? Maybe. Yes. But there are so many more sides to choose from than she used to think.

The agent waves off his own question. "You're here because you have information that might assist us." He stops twirling the pen, daring Maxine to tell him something he considers worthy of committing to his pad.

She can't bring herself to say Thaddy's name. If Zach is the only person to whom Thaddy confided his location in Montana, won't he guess Zach betrayed him? What if Thaddy is condemned to death? How will she and Zach bear knowing Thaddy is being strapped to a gurney, injected with those terrible drugs, left to writhe and die in agony? Maybe she will visit him and apologize. Not for turning him in. For her earlier failure to credit his pain. To hug him. Will she talk to him through one of those glass dividers? What will happen if she meets Thaddy's mother? Would Thaddy's mother have turned in her own son? Would Maxine have turned in Zach?

She opens her mouth and explains to Special Agent Burdock how, when she read the bomber's manifesto, certain of his phrases struck her as familiar. How, as soon as she had the chance, she dug up her former student's essay and noted his references to the Conrad novel.

The agent stops her. "You have this student's essay?"

She removes it from her backpack. "I've circled the similarities. The places where the student's language echoes the bomber's. Some of the parallels aren't exact. But I think you will find these passages to be convincing." She hates any pleasure she might derive in turning the screws on Thaddy's shackles tighter. As if finding these similarities reflects well on her.

"Excuse me." The agent pushes back from the desk. "The supervisory agent who has been handling the Technobomber case for us . . . I would like to see what he makes of all this."

Special Agent Burdock is gone a long time. The walls are solid—no two-way mirrors. But Maxine can't shake the sensation she is being watched. She peers out through the Venetian blinds. On the sidewalk, behind a metal fence, someone has set up the sort of picnic table and patio furniture you would find in a suburban yard. The area is shrouded with plastic greenery; apparently even the FBI is afraid of being watched.

Another half hour passes. She imagines Special Agent Burdock googling to see what he can turn up about Professor Maxine Sayers. She has googled herself often enough to know the answer: her book, *Empty Attics: How the Digital Revolution Is Robbing Us of Our Most Resonant Objects*, currently rated a million and a half on Amazon; six articles in social-science journals, which she intends to collect and publish as *The Pros and Cons of Immortality*; an editorial about the limits of artificial intelligence she penned for *The Washington Post*, along with the hateful responses she received from readers who seemed offended that a woman dared to express her opinion on technology; a handful of caustic put-downs on RateMyProfessor.com from students who found her grading to be too harsh (although she rarely gives anything lower than a B), her jokes unfunny, her opinions old-fashioned, her clothing too frumpy (although two students, bless their hearts, awarded her the chili-pepper symbol that indicates she is hot, or was hot, when the last of the chilis was awarded ten years earlier).

The door opens and Special Agent Burdock comes back in, followed by an associate he introduces as "Supervisory Special Agent Chance," although when the agent hands Maxine his card, she realizes the name is "Shauntz." Darker and heftier than his colleague, with a rectangular face and hair so shiny and black Maxine assumes he dyes it, Supervisory Special Agent Shauntz reminds her of the star of the detective series her mother used to watch in the 1970s. It's as if the detective on that show screwed up and was transferred from Hawaii to this far less glamorous department in Detroit.

But Shauntz is anything but a screw-up. As Burdock explains, his superior officer was one of the first agents assigned to the case, a profiler who, with his training in psychology, would surely have solved the crime if only their higher-ups in Washington hadn't shifted the investigation to the West Coast. Clearly, Burdock is in awe of the man, to the point where he seems to fawn on his every move.

Seeing that his boss has nowhere to sit, Burdock goes out and returns with a third metal chair, which Shauntz twirls backwards before he sits, leaning across his arms in such a casual way Maxine feels he is trying a bit too hard to make her comfortable.

"So," he says. "Professor Sayers. Agent Burdock here tells me you have reason to believe you know the identity of our friend who is sending all these exploding gifts."

She begins at the beginning and tells Supervisory Special Agent Shauntz everything that happened in the past few days. At relevant points, she extracts from her backpack the evidence that supports her point. So compelled is she to convince Shauntz she is not another wacko that she plunges into a description of how lonely Thaddy was in graduate school, how alienated, how depressed, how starved for female contact, skidding to a halt only moments before she would have offered up the story about Thaddy's aborted attempt to convince a psychiatrist to change him into a woman so he might find comfort in a woman's touch. She won't cheapen his pain by serving it up as an anecdote. Although later, driving home, she will realize this is precisely the sort of testimony that might soften a jury and allow them to sentence the defendant to life in prison rather than death.

From then on, she is circumspect about what she chooses to include. She avoids mentioning Zach, except to say Thaddy and her son spent time together when Zach was a boy. Only when she needs to tell Shauntz about the package in which springy snakes and talcum powder simulated the bomb that otherwise might have killed her does she feel compelled to explain why Thaddy wanted her to assume her son sent the box. Why Thaddy might be angry at Zach. Why he might feel betrayed by Zach's refusal to run away with him. Why, instead of heading to a cabin in Montana with his former friend, Zach quit his job and took off with his pregnant girlfriend to spend seven months in the family's cabin in northern Michigan.

When she explains about Professor Hertz, Burdock no longer is able to maintain his calm façade. "Hertz! Your son's teacher at MIT was Gordon Hertz?"

Shauntz leans forward even farther, pounding his trousered knees. "When?" he says. "When can we talk to your son?"

Her son, Maxine explains, is driving down from the Upper Peninsula. He will come in the following morning and tell them everything he knows.

"Tomorrow?" Shauntz says. "No. Not tomorrow. We would very much like to speak with him right away. He's on the road? You live in Ann Arbor? That's where your son and his girlfriend are heading? We'll have our agents there to meet him. Just to talk to him. At this point. And search his room."

The thought of FBI agents snooping around her house, inspecting the books on the shelves, the posters on the walls, especially in Zach's bedroom (where, she hopes, they will find nothing more incriminating than Zach's old drawings of his favorite Pokémon characters) makes her so anxious she insists on the original plan. Zach will be too tired tonight, she says. His fiancée is pregnant and needs her rest. What she doesn't say is she won't allow her son to talk to the FBI without a lawyer. That might make the agents suspect Zach is more involved than she made him out to be. They haven't caught on that if she had come in earlier she might have prevented the most recent bombing. But these men aren't stupid. They will put the timeline together. She will need to speak to a lawyer, too.

"Sorry, professor," Shauntz says. "We have an active serial killer out there threatening to blow people up unless we meet his demands. We'll need a list of the other students who took your seminar. Anything, no matter how seemingly irrelevant. Although for now, I'm going to ask that you sit tight while we make arrangements."

Arrangements? She didn't think she could feel sicker than she has felt for the past few days. "Can't I leave?"

Shauntz rubs his forehead. "The answer to that is yes. But we would much prefer if you wouldn't. We appreciate your coming in. We do. But you can understand the exigencies here. You can call a lawyer, but no one else. And now, I'm very sorry, but you will need to excuse us. Please don't leave the room."

He and Burdock go out. Maxine picks up the landline on the desk, but she can't get a dial tone. If she still had her phone she would call Rosa and ask if Mick has found a lawyer for Zach. But she is too exhausted and upset to think clearly about whether she needs a lawyer of her own. Why would she? She can't be held responsible for Thaddy's actions. She is a citizen who has come forward to provide evidence to solve a crime.

She lays her head on her arms, the way she used to do at naptime in elementary school. When the door opens, she startles awake to find that Burdock has come in with an agent in a yellow tie. They don't shine a light in her eyes, don't beat her with a rubber hose. But they ask their questions brusquely. Is she certain she hasn't seen Thaddeus Rapaczynski since, when was it, December 2002? Not once in the past nine and a half years? Not since the end of the semester in which she taught him? Even though he remained in town another year? Yet she retained in her possession the essays he wrote for her class? Isn't that unusual? That a professor of her status would keep a paper written by a student who took a single class with her nearly a decade earlier? How does she know so much about this former student's mental and emotional state? How many times did they meet? Only in her office? Nowhere else?

She reminds herself to remain calm. The good cop, Shauntz, must be waiting in another room while these bad cops give her a going over. Then Shauntz will return to regain her confidence.

The agent with the yellow tie confiscates whatever papers she brought, the fragments of the exploding package, the felt-covered snakes. She thinks of asking for copies of Thaddy's essays, wonders if this will annoy the agents, decides she doesn't care and asks. Burdock ignores her request.

The two agents exit. And sure enough, Shauntz comes back in. "What, those chuckleheads left you alone? Here you've done us the service of coming in with what appears to be highly significant evidence in one of our highest-priority unsolved cases . . . We don't usually allow visitors access to the upper floors. But what say I take you up. I can offer you the chance to stretch your legs and enjoy a look behind the scenes."

This is a strategy, Maxine knows. But what choice does she have? Shauntz leads her through another maze of halls. They pause at an amateur painting that celebrates the agent who was slain in the line of duty. "Not exactly a Rembrandt," Shauntz admits. "But the guy who painted this was the agent's partner. A lot of heart went into this portrait. Makes up for any deficiencies in talent."

Shauntz pushes the button for the elevator. The sleek metallic box lets them out on one of the uppermost floors, where agents' heads bob above a rats' nest of cubicles, file drawers, and computers. In the front area, a rotund male agent is packing away paper snowflakes, candy canes, and red stockings—odd, Maxine thinks, that the FBI would be so inefficient in changing from one holiday to the next. Shauntz introduces Special Agent Ortega, who explains he is belatedly clearing away the remains of the agency's winter toy-drive and getting ready to move on to the spring golf event, which will raise funds for the victims of violent crimes.

"You must be pretty important," Ortega jokes. "Shauntz doesn't bring just anyone up to meet us." He smiles a smile so genuine Maxine understands why he has been chosen to hand out toys and kibitz with the participants at the annual golf fund-raiser.

The female agent standing beside Ortega extends a manicured hand. "Don't mind them. I'm Special Agent Markham. Jill." A polished brunette, Special Agent Markham—Jill—wears a tailored suit whose skirt is shorter than Maxine imagined an

EILEEN POLLACK

FBI agent would be allowed to wear, an amethyst choker, and heels so high she would never be able to track down a fleeing criminal. Obviously, Shauntz called ahead and requested the services of these two agents to present the smiling, gender-diverse faces of the FBI. Still, Maxine can't help but be charmed.

Special Agent Markham—Jill—unlocks a cabinet and shows Maxine the items the agency sells or gives away—jackets, hats, fake-leather briefcases imprinted with the agency's logo, pens inscribed with the words I STOLE THIS PEN FROM THE FBI.

"Want something?" Ortega offers.

"Hard to choose," Maxine says. "Which one's your favorite?"

The agents exchange glances.

"Uh, no one who works for the agency would be seen with anything that identifies him or her as an employee," Ortega explains. "Anyone who works for law enforcement is making himself enough of a target."

"And we can't let our kids wear any of this stuff," Markham says bitterly.

"Hey," Shauntz says. "You gotta take in the view from up here." He leads her to the windows like a maître d' ushering a customer to a table. Beyond the city's desolate outskirts, the nation stretches west. Maxine squints into the setting sun and can almost see Thaddy in Montana, the same clean-shaven young man she used to teach, in a short-sleeve white shirt and ironed chinos. He stands beside a workbench. A set of tools— drills, drill bits, wires, hacksaws, wire cutters—lies beside a box, the way Maxine's father kept his pliers, screwdrivers, and spools of soldering wire fanned out beside whatever appliance he was working on. Could she wire a bomb? She would need to look up the procedure on the Internet. But she's had the necessary skills

[179]

since she was twelve. How satisfying to fashion a weapon from such innocent ingredients. Matches, she thinks. Wires. Batteries. Zinc, aluminum, lead, ammonium nitrate. To mail it off and read about the explosion in the national press. So much more satisfying than trying to persuade a human female to wrap you in her arms and say she loves you.

Once, Thaddy told Maxine about the time he took a young woman in his high school calculus class to a movie. He couldn't find a parking space that didn't require putting a coin in the meter every half an hour. Panicked at missing the film, he bought tickets and escorted his date to their seats. Then he excused himself and ran down the block, fed a quarter to the meter, and ran back, sweating. Naturally, his date thought he was strange, especially when he wouldn't admit where he kept going. Humiliated, he took her home and never dared speak to her again. It occurs to Maxine that most parents do a terrible job preparing their children to live their lives. When Zach was four, his preschool teacher pointed out it was lovely he knew how to add, subtract, and multiply, but didn't Maxine think it would be a good idea to teach him to tie his shoes? Even now, she can't reconcile her feelings for Thaddy with all the carnage he inflicted. She still feels sorry for the guy.

"Told you it was a nice view," Shauntz says. "Good thing my office doesn't have a window or I would never get any work done." He leads her along the far edge of the cubicles and opens the door to a small, spare room. Above his desk hangs a graduation portrait of a teenage girl. This has to be Shauntz's daughter, but there is no photo of a woman who might be his wife. Tacked to a corkboard is a quotation printed on fanfold computer paper in huge dot-matrix font—ANYONE CAN BE COOL BUT AWESOME TAKES PRACTICE.

"I've been on this case almost from the beginning," Shauntz tells her. "The first and third packages, they went to professors, one of them here on my home turf. To me, that was a clear indication the perpetrator had some connection to a university. To me, that meant you tried to find some disgruntled graduate student, some science genius who engaged in a tussle with his adviser and left without his degree. Or the guy was older and, for whatever reason, the department denied him tenure. Or his supervisor took the credit for some discovery, published the paper, patented it, made a fortune.

"Me and my team, we put together a comprehensive list of the possibilities. You would be surprised, at a university, how many students and employees feel disgruntled. The women, they usually give up quietly. Maybe they kill *themselves*. But the men? They get angry. They get even. If the higher-ups had given me a little more time. A few more resources. Your friend there, Rapaczynski? I just checked, and he was on my original list. But he didn't sufficiently arouse our suspicions. He got his degree. He won an award for his dissertation.

"And the bomber, after that first incident at the university, he switched his targets. He sent packages to psychologists. Environmental polluters. Airline executives. Not only in Michigan, but in the Bay Area. Chicago. Colorado. Utah. Massachusetts. And he sent letters to his victims. Diatribes against medical science. The despoiling of the environment. Everyone at the Bureau, the DOJ, the ATF, everybody, they were sold on the theory he must be an ideologue. Some PETA extremist. Some environmental warrior. They moved the task force to San Francisco. I tried to stay on top of things. But the hard-liners never trust eggheads like me. Profilers. They think anything psychological is New Age voodoo. Girly stuff. 'Intuition.' But if you don't pay due diligence to that type of thinking, there's so much you might be missing. So much you can learn about the UNSUB—sorry, that's the unknown suspect. You can learn a lot about his personality by studying crime-scene indicators. The construction of the bomb. Who he chooses as his victims.

"And nothing about this UNSUB's profile is telling me he's doing what he's doing to promote some ideology. How do I know this? If it's such a passionately held belief, how come he's not willing to die for it? A jihadi, he puts on a suicide vest, he believes in what he's dying for. But you're sitting in your living room, reading about the effects of your brilliantly constructed explosive device, you're in it for the kicks. Or you're getting back at someone. Mommy and Daddy, who didn't love you enough. Your teachers, who didn't recognize what a genius you are. All those hot women who didn't notice your inner beauty.

"So that was my guess. My professional assessment. The bomber would turn out to be some guy who hated science *because he was a scientist*. Not some crunchy environmental type who hates technology because it's ruining the earth. He hates science from the inside. Because his parents made him do his physics homework when he would rather have been outside playing ball. Most of these guys, they end up as computer nuts. But this guy, he's no lover of computers. He's a scientist who hates computers. And other scientists. Especially behavioral types. Maybe he saw a therapist? And the therapist didn't do anything to help him feel less alone? Or he hates professors who study how a human mind can be controlled. How misfits can be trained, conditioned to conform. Because that's what scares him. The need to fit in. To be like everyone else. Of course, deep inside, he wants to be like everyone else. To have their confidence, their personality. But he also likes *not* fitting in. He feels inferior, and he feels superior. He knows he's Superman, but everyone keeps treating him like Clark Kent."

Shauntz has been saying all this with his eyes trained on her face. Is he getting hotter? Colder? She can't help but be impressed. Why did she think government agents couldn't be this eloquent, this worldly, this perceptive? But something prevents her from complimenting Shauntz on the accuracy of his predictions. He thinks he knows Thaddy because he has figured out a few salient details about Thaddy's character. But Shauntz is confusing an actual person with this "profile." How could anyone know Thaddy unless Thaddy had sat in her office, crying? Thaddy has become a test for Shauntz's skills. A challenge to his ego. Still, she admires his professionally honed clairvoyance, the way she admires Rosa's ability to assess a person's character based on her intuition and a pack of cards.

"Like I said, the Bureau moved the task force to San Francisco. But every few months, I would call and talk to the guys in charge. They were out there looking at all these ideologues. And yeah, maybe the UNSUB cared about the environment. Not in a political way. For more personal reasons. Maybe his old man took him camping. Makes sense the guy would be holed up in the woods. Where else could he carry out his experiments with the explosives and detonators he was developing?

"But I still thought the guy might be hiding in northern Michigan. If this investigation had been left to me, I would have ordered the team to visit every library north of Mackinac. Think about it. You've got this brainiac professor cooped up in a cabin. He's going to be taking a shitload of books out of the town library. And not the typical potboilers and bodice rippers. The librarians up there, they'll remember the guy. I did some of that leg-work myself. On a vacation up north. But nothing turned up."

He falls silent, staring at her, chin resting on his hand like a camera on a tripod. He knows she has been visiting her family's cabin in the UP. Knows her son has been holed up there all winter. Knows that until recently she wasn't sure where that son might be.

"I was planning on going back up there this coming summer. Then the UNSUB published that manifesto. The editors weren't keen on printing it. But we told them to go ahead. We knew . . . we hoped . . . someone out there was going to read the bomber's rantings and turn him in. A classmate. Maybe his own family." Shauntz holds out his palms. "And here you are."

Yes, she thinks, *here I am*.

"You're not saying much. But I'm getting a vibe here. Don't get me wrong, we are very, very grateful. This may be our man. But there's something you're not telling us. Maybe you still like the guy? A former student, it's understandable. He was young. He wasn't who he became later. And you weren't there when those bombs went off. You haven't seen the pictures from the autopsies. I've met that guy, Schlechter. And, okay, he's no one's idea of fuzzy and warm. But what happened to Arnold Schlechter was pretty terrible. Your student, he hadn't gotten his A-game together yet, but that explosive device did a pretty good job ripping Schlechter up. Then your man Rapaczynski improves his design. One of the victims he targeted? The blast blew a hole in the man's chest—you could see all the way to his heart."

He thinks she is withholding evidence. Maybe Thaddy is hiding up there in the UP. Maybe her son is involved. Didn't she suspect this to be true herself? She is so, so very tired. Everything is bollixed in her mind. She didn't know Thaddy was the bomber. Did she? All these years?

No. All she is guilty of is protecting her son. Zach might have corresponded with Thaddy. But Zach had no way of knowing Thaddy was a murderer. Did he? Then why does she feel so anxious? Maybe Zach is no longer lying, but he hasn't yet told her the entire truth. And if the agents persuade him to confess . . .

Shauntz's cell phone rings and he takes the call. Nods. Puts his hand over the mouthpiece and tells Maxine, "Your son and his girlfriend are on your property. As of this moment, they are still in your front yard. No one is in handcuffs. All we want is to talk with him. So, could you tell him it's all right to go with our agents? We have an office in Ann Arbor. In the same building where you go to mail your mail. And while he's there, we would very much like permission to search your house. We can get a warrant. But if you give us permission, we can get all this over a lot quicker. We can have your house and your office searched by tomorrow morning. Or I believe you said two offices? You must be pretty important to have two offices. Even so, we can get your house and both your offices searched in no time. Professor?" He holds out the phone. "Do you think you could do that for me? Advise your son to cooperate? Ask him to unlock your house? Then go with our agents to our offices in Ann Arbor?"

She feels frozen to the chair.

"For now, we just want to talk to your son. There are innocent victims out there, and the bomber is planning to do them harm. You will just need to trust me. Okay? Can you do that? Professor?" He hands Maxine his phone.

She imagines Zach and Angelina at the center of a circle of FBI agents with their guns drawn and pointed. Are the neighbors staring out their windows? Are the agents wearing jackets that identify them as FBI? No, Ortega and Markham said they walk around incognito. Or is that only when they're off duty? Oh, who cares what the neighbors think! Zach must be terrified.

And poor Angelina! Maxine ought to make the agents obtain a warrant. She needs to call Rosa and make sure Mick found Zach a lawyer. But that could take all night. She and Zach have nothing to hide. If she doesn't give permission for the search, they might take Zach somewhere more upsetting than the Federal Building in Ann Arbor.

"Zach," she says. "Sweetheart. Are you there? Do what they tell you. Okay? Tell them whatever they want to know."

She waits to hear her son's voice. Instead, she hears a man say, "Ma'am? Ma'am? If you would please put Agent Shauntz back on the line?"

Shauntz takes his phone. After a while, he hangs up. "Everybody's fine. Your son unlocked the house. He and his girlfriend are safe. You did a nice job, professor."

He moves from behind his desk. Takes Maxine's hand. The contact is less sexual than governmental. Still, she wants to close her eyes and rest in those burly, suited arms.

"So," Shauntz says. "What would you die for?"

"Excuse me?"

"I didn't mean to startle you." Although she guesses he intended to do just that. "It's something a profiler wonders. What would a person die for? This Rapaczynski character, given the pains he takes to keep his distance from his crimes, the answer seems to be not much. But the rest of us . . ." He opens his arms to indicate everyone in the building. "Any of us agents would die to defend our country. To uphold its laws. As individual human beings, we would die to protect our families. So, I'm asking you. What do you hold so dear that you would put your personal safety in jeopardy to protect it?"

For the first thirty-one years of her life, Maxine would have answered: Nothing. She was so scared of dying, she would have given up zero minutes of her life to stand up for a principle. Then she gave birth to Zach.

"My son," she says. "I would die for my son."

"And you thought he was mixed up in all this, didn't you."

She mustn't answer without a lawyer. But for Zach's sake, she tries to remain cooperative. "I'm sorry. I'm so tired and hungry, I can't think clearly."

Appalled at his lack of gallantry, he offers to bring her sandwiches. "Or look. It's going to be a long night. Your son is absolutely safe. Why don't the two of us get some dinner? There's this place nearby that makes incredible barbecue. Slows. A Detroit institution. I don't know how you feel about brisket or ribs, but for a Kentucky boy like me . . ."

She knows this is a setup. But would anything be so wrong if she allowed Supervisory Special Agent Shauntz to take her out for dinner and a drink?

"We aren't your enemy," Shauntz says. "You might even consider coming to work for us." Recently, the agency hired a female futurist. "This woman—Meyer, Breyer, something like that—she analyzes whatever statistics the data-heads collect. Then she uses it to predict any crime trends that might be coming at us down the pike. More and more, the bureau needs futurists to head off attacks from groups that aren't yet on our radar. Me? I think the future might be too big for just one person. Maybe you and Meyer, Breyer, the two of you could head up a new division. You've already got a great start, helping us solve one of the most notorious serial bombings in history."

The job seems even more thankless than directing an institute that attempts to predict the effects of technological change on human society. If you accurately predict a terrorist attack and the government heads it off, how will you get the credit for heading off an attack that never happened?

"So, what about that dinner?"

She is saved from declining his proposal by the return of the agent who reminds her of her old music teacher. Burdock lays out duplicates of Thaddy's essays, so perfectly copied she can't distinguish the Xeroxes from the originals. Somehow, this upsets her. She wants to hang on to the papers Thaddy touched. The ones with the comments she penciled in the margins. The ones with the rusty echo of the paper clip, not a Xeroxed echo of the echo.

She inserts the copies in her backpack. Thanks Shauntz for the dinner invitation. Asks when she will be allowed to get back in her house.

"My guess is this," Shauntz says. "Your son is in for a long night. And your house is going to be filled with agents. Maybe you have a friend you can stay with? Or you could check into a motel. By morning, if everything is as you described it, your son and his lady will be home and eager for a home-cooked breakfast. Here is my direct line and cell phone number. Feel free to use it—any time, for anything."

She had been hoping Shauntz would be the one to escort her back down to the waiting room. But Burdock fulfills that role. The man with the fedora and the woman with magenta hair are gone. In their places sit a woman in a hijab and a dark-skinned teenager in a gold tracksuit. Are they here to inform on their neighbors, or on their families?

Burdock leads Maxine to the security booth, where the guard returns her phone.

"The system," Burdock says, "it works. We know things you can't imagine we know. Shauntz is . . . You have no idea what kind of man Roland Shauntz is."

Burdock says this as if he is in love with his superior. Which, why not, of course he could be. Maxine gets the idea Burdock pledges his fealty more to Roland Shauntz than to the agency. She is less certain why Burdock sees her as a threat to this allegiance.

"The guy is a genius," Burdock says. "He would have figured out the identity of this individual. If the agency had given us the resources he asked for, we would have brought in this Rapaczynski years ago, on our own."

. . . Watches History Repeat Itself

The Buick is the only car in the lot. The guard has abandoned his booth. But Maxine sits in the dark, using her newly restored phone to call Rosa. Zach hasn't committed any crimes. Unless getting his girlfriend pregnant is illegal. But she was right to suspect her former student has become a terrorist. And Zach quite possibly knows where the man is hiding. The FBI is questioning him now. The agents will be holding him overnight.

"Jesus," Rosa says. "You must be going out of your mind. Try to stay calm. Mick found you the legal equivalent of Muhammad Ali. You remember Stuart Greenglass? He defended everybody from the White Panthers and the Chicago Seven to Angela Davis and Daniel Ellsberg."

Maxine reminds Rosa her son isn't exactly Abbie Hoffman. The FBI might associate this Stuart Greenglass—and therefore Zach—with those earlier and more notorious radicals. But the idea of such a prominent lawyer working on her son's behalf silences her objections. Rosa gives her the lawyer's number. "Thanks," Maxine says. "I feel so alone in all this." She starts to tear up—from gratitude, from exhaustion.

"By the way," Rosa says, "congratulations on becoming a grandmother. Isn't that something? You and I are both going to be raising grandkids. That should give us something to look forward to, don't you think?"

To be honest, this is nothing Maxine feels cause to celebrate. She sees herself pushing a swaddled, faceless lump in one of those swings that resembles a rubberized diaper. She will be caring for her grandchild so her son and his wife can get on with their future. Her own future will be in the past.

She doesn't say any of this to Rosa. She thanks her again for arranging the meeting with Stuart Greenglass. She hates to ask, but while the government is searching her house, can she spend the night at Rosa's? When Rosa says yes, of course, Maxine hangs up and calls the lawyer. He sounds distant. Gruff. No doubt she interrupted his dinner. But once he understands the case involves the serial bomber whose manifesto was printed in *The New York Times*, he says, "Yes! I see!" And his voice becomes the voice of a man hanging on her every word. He will get right down to the FBI's offices in Ann Arbor. If all goes well, he may have Zach out in a few hours. Depends on what Zach is telling them. If they want, the agency can just keep moving the kid around until Greenglass manages to get to a judge. Unless Zach invokes his right to counsel, in which case Greenglass will sit there with him all night while he's being questioned. "I'll keep you apprised of the situation," Greenglass promises, and then, when she hears him disconnect, Maxine hangs up, reluctantly, because now she has nothing to do but worry.

She gets on the highway to Ann Arbor. It is after rush hour, but there must have been some tie-up because no one is rushing anywhere. When the traffic on I-94 clogs to a halt, Maxine lays her forehead against the steering wheel and closes her eyes.

The car behind her honks. Has she been asleep? She opens the window and drives as fast as she can. When she makes it to Ypsilanti, she finds Rosa's house, knocks, and collapses in Rosa's arms. After dinner, she asks if she can take a bath, then strips off her wrinkled skirt, her fetid blouse, her disgusting underwear, and plunges gratefully into the hottest water her skin will tolerate. She scrubs every square inch. Lathers her scalp. Slides beneath the surface and holds her breath. When she comes up, she is as surprised by her breasts as if two soft, aquatic creatures had found their way into the tub. When was the last time she saw them? The last time she enjoyed an orgasm, even one she supplied herself? The skin on her chest is developing that wrinkly crepe that always made her think a woman was truly old. How little time is left before she is ashamed to take off her clothes? She remembers Sam going down on her, the whirlpool of thinning hair at the very top of his head, which she otherwise never saw. Then it is Thaddy between her legs, not for her own pleasure, but so she can instruct him on how to please a woman of his own. She replaces the image with Jackson Sparrow, who seems to be showing off, demonstrating that age can be not a liability but an advantage.

Maybe Jackson is right. If we survive to a trans-human age, won't we mourn the loss of our organic bodies? Maybe our digitally enhanced skin will simulate such exquisite sensation our enjoyment of sex will be off the scale. But that only makes her more desperate to enjoy her body while she has it.

She puts on the sweatshirt and sweatpants Rosa left by the tub—her son Jamal's castoffs. Rosa has made up the bed in Jamal's old room. As worn out as she is, Maxine can't believe she will be able to sleep. Not with Zach in custody. But when she is awakened by the chirping of her phone, it's seven-thirty.

"I didn't manage to see him," Greenglass says. "But they agreed not to charge him."

"Charge him! What would they charge him with!"

Greenglass calms her. Zach ought to be arriving home in another hour. He should have just enough time for a shower and a hot meal before he needs to return to Detroit for further questioning.

She hangs up, thanks Rosa, hurries home. The lock on the front door is intact—Zach used his key to let in the agents. And very little in the living room or kitchen has been disturbed; except for some muddy footprints, she barely would have noticed the intrusion. Upstairs is a different story. The ancient Dell PC from her bedroom is gone, as is the equally obsolete Gateway from Zach's room. Good luck getting either machine to boot up. Her cabinets and drawers have been rifled through. There are gaping spaces on her son's bookshelves; no doubt the agents confiscated his Howard Zinn, among other incendiary volumes. The video games and board games—some of them designed by Norm—have been thoroughly ransacked. But the disruption seems less severe than she expected.

She hears a commotion outside. From the upstairs window she can see Zach and Angelina climb from the back seat of a black Ford Bronco. A second black car pulls up behind the first.

Maxine runs down and opens the door. "Are you okay? They didn't hurt you, did they?"

"Sorry, Mom," Zach apologizes. "I didn't mean to put you through all this," as if she is the one who spent the night being questioned. He nods to the cars at the curb. "For our protection, they said. But it's more like house arrest. One of the agents— that beefy guy with the black hair that comes to a point on his

THE PROFESSOR OF IMMORTALITY

forehead?—he said he promised you he would have us home by morning. Otherwise, I'm pretty sure we would still be there."

The "we" makes Maxine remember Angelina. Maxine helps carry their bags up to Zach's bedroom. Following behind, she sees how badly Angelina wobbles—from the stress, the lack of sleep. She swings her left leg and left crutch to the side before she plants these on the step above. Then she repeats this with the other crutch and the other leg. Maxine hovers behind in case she misses her footing and tumbles backward. This must be how protective Sam felt toward Maxine, all those years ago, hovering behind her as she limped up the three flights to her apartment. But of course Angelina is an experienced stair-climber and doesn't fall. Zach ushers his girlfriend into his boyhood room, with its slanted stucco ceiling and the childish paintings tacked to the walls with dried-out putty. His posters of Pokémon characters. The cartographer's map of the world his father gave him so Zach could follow his travels.

Angelina picks Zach's yearbook off a shelf and begins to leaf through it. "Oh, Zach! Everyone else in this photo is laughing, and there you are, scowling. Didn't you have any fun in high school? What about kindergarten? Are there photographs of you scowling in elementary school?"

Watching the two of them giggle and nudge each other, Maxine wonders if she should offer to let them stay in her room. Zach is six feet three inches tall. His fiancée is seven months pregnant. How will they both fit in Zach's childhood bed? Thinking this, she can't help but picture her slim, handsome son making love to his big-bellied, big-breasted fiancée. The image is so novel she allows it to linger longer than she should. Every child tries to keep from imagining his parents having sex. And every parent—at least the ones who aren't monsters—tries equally hard not to imagine his or her child making love. Which means every generation misses out on imagining the people they love best at the moment they are the happiest.

She leaves them sitting on Zach's bed, laughing at his yearbook, and goes downstairs to call Greenglass to update him. Later, she listens to make sure she won't be interrupting anything, then summons Zach and Angelina down to eat. She allows Zach to set the table, then watches the two of them scarf down the English muffins and cheese omelets she has prepared—the calcium in the cheese will be good for the baby's bones. She feels like Job, getting back, if not her original family, then a new one. Zach and Angelina and the baby will come to dinner often. Maxine will drive to Detroit to babysit. Her son and his wife will spend Christmas and Easter with Angelina's parents. But Maxine will hold Thanksgiving and Passover in Ann Arbor. If everyone lived forever, would children experience the same incentive to spend holidays with their parents? Would they bother visiting their parents at all? She considers blogging this idea on www.professorofimmortality.com, then remembers she shut down the site.

As they fork up the last of the omelets, Zach talks about their plans for the day. Angelina will rest while he and Maxine drive to Detroit to talk to the FBI, which Zach thinks won't take more than another few hours and Maxine hopes won't consume the rest of their lives. They talk about Angelina's plans to call her parents. Until now, the Ruizes have welcomed Zach as an upstanding young man who treats their daughter with respect. Now, he will need to convince them he isn't a terrible person for getting her pregnant and dragging her into this mess. Hopefully, they will be pleased at the couple's decision to get married, their plans to start a business Angelina's father can understand

THE PROFESSOR OF IMMORTALITY

because, like his own, it involves growing and raising plants.

"Professor Sayers?" Angelina says. "You mustn't think Zach is going to need to take care of me. I can do anything anyone else can do. If our plan doesn't work out, I will help to support our family. You won't ever need to be ashamed of having me for a daughter-in-law."

"Ashamed!" That Angelina can even imagine such a possibility makes Maxine want to prostrate herself before her future daughter-in-law. Instead, she wraps her arms around Angelina's bare shoulders—which feel much sturdier than they look. "Don't even think such a thing! And please, if you can't bring yourself to call me 'Mom,' could you at least try 'Maxine'?"

Zach and Maxine drive to Detroit, followed by one of the two black sedans—the other remains behind, as if to protect Angelina, or make sure she doesn't run off. They meet Greenglass in the lobby of the Federal Building. A compact man in his mid-seventies, with bright red reading glasses dangling from a leather cord around his neck, Greenglass is all business. He also is black, rather than the New York Jew Maxine expected from his name and flat, nasal intonations. (Later, she will learn Greenglass attended the Bronx High School of Science and CCNY before he moved to the Midwest to attend Wayne State Law School.) He shakes her hand, then shakes Zach's hand, puts on his glasses, and inspects them both.

"Did you ever invoke your right to counsel last night?" the lawyer asks Zach.

Zach purses his lips. "I didn't think I had anything to hide."

Greenglass cackles. "If I laid end to end all the people who thought they had nothing to hide . . ." He slaps his palms against each other, as if rubbing off whatever damage might have accrued. "Done is done." But Zach is finished talking to the cops until Greenglass has the chance to review the facts and evaluate his client's potential jeopardy.

"I'm sorry," Maxine says. "I can't live through another day of this. I can't have it on my conscience if the bomber sends out another bomb and another innocent person gets hurt or killed. If Zach and I were going to incriminate ourselves, we already did."

But Greenglass refuses to represent either of them unless they spend at least a few hours discussing Zach's testimony. He pulls out his phone and dials. "Shauntz? Greenglass. Give my boy a couple of hours. Can you do that?" He listens. Grunts. "We've got two hours," he tells Maxine. "Assuming I have no reason to convince you not to show up at all."

The appointment leaves little chance to get back to Greenglass's office. The streets around the Federal Building are stark, with nowhere to eat except the Rosa Parks Transportation Center, a futuristic mess with sails and what appears to be a satellite antenna, as if a space station has spiraled to a crash landing in downtown Detroit. The People Mover floats above the station on its monorail, making endless circuits around the nearly empty city, the giant Michelin tire man plastered across its side like a grinning ghost.

The three of them cross the trash-strewn intersection and enter a bus station that, despite being named for the champion of integration, is so segregated that Maxine and Zach comprise one hundred percent of the Caucasians present. A sign forbids loitering, but many in the throng appear to have been waiting at the station for hours, if not weeks. Never mind the future; these Detroiters are waiting for amenities their fellow citizens have taken for granted for fifty years. They wait and wait, and no one sees fit to announce that the future they are waiting for isn't coming.

Maxine excuses herself to use the restroom. A broken changing table dangles from the wall. The toilets in three of the stalls are fetid. After waiting to use the fourth, Maxine emerges to find the woman who used the stall before her waving her hands to dry them—the facility hasn't been provided with paper towels or a working blower.

Back in the lobby, she follows Greenglass up a set of metal stairs to what a hand-lettered sign advertises as the FOOD COURT. An old man naps with his head on one of the three steel tables. A second table is festooned with a pair of soiled green undershorts. The only functioning eatery offers Louisiana Creole takeout; the décor consists of a painted wooden alligator on a serving cart, as if the staff might be preparing to carve up the scaly beast for the lunchtime crowd. Greenglass makes a trip to the counter and brings back a sack of biscuits and three cups of coffee. He removes his overcoat. Takes out a pen. Asks Maxine to repeat, from the very beginning, everything she told the FBI. She drags out copies of Thaddy's papers. Greenglass takes copious notes. "Is that all?" he keeps asking. "Is there anything else?"

When she finishes, he looks Zach hard in the eyes. "All right, young man. I want every single detail, no matter how minute, about your interactions with this Thaddeus Rapaczynski."

Zach puts his palms to the table, scowls, and moves his lips, as if, should he say what he has to say, his words might lay waste to all around him. ("Look out," Sam used to whisper. "He's making his Ralph Nader face again.") Her son's only crime is being overly earnest in the pursuit of purity. But the lawyer might get the impression Zach is a rageful young man who has something to hide.

Zach scowls a while longer. Then he stammers an explanation

of his relationship to his mother's former student. First as an adolescent. Then as an undergraduate at MIT, where Thaddy wrote him letters. Later still, as an employee at the company where Zach worked until Thaddy showed up and insisted on camping on the sofa in Zach's apartment. For a week. Maybe it was ten days. Maybe longer.

"He stayed a week?" Maxine says. Her impression had been that Thaddy put in a brief appearance before his failed attempt to persuade Zach to run off with him to Montana.

"I shouldn't have let him hang around that long," Zach says. "My roommates were totally pissed. Thaddy got in this really ugly argument with my friend Jordan," Jordan being Zach's African-American roommate from MIT, who also had found a job in Silicon Valley. "Jordan is already pretty high up at Facebook, and Thaddy went on and on about how the company is keeping tabs on everything we buy or click on and is selling the data to corporations and to the government. Thaddy hammered Jordan that he shouldn't let himself get co-opted into becoming a slave to the new technology. Thaddy thinks liberals are only facilitating the transformation of the black and Hispanic underclass into capitalist drones." Unexpectedly, Zach laughs. "Thaddy kept trying to act all cool and hip with Jordan, but it was pretty painful to watch. 'Man,' Thaddy said, 'you're too *human* to let yourself become a cog in the white man's machine. Man, you've got too much *soul* for that.' Jordan just rolled his eyes. Then Thaddy got under his skin and Jordan really let Thaddy have it. That's when I told Thaddy he had to go."

Maybe Greenglass will like her son more now that he knows Zach had a black roommate. Maybe he will see Zach as less humorless, less stiff. But Greenglass closes one eye and stares sideways at Zach. "Are you sure you're the one who asked

Rapaczynski to leave? It wasn't this roommate of yours, this Jordan? And you asked him to leave because of political or ideological differences in your points of view?"

Which leads Maxine to wonder, if not for this nominal difference in their ideologies, would Zach have run off with Thaddy?

And the answer is yes. How could she have been so dense? As alienated as Zach was from his job in Silicon Valley. As impressionable as he has always been. As inclined to the hermit-martyr's withdrawal from society. Zach would have been appalled when he discovered what Thaddy was doing in that cabin. When Thaddy asked for help in designing a better bomb. But would Zach have ratted Thaddy out? Yes, Maxine thinks. Of course. Trying to convince herself that he would have.

"It wasn't only the politics," Zach says. "He was furious I was even thinking of getting married. He made some awful comment about how Angelina only loves me because she's a cripple and no other man would have her. If you want the truth, that's as much why I asked him to leave as he was driving Jordan nuts."

What he doesn't say is that this is also why he has been avoiding his mother—because, like Thaddy, she once implied the only reason Zach would be dating the woman he loves is that he pities her.

Greenglass tilts his pen toward Zach. "Something fishy is going on. I think you became more involved with your houseguest than you are willing to admit. Maybe you went with him to his cabin. Where was it, in Montana? And that's why you know the name of the town. Maybe these were plans you and he made together. To wage a campaign of fear against those you regarded as despoiling the environment. For you, those plans were mostly fanciful. Once you realized your partner was actually carrying out those plans, you developed cold feet."

On he goes, needling Zach, trying to satisfy himself that his client isn't hiding some involvement in the bombings. Or to make sure Zach can refrain from losing his composure under the aggressive questioning that will come after the agents have analyzed the sleep-starved statements he gave them last night.

The coffee grows cold. The biscuits have left greasy blotches on the cardboard plates. Greenglass emphasizes that both of them need to tell the truth. The agency will want them to remain available for any follow-up. They mustn't discuss the case—not with a best friend, not with a cousin, not with a nosey neighbor, not with a sympathetic girlfriend. Above all, they mustn't speak to anyone from the press. "Neither of you seems the type to go calling Oprah, but I don't care if it's what's-her-name, Nina Totenberg from NPR, you say, 'I'm very sorry, but I am not at liberty to comment right now.' And you hang up or you shut the door."

Greenglass caps his pen and clips it to his pad. He rises from his seat and puts on his coat. Then he says, "Tell me again, Professor Sayers, why you didn't go directly to the FBI. Why you drove all those many hundreds of miles, way up north, to your family's cabin. It wasn't because you suspected someone else might be up there, hiding with your son?" Before she can answer, Greenglass zips his coat. "No. Of course that wasn't the case. You waited because you wanted Zachary here to corroborate your suspicions. You didn't want to go off half-cocked and get your former student in trouble if your suspicions might prove incorrect." Greenglass nods at his own assessment. "Yes. That account makes perfect sense. As I have advised you both, whatever you are asked, you tell the truth. I don't think the government is going to look to bring charges against the persons who help them solve a series of crimes they have been attempting to solve without success for, what, six or seven years? But here's the deal: You don't lie. You never have to talk to an officer of the law. But lying to one is a felony."

He cups Maxine's elbow and leads her to the steel staircase, motioning Zach to go down before them. "You will have my retainer agreement this afternoon," he tells Maxine. "I want you both to sign it. I promise to go as easy on you as I can, but I am going to need a check for ten thousand dollars by tomorrow afternoon. As a down payment. Can you do that for me?"

Ten thousand dollars? And that's only the beginning. "I can do that," she says. If he asked her to drain her retirement account and sell her house, she would answer in the affirmative.

They are only a few minutes late arriving at the Federal Building, but Shauntz and three men Maxine doesn't recognize already seem impatient. Shauntz and Greenglass shake hands. Then Shauntz extends his hand to Zach, who regards it as if it were a grenade that might go off before he shakes it carefully. They pass through security. Shauntz and the other agents lead Zach to the offices beyond the door. Maxine wants badly to go in with them, the way she did when Zach had an appointment with his pediatrician, until kindly Dr. Harutyunyan suggested Zach was old enough to go through his checkup without his mother. And Zach, all of eleven, said, "Yeah, Mom. I didn't want to hurt your feelings, but even last year, I would rather have gone in alone." To which she lied and said, "My feelings aren't hurt. Of course you should go in without me."

At least Greenglass is allowed to enter. What can she do but trust Zach's essential goodness will shine through his overly serious exterior? Trust her son will realize he no longer has any loyalty to a childhood friend who has been mailing explosives to innocent victims, one of whom was Zach's professor at MIT?

She hasn't brought a book. She wouldn't have been able to concentrate anyway. A cue-ball-headed white man shares the waiting area; when he gets up to go inside, he offers her his copy of the *Free Press*. She searches for any mention of the bomber. Government officials are quoted as saying as many as twenty thousand tips have poured in on various hotlines. The authorities are pursuing leads they are confident will pay off soon. As she reads, Maxine feels her throat constrict, as if the authorities are closing in on her rather than on Thaddy. On the op-ed page, a reader disputes the decision to give a national platform to the bomber's rant, but a columnist expresses his view that as much as he deplores the bomber's violence, society needs to examine the ways technology is robbing us of our privacy. The bomber, this columnist writes, has tapped into a larger malaise in which citizens are "consumed with widespread feelings of helplessness and inferiority, beaten down by an excessive expectation of conformity to societal rules and norms, living lives far too abstract and complex and divorced from nature and reality to be satisfying." The truth, this columnist writes, is that "there is a little of the Technobomber in each and every one of us."

Maybe Thaddy has hit a nerve. Maybe he has sparked an outbreak of dissatisfaction. But one op-ed piece does not a revolution make. As she pages through the paper, she guesses most Detroiters are more concerned with the Red Wings' chances of staying alive in the playoffs, or the wild fluctuations in that spring's temperatures, or even Ted Nugent's threat that if Obama gets reelected he, Ted Nugent, will either be dead or in jail, presumably because he gunned down the president.

By three, her son has yet to reappear. She forces herself to read an article in the business section about a project to employ recovering addicts by hiring them to raise fish in fiberglass tanks in a vacant industrial lot—surely, Zach and Angelina will be interested. In Norway, a right-wing terrorist proudly proclaims that if time allowed, he would have gunned down more than the seventy-seven teenagers he managed to execute at their summer camp. In Iraq, a suicide bomber has blown up another thirty civilians. Next to these cold-blooded mass-murderers, what is Thaddy but a posturing intellectual?

Still no Zach. In the obituary section, she reads that an Ann Arborite two years her junior has died of a heart attack; she never met the man, but she knows his wife. On the comics page, she is shocked to discover that Beetle Bailey, Sergeant Snorkel, and Miss Buxley are still carrying on in ways Maxine didn't find funny even when her father explained the jokes.

Finally, the men come out—without Zach. Maxine jumps up—it's as if Dr. Harutyunyan had come back to the waiting room not with her son but with a team of surgeons and oncologists. "What's wrong? Where's Zach?" But Greenglass avoids her gaze. Given that she is paying his fees, shouldn't he report what went on?

Shauntz motions her inside. Greenglass follows. She expects Shauntz to lead her to Zach. But the room is empty except for Burdock. Greenglass takes a seat and motions Maxine to do the same. Then Shauntz asks her to repeat and clarify certain aspects of her statements from the day before. Did Rapaczynski grow close to any other professor on campus? Does she have reason to suspect he was a homosexual? No? Did he ever mention a girl-friend? Any other females with whom he might have engaged in a sexual relationship? Shauntz's persistence makes her think he suspects she and Thaddy engaged in some sort of romance.

She still hasn't told anyone but Rosa about Thaddy's screwed-up plan to become a woman. If she manages to convey how starved he was for female companionship, how he was driven to despair by the sounds of his neighbors' lovemaking, that might save him from the death penalty. More likely, any such revelation will cause Thaddy to curse her. Who will represent him? Might she ask Greenglass to act as Thaddy's counsel? But who would pay the fee?

No, she tells Shauntz. They weren't romantically involved, but she doubts any professor had a closer friendship with Thaddy than she did. She repeats the story about the Korean graduate student Thaddy followed to Ypsilanti. The agents quiz her endlessly about the details of that encounter. Then, abruptly, Shauntz asks if she has any reason to believe Rapaczynski and her son were, at any point, lovers.

"Excuse me? My son was fourteen. If anything sexual happened between them, you can't believe my son . . ."

Shauntz makes a lowering motion with his hands. "Not when he was fourteen. When your son was an undergraduate at MIT."

"I have no idea what you're talking about," Maxine says. "When Zach was at MIT, Thaddy was a professor at Berkeley. Or he was living in Montana. As far as I know, Thaddy was never in Massachusetts. At least not after he graduated from Harvard."

Greenglass sighs. "I'm afraid Zach just gave us some additional information. Something he forgot to mention last night. Apparently, he spent the entire summer between his freshman and sophomore years living in Montana. With Mr. Rapaczynski."

Maxine feels the floor give way. "But that was the summer Zach had his internship with his adviser!"

Shauntz puts on the universal expression of anyone who has ever raised a teenager. "I hate to say this, but young men have been known to lie to their mothers about their whereabouts. And your son seems to have been extremely unhappy his first few terms of college. He was put off by how many of his professors were working for the military. How little concern anyone showed for the sorts of projects he thought scientists of their caliber ought to be turning their minds to. He was especially outraged at Professor Hertz for his work on facial-recognition software. They argued. The professor failed your son. As you might recall, this is the same Gordon Hertz who was the most recent recipient of a package from your son's friend. All this while, Mr. Rapaczynski was hectoring your son with letters and phone calls, describing the life they might be living out there in his rural utopia. Your son hitchhiked west and joined him."

Maxine tries to take this in. That was the summer Zach told her his professor had invited him to spend six weeks on the Navajo reservation, collecting data from an array of solar panels constructed from some new material. She has the postcards Zach sent, one showing the Grand Canyon, another the rock formations at Monument Valley, with Zach's childish printing on the back assuring her that his experiments were going well. Then again, he could have found those postcards anywhere.

Her heart pounds in her throat. Zach didn't have any knowledge of Thaddy's activities. Did he? Had Thaddy been building bombs even then? Six weeks was a long time to keep an activity like that hidden. In a cabin that small. No, she thinks. The two of them hunted and fished and toasted marshmallows until Zach grew tired of living in the woods and returned to MIT. She wants to ask Greenglass exactly what Zach confessed to. But she is afraid to open her mouth. She is balanced on the thinnest precipice, and if she takes a single wrong step, she is going to topple into a bottomless chasm, and take Zach and Thaddy with her.

She looks at Greenglass for a clue, but his face betrays nothing. Greenglass is probably furious at Zach for lying to him. For allowing him to be bushwhacked by his client in the presence of the FBI. Will Greenglass give up on them? This can't be the first time a client hasn't told him the entire truth. But if Greenglass washes his hands of them, who will she find to represent her son, now that he truly needs representing?

"Are you arresting him?" she says. Crazily, she tries to come up with a way to implicate herself. To get thrown in prison instead of her son, or with him. "Are you keeping him for further questioning?"

Shauntz clears his throat. Their eyes meet. She refuses to turn away.

"No," he says. "I'm trusting my instincts here. Your son seems to have a propensity to . . . well, you're his mother. There's nothing I can tell you about your son you don't already know."

Does she? Know her son? Does any mother? He has a propensity to do what? Lie? Run away? Maybe what he has is a propensity to run *towards*. Where others sit and talk about the injustices of the world, her son rushes off to right them. And yes, he lies. But is that so unusual for a boy his age? Except, at twenty-four, he no longer is a boy. Maybe she is deluded, but she can't help thinking he is lying to protect her. To protect Thaddy. To protect everyone but himself.

"I'm not sure I can trust your son," Shauntz says. "But I am going to trust you. To not let him run off. Or lie to us. Again. Or hide what he knows."

She nods. She says she promises.

And, strangely, that's all it takes. Greenglass looks at Shauntz. Shauntz nods. All four of them, including Burdock, get to their feet. Shauntz accompanies Maxine to the waiting room and repeats what Greenglass told her earlier: stay in town; remain available; no talking to the press; no talking to anyone except your lawyer. He tells her that his agents will be keeping an eye on her house. Greenglass is deciding whether the FBI can tap her phone, screen her mail, monitor her and Zach's use of the Internet, or whether he will require the government to obtain a warrant.

"Oh," Shauntz says. "One more thing." He lowers his voice, although Greenglass no doubt can hear him. "You may want to kill your son but please don't. We need him. I'm sorry if we were more aggressive in our interactions than we needed to be. We are very appreciative that you and your son have come forward. I'll be in touch. One way or the other."

He lifts his meaty hand and salutes her in a gesture she finds corny and endearing. Just before she follows Greenglass to the lobby, where, she has been told, Zach will be waiting, she turns and sees Shauntz lift one corner of his mouth, wink, and make that clucking sound detectives like Humphrey Bogart used to make to signal to a dame they liked her. What she doesn't know, not actually being gifted with the ability to predict the future, is this will be the last time she sees Supervisory Special Agent Roland Shauntz, and from now on, every time she thinks of him, which will happen at least once a day for the remainder of her life, she will remember that wink, and again hear him make that ridiculous clucking sound with his mouth.

. . . Looks in a Place She Already Looked

When she sees her son, she runs across the lobby. But instead of embracing him, she hits him. Hard. With her fist. So hard his sternum gives beneath her knuckles. She hurts her fist worse than she hurts his chest, but she hits him again, harder, on his arm. Then with both fists, pummeling him wherever she can reach. She has never hit her son. Would have hurled herself at anyone who tried to hurt him, no matter how threatening the attacker. Given the difference in their height and weight, she could hit Zach with as much force as she could muster and he would barely flinch. But she wishes she could summon the strength to make him crumple to the ground and beg forgiveness. For lying. For disappearing. For putting her through the nauseating fear to which he has subjected her.

He follows her to the car. On the ride home, he sits quietly, knees propped against the glove box. In the old days, after Sam died, this was the only way she could get him to talk. The two of them making the sad, lonely pilgrimage to see Zach's grandmother in Chicago. Something about sitting side by side, staring straight ahead instead of at each other, relieved the stress of talking about his feelings.

She no longer feels guilty that she betrayed him by thinking he was more implicated than he let on. But she feels even guiltier for preferring her innocence to his guilt. He might be sent to prison for lying to the FBI. Or withholding evidence. Or even—she can't bear to say the phrase—being an "accessory to the crime." How could she have paid so little attention to all the warning signs? What was so wrong with her that her son couldn't confide he wanted to drop out of college? What did he accuse her of at the cabin? That she and Sam wanted him to care, but not care too much? That they had trained him to change the world, but without incurring the slightest risk to himself or others? Maybe she had neglected him after his father's death. And then, to overcompensate, she had become too intrusive, too protective. Or maybe Zach had been overly protective of her. Maybe he had tried to spare his grieving, overworked, widowed mother his own troubles, his own confusion.

Or maybe none of this was her fault. Mothers never knew their sons. But they took the blame for whatever went wrong in their children's lives.

"I hated it," Zach says. "That whole first year. I hated everything about MIT."

She keeps driving. Waits for Zach to tell her about the summer he spent with Thaddy. Although how can she believe what he is telling her, even now?

"You have no idea how many arrogant assholes they can pack into a place like that. So many of my professors were working on weapons for the military. And yeah, Professor Hertz and his fucking facial-recognition software.

"And the sexism! You wouldn't believe what they said about women, especially when the women weren't there. Let alone how they treated them. I hated my dorm—it was like living in a concrete bunker. The buildings had numbers instead of names. All anyone cared about was plotting these elaborate stupid pranks.

"And Thaddy . . . he kept writing me about how scientists were egotistical jerks who were ruining the planet. Ruining the way we lived. Millions and millions of people were going to die. Entire countries—poor countries no one gave a fuck about— were going to be underwater. The ice caps were melting. And no one was doing a damn thing about any of it. If you believe— if you *know*—millions of your fellow humans are going to die, if entire species are going to go extinct, aren't you obliged to act?

"And the way Thaddy described this idyllic life he was living in Montana, I wanted to drop out right then, in the middle of the semester. But how could I tell you? I knew how much you and Dad loved MIT. That's where you guys met. All those stories about the smoots . . . I just had to get away. And I didn't want to spend the summer sitting around Ann Arbor playing video games with Norm.

"So I cut out. One of the guys from my dorm was driving cross-country and said he'd drop me off near Helena. I made up some random shit about Professor Begay offering me that internship. I barely knew Curt. I'd taken a class with him, and he seemed great. You know, this Navajo guy with long hair, up there on the stage in a floppy hat and beads? But it was this huge lecture course. I barely got up the nerve to go up after class and ask a question. I told you whatever popped in my head. He did have this solar project he'd started on the reservation. Maybe I told you what I wished could be true, that he'd picked me to be his intern. I packed a duffel bag. I stowed the rest of my stuff in some basement at the dorm. I didn't have the guts to drop out. Not officially. I just left.

"Which was a good thing, because the minute I got there, I knew I'd fucked up. The minute I saw Thaddy on that bike . . . I don't think any two parts came from the same machine. He must have thought I had piles of money, because he kept asking me to buy all this stuff he needed. Groceries. Hardware. I got the feeling he invited me out there so he could use me as a sort of moneybags.

"And that cabin! It was clean enough. Thaddy was obsessive about being neat. But it was barely big enough to fit one person, let alone two. Thaddy put a sleeping bag on the floor for me, but it smelled all moldy, and mice kept running over me all night. There was a stream nearby, and he piped water so you could take a shower from these bottles hanging in the trees, but the two of us got plenty stale. And there wasn't an outhouse. Thaddy would save his shit and use it to fertilize the garden, which didn't make me want to eat those vegetables.

"Some of it, I admit, was pretty neat. Like I was Huck Finn and Thaddy was . . . not Jim, some older guy who was teaching me to survive on my own. How to catch fish and lay out traps. I wasn't big on shooting and gutting deer, but at least we weren't eating meat from some huge industrial cow-factory. And one whole wall of the cabin was books. It could have been a great summer, Mom. Hanging out in Montana, reading Nietzsche and Camus and books on Roman history.

"You know how smart he is, Mom. And Thaddy could be nice. If he wanted to be. He listened. He seemed to care. He sure went through a lot worse than I did, at Harvard. Did he ever tell you about that experiment? The one where he was a guinea pig? God, if I had been through shit like that, I might be a bomber, too.

"But Thaddy was even more arrogant than my professors. With Thaddy, everything was either right or it was wrong, and only he knew which was which. He talked big, but most of what he did seemed, I don't know, kid-like. Petty. He was angry at all the military jets flying over the wilderness, making so much noise. But shooting at them? What was that going to accomplish? We used to sneak around and slash tires on ATVs, put sugar in the tourists' gas tanks, bury the loggers' chainsaws. How was that going to change anyone's mind about the direction civilization was going?

"And you and Dad . . . he couldn't stop talking about how fucked up you both were. How everything you taught me was crap. His own parents, he blamed them for everything. Okay, they pushed him to do well in school. To be a 'good boy.' But lots of parents treat their kids that way. I can't figure out why he had it in for you and Dad. I mean Dad, okay, he was bringing technology to the masses. But you? What did you ever do to him except be really, really kind?"

Zach turns to look at her, and even though she is driving, she looks back. His eyes are clouded by the frustration she saw when he was a little boy who couldn't find the words to express his sadness. Will she ever tell him how badly she failed Thaddy? How Thaddy had come to her at his most desperate and she had been too timid, too preoccupied, to get him the help he needed?

Eventually. Not now. That her son spent six weeks living with Thaddy, listening to him rant against her and Sam, so infuriates her that she finds herself taking satisfaction in the image of the police leading Thaddy away in handcuffs. Or maybe it's her son who is being led away.

"You lied to me," she says. "Over and over." What did Shauntz tell her? Most teenage boys lie to their mothers? But not about things like this. If she didn't need to keep her hands on the steering wheel, she would hit him again.

"Okay," he says. "I lied. Out of, I don't know, sheer instinct.

To protect my friend. He might be fucked up, but he's my friend. Or he was my friend. I lied because I'm about to become a father and I didn't want to spend the first who-knows-how-many years of my kid's life in prison. To leave Angie alone with a mess like that. I guess you did what you needed to do. But you didn't trust me, Mom. You didn't trust me to take care of what needed to be taken care of. You turned me in. To the FBI. You blew up my life. You blew it all the fuck up."

No, she thinks. She is not about to let him sidetrack her. Not again. "You knew," she says. "You knew what Thaddy was doing in that cabin." The sun, setting to the west, spears her in the eyes. "You knew," she says. "How could you live there and not know?"

Zach seems to crumple in his seat. His anger dissipates. "It took me a long time," he admits. "A guy keeps a few extra batteries around his cabin, so what. But not as many as Thaddy was stockpiling. A few extra boxes of matches, okay. But whole cartons? Whole crates of wires and switches, even though the cabin isn't hooked up for electricity? And why keep your notebooks in code? Why put three locks on the door when there isn't a single thing worth stealing? Then I found these weird shoes—they had an extra pair of soles taped to the bottom, I guess so he could leave a different set of footprints from the real ones. And he had, I don't know, disguises?

"I knew he was guilty of something. But I hadn't followed much about the bombings. And Thaddy could be such a great guy. There was this old couple who lived next door. Well, not next door, but a few miles down the road. Thaddy used to play pinochle with the husband, but then the old guy died, and Thaddy and I would take potatoes and turnips to the widow. And this other woman? She lived in town. She was Thaddy's age. Thaddy tutored her son in math. And Jesus, Mom, his neighbors seemed a whole lot more dangerous than Thaddy did."

"Neighbors?" she says. "Thaddy had neighbors?"

"Not like you have in Burns Park. But he wasn't a hermit. Or maybe it was just that there were a lot of other hermits in the same woods. Militia types. Survivalists. KKK types. Vietnam vets. Ex-hippies. And you'd be surprised, all these mansions are going up there. Thaddy hated those the most. The bankers. The movie stars. The loggers. I figured he was planning to do worse than slash someone's tires. But bombs? I wasn't sure. I didn't want to get him arrested on some stupid hunch. Now I have everything on my conscience. Not the ones he hurt before I got out there. But after? I could have stopped him. Especially Hertz. Thaddy probably only mailed that bomb to Hertz to show me we were still on the same side. To get back at this professor he thought I hated. How am I going to live with any of that? How? How am I going to live with any of that on my conscience?"

He leans forward, pounds his forehead with his fists. Seeing him hit himself brings back her maternal instincts. But she is still so angry she resists the urge to comfort him.

By now, they are back in Ann Arbor. Zach goes upstairs to tell Angelina about his inquisition at FBI headquarters. Does Angelina know about the summer Zach spent with Thaddy? Does he tell the truth to her? Given they spent an entire winter cooped up in that cabin, he probably told Angelina more than he told Maxine. And yet, Angelina has such a strong moral compass, if Zach told her he suspected Thaddy of building bombs, surely she would have convinced him to tell the authorities what he knew. Is Maxine fooling herself to think her son loves her? To believe he wasn't involved in Thaddy's acts of terrorism?

Did Zach really do no worse than slash tires or put sugar in gas tanks, which she once would have considered bad enough?

Angelina and Zach are upstairs a long time; clearly, there is much Zach feels the need to tell her. Maxine finds a can of tuna in the cupboard but worries the mercury might poison the fetus. She salvages a few leaves of spinach, mushrooms, a slice of Swiss cheese, and makes yet another omelet, which she and Zach only pick at but Angelina devours in ravenous bites. Maxine brews tea and they take their cups to the living room to watch the news. It's too soon for the FBI to have acted on the information she and Zach provided, but she dreads seeing a video of her former student stepping from his wretched cabin. Aged now. Bedraggled. Hands above his head as he surrenders.

The anchor signs off. But Thaddy's reprieve is only temporary. He will get into bed not knowing this might be his last good night of sleep. *Quick!* she wants to warn him. *Get out of that bed and run!*

At nine, she leaves Zach and Angelina on the sofa and climbs the stairs. There is no one she can call. She is not willing to confess, even to Rosa, that her son spent six weeks in a terrorist's cabin and failed to turn him in. The government has taken her computer so she uses her phone to check her email. Are the agents monitoring what she writes? She answers a few of her students' messages. Tomorrow is Friday. She ought to be able to focus enough to teach on Monday. She has never missed a class, not even when she gave birth to Zach.

She gets into bed and turns on the radio. Listening to the same news being broadcast over and over—the same weather report, the same interview with the conductor of the local symphony— acts as a soporific. When she awakes, she assumes Zach and Angelina will still be sleeping. But there they are, bleary-eyed, in their clothes from the night before. Did they ever go to bed? Did they have a fight? Angelina seems unusually detached— she is staring out at the trampoline in a neighbor's yard while Zach sits in an armchair, studying her back.

Maxine tiptoes past them, makes regular coffee for herself and Zach and decaf for Angelina. After breakfast, Zach suddenly recalls he has a grandmother.

"You'd better prepare yourself," Maxine warns him. "She's taken a real nosedive since the last time you saw her." She regrets having twisted the knife. But why are young people so concerned with showering kindness on everyone except those who love them?

"Do you think she'll be okay about . . ." Zach gestures toward Angelina, who is still staring out the window.

Maxine shrugs. "She didn't make a fuss when I married someone who wasn't Jewish."

"That's not what I mean. Ever since I was in, like, seventh grade, she's given me lectures about not ruining my future by getting some girl pregnant. I thought she was nuts. Like any girl would want to have sex with me."

Maxine doesn't have the heart to say his grandmother might not have the strength to express her displeasure. Besides, if he is old enough to be a father, he is old enough not to cringe in fear of his grandmother's lecture on responsibility.

An hour later, they pull up to Sunrise Hills. Maxine signs the logbook. But as they head to the elevator, the guard summons them back.

"You need to sign in all three names."

As if Maxine might have been trying to smuggle her son and his fiancée into the home illegally. *Zachary Pardue*, she signs. Then *Angelina Ruiz*, wondering if Angelina intends to keep her surname or take her son's. Maxine doesn't care. But it occurs to her that the Sayers family name will die out with her.

They take the elevator to the fifth floor. Like most young people, Zach and Angelina haven't yet convinced themselves that banishing one's elderly parent to a nursing home is ever justified. Passing the lineup of quivering, moaning invalids clearly tears at their hearts. But even this gauntlet of horrors doesn't prepare Zach for stepping into his grandmother's room and seeing what's left of her propped up in her bed.

"Grandmom?"

Her eyes focus. She jerks her hands to her head, attempting to pat her hair into place. "Oh no!" she cries, any joy she might have taken in seeing her grandson destroyed because she hasn't had time to primp.

Zach leans down and kisses his grandmother. "I'm really sorry, Grandmom. I've been —"

She cuts him off. "Men don't *apologize*." She peers at Angelina. "Is this your wife?" And before Zach can stammer that they aren't yet married, but plan to be, very soon, she says, "She isn't white, is she."

Horrified, Maxine steps between her mother and future daughter-in-law.

"And there's something the matter with her. Some kind of defect?"

"Mother!" Maxine scolds. Her mother has never been racist or mean-spirited; the Parkinson's has loosened her inhibitions. Maxine explains all of this to Angelina, not caring if her mother hears, but Angelina shakes her head, as if it is her place to accept whatever judgment her husband's grandmother passes. Maxine, who spent years accepting her mother-in-law's negative judgments of her, makes a note to tell Angelina she doesn't need to take crap from anyone, not even from Zach's grandmother. Or, for that matter, from her.

"Grandmom," Zach says, "if you love me, you'll love Angelina."

"Of course I will," his grandmother snaps. "I was going to say, if she isn't white, and she has whatever else is wrong with her, and you still want to marry her, she must be a wonderful person." With great difficulty, she lifts her head from the pillow and squints at Angelina's belly. "Unless she is taking advantage of your good nature by shaming you into marrying her."

"Mom!" Maxine lifts her hand to her mother's mouth as if to deflect further insults, but Angelina takes Maxine by the arm and gently pulls her back.

"It's all right," she says. "I have a grandmother, too. Sometimes the things she says . . . I wouldn't want Zach to hear those either."

Zach sits on the edge of his grandmother's bed. "We're moving to Detroit, Grandmom. We're going to start a business." He explains about buying the empty property and converting it to a farm. Maxine isn't sure how much her mother understands. But she understands enough to smile and tell Zach he sounds like his grandfather.

"Just don't let anyone take advantage of you," her mother warns Zach. "The way your grandfather let those miserable 'partners' take advantage of him. You make sure this young woman gets everything she deserves. She grew up poor, didn't she? Like me. She deserves to be treated like a lady." She closes her eyes. "And I am going to be right there. Clapping my hands off. When that baby graduates from college."

What delusion the human mind is capable of! But hasn't Maxine, at some level, believed she would never die? The truth is, she won't live to witness the Age of the Messiah. She might not even live to witness her grandchild receive his or her high-school diploma. And she won't be observing her deadness from somewhere else. Won't be there to comfort Zach in his mourning. The books and articles she has written, the institute she directs, her work on the effects of extended lifetimes—these have been nothing but her own form of terror management.

"Why are you crying?" her mother demands. "I'm the one who's sick!"

Maxine pulls a tissue from the box, glad for the aloe in the fabric.

"Zach," her mother says, "you didn't kill anyone, did you?"

Maxine can sense her son's shock, that his grandmother would even ask.

"No, Grandmom. I haven't killed anyone."

His grandmother's expression isn't relief so much as satisfaction. "Your mother thought maybe you had. But it was that other one. The one you were afraid of. I kept telling you not to spend so much time with him. No one ever listens to me."

Zach takes his grandmother's hand and pats it. "You're right. He was a very disturbed person."

"Hah!" she says. "That's not the only thing I was right about. It's here. The letter from Cousin Joel. You promised, Maxine! You promised you would look. Not pretend. Really look. Zach, you help her."

Maxine shoots Zach a look to convey they need to humor his grandmother. First, she picks up the tissue box. Nothing hidden there. The manicure set. The mirror. The crossword puzzle book her mother hasn't opened in months. The makeup kit. The menu for the following week, beneath which Maxine finds the schedule of activities, and, beneath that, the issues of

Vogue that, until recently, her mother enjoyed browsing. At the bottom of the pile Maxine pulls out the tattered manila envelope in which her mother has preserved the letters and cards Zach sent her over the years. The letter from Cousin Joel won't be in this envelope, but Maxine will enjoy reminding herself how thoughtful her son has been.

She lifts the flap and pulls out the cards—for Mother's Day, Valentine's Day, her mother's birthday. A postcard shows the Golden Gate Bridge; on the back, Zach has printed that he is enjoying his job (a lie!), thinking of his grandmother (who knows, maybe he was), sending his hugs and love. She reaches the last card and shuffles the pile back into the envelope. But in doing so, she notices a thin sheet of onionskin paper, folded twice, wedged inside a card whose glittery surface must have caused the paper to adhere. The brittle stationery is printed with the faded address of Cousin Joel's law office in Albany—not that Cousin Joel has practiced law in decades. When Maxine unfolds it, a typewritten letter explains to her mother that her husband's former employee and business partner, Spider Macalvoy, a few weeks prior to his death, confessed to his youngest daughter, Caitlin Garrity, of Orlando, Florida, that he and Dr. Simon and Dr. Vincent, formerly of Fenstead, New York, had been aware that Maxine's father had been planning to sell his cable television company to the TelePrompTer corporation for twenty million dollars. When they offered to buy Maxine's mother's share for a mere fifty thousand, they had cheated her. A good Catholic, Spider couldn't die with that deception on his conscience. As a result, he has left Maxine's mother an additional twenty-five thousand of his remaining share.

Maxine grips her mother's fragile wrist. "Mom! You were right!"

"I know!" Her mother shakes her wrist free. "About what?"

"Spider. He confessed on his deathbed. He left you another twenty-five thousand dollars." Which is only a fraction of what her mother should have gotten. Most of this will go to pay Stuart Greenglass. But her mother's lawsuit paid off.

Her mother is silent a long time. Should Maxine try to rouse her? Finally, her mother says, "He could cheat a poor widow. And his partner's little girl. But then, on his *deathbed* . . ."

She can't finish the thought, but Maxine fills in the rest. Spider could have gone to his grave with no one the wiser. Instead, he invented a God who would chastise him with a vengeance Spider hadn't managed to turn on himself and consign him to torment for eternity. If the human race ever became immortal, would deathbed repentance become irrelevant?

Her mother asks Maxine to reread the letter. When she finishes, her mother repeats, "I won?" Her tone sounds disappointed, as if she will no longer have a reason to live.

"Wow, Grandmom!" Zach says. "Twenty-five thousand dollars!"

At one time, her mother might have used such a sum to pay Maxine's tuition. Or redecorate the house in Fenstead. Or travel to France.

Then again, the lawsuit was never about the money. Her mother sued to avenge Maxine's father's honor. She sued because Maxine's father would have wanted the proceeds from his invention to go to the daughter he loved, to finance whatever project she chose to undertake to bring about the age of a messiah she no longer believes will come.

. . . Eats a Hot Dog with a Dying Man

Sunday evening, Zach and Angelina get ready to drive to Ypsilanti to have dinner with her parents. They will break the news that she is pregnant. That she and Zach are getting married. That they will be moving to Detroit to start a business.

"I can't do this," Angelina says. "My mother . . . my father."

Maxine takes Angelina's hands. "They're your parents. They'll be hurt you didn't tell them the truth. But they'll forgive you. They'll keep loving you, no matter what."

After the two young people drive off, she tries to concentrate on preparing for the class she needs to teach the next day. But she can't keep her mind off Thaddy. At ten, she tries to sleep but can't. Did she once want to live forever? She barely can make it through another sleepless night. The next morning, she trudges downstairs to find Zach making waffles for Angelina. Or rather, he has pulled the waffle iron from the top shelf and is rummaging through the cookbooks beneath the microwave.

"Where's the recipe Dad used to use?"

She nudges him aside and finds the card. Floury. Yellowing. Fragrant with vanilla. At the bottom is a chocolate fingerprint that must be Sam's. It's all she can do not to stuff the card in her mouth and eat it.

Settled deep in her tatty orange robe, she watches her son

heat the iron and produce a perfect chocolate-pecan waffle for his future wife. Angelina wears a striped maize-and-blue rugby shirt that used to be Zach's; it barely contains her belly. That another life is being lived invisibly so near her own makes Maxine feel as if her house is inhabited by another family, curled up in some fifth dimension. Why didn't she and Sam have a second child? At the beginning, she wanted to enjoy Zach's babyhood. Then she needed to finish her book so she wouldn't look foolish when she came up for tenure. Then she needed time to set up her institute. After that, Sam had been on the road so often. Did they believe the limits of a woman's fertility didn't apply to them? Would it have been better if Sam had left not one but two children without a father?

"How did it go last night?" she asks Zach.

"I was a coward," he says. "I just sat there and let Angie's parents yell and carry on as if I weren't there."

"That isn't true!" Angelina scolds him. "Zach stood up for me. He stood up for *us*. My parents were upset. Because we had lied. But like you said, they couldn't stay angry. Not when they thought of their first grandchild coming—so soon! And the three of us living so nearby."

Angelina continues about how much her parents love and respect Zach, how willing they are to accept him into their family. Maxine asks about their wedding plans. Having married a man who wasn't Jewish, she can't very well require her son to find a rabbi. (She and Sam ended up asking a classmate of Sam's who received his ordination from the Universal Life Church. A jovial, bearded Jew, this classmate allowed Maxine's mother to imagine her daughter was being married by a rabbi, an illusion reinforced by the canopy beneath which she and Sam stood in the chapel at MIT, while the absence of any overtly Jewish symbolism minimized Sam's mother's sorrow that her son wasn't marrying a gentile debutante.) Maxine listens as Angelina excitedly describes the ceremony she and Zach are planning in her parents' backyard, the vegetarian organic Mexican food Angelina's friend Suzanne's fledgling catering company will be providing. Sam's mother might or might not attend. Maxine's mother, if she makes it that long, will be too infirm to get out of bed. Rosa, Mick, and a few other Ann Arbor friends will show up. Plus a few of Zach's childhood friends, like Norm. But Zach will miss his father, the way Maxine missed her own father as she walked down the aisle on her uncle's arm. The way her mother missed her father at the same event.

Angelina forks a wedge of waffle in her mouth and moans in pleasure. But the moan turns to a grunt and she grabs her side. "Oof. Feel that. That has to be an elbow."

Zach allows Angelina to place two of his fingers to the spot where their child elbowed or kicked. His face lights up with astonishment. Then he kisses the bump. *Oh!* Maxine thinks. *I get it! Part of the joy of being a grandparent is watching your child experience the bliss you experienced raising him.*

She lingers as long as she can. Then she excuses herself and hurries upstairs to dress. It's Monday; she needs to teach. But she doesn't intend to stop by either of her offices. She hates to think of Special Agent Burdock paging through the hundreds of letters of recommendation she has written, shaking his head at the vacuous praise, the laziness of repetition. Snickering over her student-evaluations. Judging her lecture notes to be esoteric, boring. Then again, whose life would bear up under investigation by the FBI? Maxine has gossiped. She has made politically suspect jokes. She has made catty remarks about her colleagues. If her emails are released to the public, will she retain a shred of self-respect? Or a single friend?

Zach and Angelina are driving to Detroit to gather details about the mortgage they will need to buy that delinquent property. She waves at their departing car, then sets off for campus. As she crosses the Diag, she notices Jackson Sparrow heading toward her. He is wearing one of those flat black caps that remind her of the headgear on a Depression-era newsboy, or maybe Lenin. His left cheek is covered by a bandage the size of an address label.

"Maxine! I was about to grab a hot dog from the cart. See that nice patch of grass? Why don't you save it and I'll be right over. Mustard? Sauerkraut? And, what, a Diet Coke?"

Before she can refuse, he is off to buy their hot dogs. The spot of grass Jackson pointed out is so green and lush she is tempted to drop to her knees and graze. She settles to the ground and lifts her face to the warmth and light. Jackson rejoins her, handing down the four hot dogs, the two bags of chips, the two cans of diet pop.

"Better watch out." He motions toward the sun. "You wouldn't want to get one of these." He taps his cheek. "All those summers I spent working outdoors. Construction."

She squints up at him. "Was it . . ." She can't say the word "malignant."

"Not as if I had high hopes of winning a beauty pageant anyway." He eases himself down. Even with the bandage, he has the edgy, intelligent face some scrawny Jewish men are surprised to find themselves blessed with as they age. But his skin is so thin she can see the veins. His hair is translucent, the scalp pink as a baby's. When he smiles, she glimpses his receding gums. How could she fall in love with a man with gray teeth? A gray tooth is a dead tooth. The man has dying teeth because the man is dying!

"I appreciate the concern, but it's not as if I'm about to kick off right here at our picnic."

No doubt he is minimizing the seriousness of what he has been through. With a bandage that size, the surgeon must have gouged a considerable chunk of Jackson's flesh. Still, he is motioning her to eat, so she bites her hot dog. Compared to the bland, squishy tofu pups she used to buy for Zach, this perfectly charred all-beef frankfurter stimulates senses she forgot she has. The skin bursts between her teeth; juices shoot out on her tongue. She registers the tang of mustard. The vinegar of sauerkraut. Adds the salty crunch of a potato chip, then washes everything down with the metallic sweetness of the Diet Coke.

"Mmm," she murmurs, taking another bite and chewing.

"My doctor keeps telling me these things will kill me," Jackson says. "But if I can't eat a Coney or two for lunch, why would I want to live?"

She stuffs the last of the second hot dog in her mouth, then licks her fingers. Jackson reaches with a napkin and wipes mustard from her cheek.

"Wouldn't want you teaching your class with schmutz on your face. Almost as bad as teaching with your fly open."

"Thanks." She smiles, afraid he will take the smile for more than it is.

"You know, I really am very attracted to you. And you can't tell me you're not lonely. You live just down the street. I see you. Wouldn't you rather be watching the news curled up on the sofa with me than all alone? Are you going to tell me you never want to be made love to again?"

"I have a lot on my mind right now," she mutters, vaguely creeped out that he has been watching her watch the news.

"He's not coming back," Jackson says. Which might strike

her as a non sequitur if she didn't know whom he meant. "Sam won't be jealous. He would be jealous if he were alive. But he's not alive." Jackson wads his napkin and tosses it in the can. "You think they're coming back. You think, well, she died, that's very sad, she's going to be gone for a year, or two, maybe even three. Then she'll show up, and we'll have missed a few good years, but we'll be together for the rest of our lives. Except that's not how it works. The dead stay dead. That's how one of my poet friends put it. 'You think their dying is the worst thing that could happen. Then they stay dead.'"

When she was in college and grasped some physical law that kept the galaxies spinning or predicted the decay of a radio-active particle, she would literally gasp at the beauty of such a truth. And these few lines of poetry seem even truer than that.

"We miss them," Jackson says. "But when they were alive, they weren't as perfect as we make them out to be."

This, too, is true. Sam didn't need to go to Africa to find people who could benefit from low-cost technology. He traveled so much because life in Ann Arbor bored him. His life with her. His life with Zach. He put too much of a burden on their son. He clipped his toenails in bed, no matter how many times she asked him not to. Unfortunately, remembering these flaws makes her miss him even more.

"You think poets are ignoramuses," Jackson says. "Would you respect me if I told you I have a physics degree from Cal Tech? Would that make you want to fuck me?"

"Do you?"

"Do I what?"

"Have a physics degree from Cal Tech?"

"Are you crazy? The only thing I'm an expert on is beauty.

And longing. And loss."

Maybe Rosa was right. Maybe a poet is exactly what she does need.

"What is it?" Jackson asks. "Why won't you give me a chance?"

She can't think of a lie, so she tells the truth. "You're too old. I'm afraid I'll fall in love with you and you'll die."

He exhales. "Got me there. I fool myself into thinking I'm still a relatively young man." He bares his arm and strikes a pose like Popeye. "Not quite as muscular as when I worked at the GM plant. But I take good care of myself. Besides, you might be the one to die first. That's what happened to the poet who wrote those lines. Donald Hall. Married a woman twenty years his junior—wonderful woman, Jane Kenyon, grew up not far from here. Don got colon cancer. Metastasized to his liver. Doctors gave him a one-in-three chance of surviving. And what happened? Jane came down with leukemia and was dead in eighteen months. And Don? He's still ticking, well into his eighties, writing poetry about how much he loved Jane, how no one will ever take her place. Although, to be honest, he chases any woman who will have him."

Maxine wants to say this poet and his dead wife have nothing to do with her. But Jackson's story proves her point. "Who cares which one of us dies first? One of us will get sick, and the other will need to go through . . . I could never stand it again. I would have *two* husbands to miss, and that would kill me."

Despite the graying canines, his smile is winning. "What if I told you my brother-in-law is an actuary for a major insurance company and he's given me a seventy-five percent chance of living another fifteen years?"

"That isn't true, is it?"

"No. Whenever I use a percentage, you know I'm lying."

She gets up. "I have a class to teach. But maybe we can go for a walk. When everything settles down." Although she realizes he doesn't know what she means by "everything."

Jackson cranes his withered neck to look up at her. "Go on. I don't want you watching how difficult it's going to be for me to get to my feet."

She thinks of offering him a hand. But she doesn't want to rob him of his manhood. She thanks him for the hot dogs and turns to go. But she can't help glancing back. He gets up on all fours, like a dog, and struggles to stand from there. This breaks her heart. From pity? From love? Sometimes, it's difficult to tell the difference. But in this case, yes, she is beginning to think the latter.

When she arrives in the classroom, the early birds are busying themselves with their phones. They can't know about Thaddy. But she gets the impression they are avoiding her. Narissa Hymes saunters to Maxine's desk, lifts her sunglasses, and asks for an extension on the paper due that afternoon. "You can't imagine what my weekend was like. My laptop crashed. Then someone borrowed my car—really, it's my parents' car—and totaled it. So I'm hoping I can have an extension until, like, Thursday?"

Maxine refrains from pointing out her own weekend has been even more eventful than Narissa's. To make up for her lack of generosity, she gives Narissa until tomorrow to turn in the paper. The students stow their phones and take out the readings Maxine assigned. A few open the material on their laptops, although for all she knows they are using their computers to shop or watch videos of dancing cats. What does she really have to teach them? Where will these young people be in twenty years? As much as she cares for them while they are in her class, she rarely keeps track of them once they graduate. Oh, some students email her later to ask for letters of recommendation. But once they find a job, they rarely remain in touch.

Then again, which of her professors kept track of her? Is she only faking her concern for Patti or Obayo? How can anyone predict the future of the human race when predicting the path of even one student remains impossible? Like her, most of these young people will stumble toward their destinies. A detour here. A setback there. In all her years teaching, she has never seen so many students so apprehensive about getting into medical school, law school, business school. An alarming number have developed anxiety disorders—some so severe they end up in the hospital. They tell themselves if only they get good grades, they will be able to afford a decent house, a nice car, enough gadgets and games to distract them. But they aren't convinced they will be happy living the lives their parents have tried to persuade them they want to lead. Nothing she says in Intro to Future Studies will help them get into graduate school. And yet, they enroll in her class. They want someone to advise them. How can they find meaningful work? Contentment? Courage? Love? She wants to tell them a young man once sat in these same seats, and if she had been a wiser teacher, she might have been able to make him see that his arguments were flawed, his extremism wasn't warranted, his anger needed to be tempered by compassion.

Instead, she launches into the lesson she has planned on genetic engineering. Recent advances in biomedical science will allow doctors to insert specific genes into a set of chromosomes and create a child who will exhibit selected traits, whether blue eyes, an impressive height, or certain types of athletic or intellectual ability. Most traits remain far too complex to select for. But, for the sake of argument, she asks the students to take out a sheet

THE PROFESSOR OF IMMORTALITY

of paper and list the traits they would select if they had a child.

Most sit biting their pens. One student asks her to repeat the question. A few begin scribbling furiously.

"Now," she says, "I want you to list the traits your parents would have chosen if they could have designed you."

She has never asked this before, has no idea how the exercise will turn out. The silence hangs heavy. No one is writing anything.

"Can you select for your kid to be a nice person?" Marcos Costello asks. "I guess you could ask for your kid to be smart *and* nice. But if my parents had only one choice, I think they would have wanted me to be smart. If I get to choose *my* kids, I would choose that they not feel crappy all the time about how badly they're fucking up and disappointing all their relatives."

"Yeah," says Tommy Bruce. "My mom, all she cared about was I be a good person. She cheered for me, no matter what happened on the field. But my dad, he would have asked the genetics person to select for more muscle. More speed. He would have wanted me to make the pros."

Then she hears someone sobbing. It is sweet, Gothed-out Margo Korck, her black eye-makeup distorted by her tears. "Why do you always make us think about upsetting things? If you want to know the truth, my parents probably would have checked the box that I shouldn't have been born at all."

Somehow, after she and the rest of the class have convinced Margo she is a lovable, worthwhile person, Maxine makes it through the rest of the day. Maybe the FBI hasn't found Thaddy's cabin. Better yet, the agents found him, conducted a painstaking search, interrogated him thoroughly (but not too harshly), and concluded any claim he might be the bomber is ridiculous. Thaddy has been living quietly. Growing vegetables. Raising goats. He found a shy Montana girl who is awed by his intelligence, his good looks, his gratitude for the simplest kiss.

And so, when her phone rings and the female voice introduces itself as belonging to Special Agent Jill Markham, Maxine expects to be informed that Thaddy has been checked out and cleared. Instead, what Special Agent Markham says is the agency's investigations intersect on the very real possibility Mr. Rapaczynski is the serial bomber for whom they have been searching since 2006, and Maxine's son is needed in Montana to help the agents be absolutely certain the cabin they are keeping under surveillance is Mr. Rapaczynski's. More than one cabin fitting the description Zach provided is located in the vicinity, and the last thing the agency wants is to rush in and find out they have targeted the wrong structure, thereby allowing the suspect to be alerted, destroy the evidence, and take off into the Montana wilderness. In addition, the agency would like Zach on hand in case they end up in a standoff. If Thaddy is alerted to their presence and refuses to leave his house, they might need Zach to talk Thaddy into surrendering.

"We have a flight leaving tomorrow morning from DTW. We will be sending a car for your son, so if he could be ready at four-thirty a.m.—sorry, I know that's not ideal—that would be of tremendous assistance."

Maxine feels sick that Zach will be called on to inform on his former friend. But this might provide him with the opportunity to work off his guilt that he didn't turn Thaddy in earlier. Then again, with Zach in Montana, so much might go wrong. What if he gets caught in the crossfire? What if Thaddy finds a way to exact vengeance for what he can't help but perceive as the most intimate of betrayals?

"I need to go with him," Maxine says, although she isn't sure what argument she can offer. Maybe, if Thaddy barricades himself in his cabin, she could be the one to persuade him to give himself up.

"Actually," Special Agent Markham says, "we were hoping you would be willing to travel to Helena with your son. We might need you to persuade the judge issuing the warrant that the language in the manifesto justifies our belief that Mr. Rapaczynski is the bomber."

"Of course," she says. "We'll be ready on time, I promise."

As soon as she hangs up, she is paralyzed by indecision. Should she call Zach? Why does she think if she tells him what the FBI wants him to do, he will refuse? Run away? If she waits until Zach and Angelina get home, Angelina will take Maxine's side. Won't she? But what if they don't get back until very late? Or tomorrow? In the end, she calls Zach on his cell and, when he doesn't pick up, leaves a message that he needs to come home right away, she will provide the details when she sees him.

Then she runs upstairs, pulls out a suitcase, and tries to figure out what to pack. Jeans. A few long-sleeve shirts. Toiletries. She checks the weather in Montana, then adds a sweatshirt and heavy socks. And for Zach? She hasn't packed for him in years. Not that it would matter. He could get by with the same pair of jeans and underwear for a month.

She goes back downstairs and remembers to call Greenglass, who tells her that she and Zach should do whatever the agents tell them to do, nothing more, nothing less, and she should call him any time of the day or night if she has questions. By the time Zach and Angelina get back from wherever they have been, it's after ten. When she tells them what the agent told her, Zach says, "So Thaddy will see me? He'll know I was the one who turned him in?"

She starts to say this isn't the same as ratting out some kid who set a playground on fire, but Angelina steps between them and says Zach has made his peace with what he is being called upon to do. And then, to Zach, "Why don't you go upstairs and pack? Then you can drive me to my parents' house so I can stay there while you and your mother are in Montana."

He nods and kisses her and climbs the stairs, but instead of going into his bedroom, he slips into the bathroom and shuts the door. This is something he used to do when he was a kid. On the outside, he seemed indifferent to whatever calamity had befallen him. A failed exam. Some argument with his father. But he would retreat to the bathroom, lock the door, and give in to the demands of his volcanic insides.

"Professor?" Angelina has come up beside her—they stand looking up the stairs. "I know Zach has to do what the FBI is telling him to do. But I have this very bad feeling." She puts her hand on her belly. "If something bad happens to Zach . . ."

Maxine lays her palm to Angelina's surprisingly hot cheek. "I won't let them put Zach in danger. They wouldn't anyway. They don't let civilians risk their lives." At least, she doesn't think they do. "And if anything did happen, which it won't, I would take care of you and the baby. For the rest of your lives."

Angelina nods, kisses her, thanks her, but says Maxine misunderstood. "I don't need anyone's help to raise my child. If I do, I have parents of my own. I only meant my baby would grow up without a father, the way Zach grew up without his father, and that did such terrible things to Zach. You think his troubles are because of you. But most people . . . their troubles are because of what is missing in their lives. And there is no way you could make up for that."

. . . *Embraces Reality*

The next morning, Maxine and Zach step outside into the gray predawn murk to wait for the black sedan that picks them up. Zach must have cut himself shaving—Maxine is tempted to lick her finger and wipe the blood oozing from his chin.

At the airport, they proceed to the executive terminal, where Special Agent Burdock stands tapping his foot and glancing at his watch.

"I just want you to know," he says, "I'm not in favor of either of you flying out there."

In broody silence—not that Maxine is dying to make small talk—Burdock leads them to the tarmac, where a military plane awaits them.

"We're hitching a ride," Burdock says. The plane seats about twenty; everyone but Burdock, Maxine, and Zach is in uniform.

Zach tucks himself against the window, plugs in his earphones, and slips into real or feigned sleep. Which leaves Maxine to watch Burdock take a magazine from his carry-on and read it cover to cover before completing the crossword at the back—in pen.

"You know," Burdock says, folding the magazine, "he worked his way up from a beat cop. Back when he got his degree, profilers weren't taken seriously. After all the time he put in, they took away the case and moved it to San Francisco. And then, who ends up breaking the damn thing wide open? Even now, he had to argue to be included in the stakeout."

"I've only just met him," Maxine says. "But I can see where you would feel . . . I can see why he would want to be there."

Burdock snorts and reverts to silence. Out of ideas for passing the time, Maxine curls against her son and pretends to sleep. Maybe she does sleep. Or maybe the flight is shorter than she assumed. As they skim in over the misty, snowcapped Rockies, the view is so sublime they might as well be landing on Mt. Olympus. The name of the city—*Helena*—gives her the sense they are arriving at the launch of a battle between the mortals and the gods.

When they land, it is still midmorning, Montana time. She has on jeans, hiking boots, and a parka that once belonged to Zach, which is a good thing because the temperature is a good thirty degrees colder than in Ann Arbor, as if Thaddy, by his mere presence, has managed to fend off global warming. A female agent in a white Bronco drives them to downtown Helena. On the third floor of an unassuming building, the FBI maintains a fusty office. Dozens of agents in down vests, hiking boots, and fanny packs stand around consulting documents and each other. The atmosphere is both tense and relaxed, if that is possible. Shauntz is nowhere to be seen.

Burdock leaves them standing against a wall. When he returns, he tells Maxine they won't need her help persuading the judge to issue the warrant; the agency's lawyers and the US attorney managed to make the case without her. But they still might require her assistance in talking Rapaczynski out of his cabin; Maxine can't figure out if she hopes they do or she hopes they don't.

He leaves them awhile longer. Someone brings them sandwiches. Zach tells his mother he isn't hungry, but Maxine urges him to eat, as she used to do when he was a little boy. "You don't know the next time you'll get the chance," she says, and he makes a show of taking a few bites, to please her. Then the agent who drove them from the airport requests they come with her. She is a petite woman in chinos and a blue FBI windbreaker; her dark hair seems to have been cut in the shape of a cereal bowl. They get back in the Bronco, Zach in front, Maxine in the rear, and the agent drives them out of the city along a two-lane highway on which the traffic quickly thins. Zach tips his head against the passenger window and peers out, no doubt comparing who he was the summer he spent here with Thaddy with who he is now. His lips move, as if he is arguing with himself. Or maybe he is wishing he were back in bed with his future wife.

The driver must be local; she can't help commenting on the landmarks, the names of which come straight out of the westerns Maxine's mother used to watch. The Continental Divide. Lewis and Clark National Forest. Little Blackfoot River. Whiskey Gulch. Patches of snow stipple the muddy, matted fields. The narrow highway passes over a lake the same color as the sky. Up seems down and down seems up.

They turn west on Route 200, which becomes the main thoroughfare of downtown Lincoln. They pass the library and public high school. A store called Grizzly Hardware—Maxine wonders if this is where Thaddy buys the components for his bombs. A grocery store. A shack called Coyote Coffee—it's not Starbucks, but she hadn't expected Thaddy to live within biking distance of a café where he could, if he so desired, pick up an espresso. They turn right at Lambkins Restaurant Lounge Casino—a sign out front promises "karoke," but Maxine can't imagine Thaddy stopping here to show off his singing skills. A hundred yards farther, their driver pulls in at the Hotel Lincoln. The hotel appears to be made of logs, whether because Abraham Lincoln grew up in a log cabin or the local businesses are trying to play off the whole wilderness vibe. The agent checks Maxine in, then says she hopes Maxine won't be bored but she can get dinner at the hotel—the sign here advertises something called the DUCKS UNLIMITED BANQUET.

"On my own?" she says. "Where will Zach be?"

"Sorry, ma'am. My orders are to bring your son to our observation post. We need him to positively ID the cabin. And we want him close by in case the situation goes south and we need to communicate with the UNSUB."

She can't come? They're taking Zach and leaving her here, in the middle of nowhere? With nothing to do? Powerless to influence the outcome of events, to protect Thaddy, or her son?

"Don't worry," Zach says. "Thaddy's cabin isn't far."

Maxine looks up at him. The nick on his cheek is no longer bleeding. The bright red spot has darkened and scabbed over.

"It's okay. Really." Zach's hug is unexpectedly fierce, as if he is planning to run off, or to warn or rescue Thaddy, and he might never see her again.

She walks them out to the parking lot and watches the Bronco disappear down Stemple Pass Road. Other than running after it, she has no idea what to do. Back inside, she wheels her overnight bag down the log-lined corridor. Her room is decorated with a designer spread and pillow shams that might have come from Pottery Barn and an artsy wilderness photo above the headboard. She washes her face and brushes her teeth but can't force herself to stay put. Out behind the hotel, Adirondack chairs line a stream. She sits watching the firs sway, the light filtering through the clouds. A mother duck and her fledglings waddle along the shore, then slip into the current, where Maxine hopes they will evade whoever might otherwise turn them into an unlimited banquet.

She has been up since three-thirty a.m., Ann Arbor time, but now, in Montana, it is barely five in the afternoon. What do they expect her to do, grab an early dinner and spend the rest of the night watching TV? No one ordered her to remain at the hotel. If she goes for a walk, what are the chances she will run into Thaddy? Would he even recognize her? What would happen if he did? What would she say? *I'm sorry I didn't pay more attention to your misery? The FBI has your cabin staked out, get away while you can?*

She walks the length of Main Street, all the way back to the public library, which is shut tight for the night. The antiques shop is also closed, as are the hardware store and vintage clothing shop. She is so jumpy she doubts she could eat. Instead of heading into the restaurant or back to the hotel, she turns down Stemple Pass Road. The trees are nothing like the birches, aspens, maple, and spruce her father taught her to identify on their long walks in the Adirondacks. Still, the scent of damp bark and the musk of fungus remind her of the forest that surrounded her in her childhood. A woodpecker beats out a code so insistent she nearly turns back. A pair of crows swoop down and walk beside her like black-clad FBI agents with their hands behind their backs, their beady eyes monitoring her every move. Zach said Thaddy hunts, so she knows these woods are populated by deer and bear, maybe elk or moose. Every snap or whistle in the leaves causes her heart to lose a beat. At any moment, Thaddy might go pedaling past her on his bike.

She reaches a turn-off where Stemple Pass Road continues in one direction and a narrower road cuts to her left. She stands like Dorothy in Oz, waiting for some helpful scarecrow to advise her. She cocks her ear, listens. If, as the agent said, "the situation goes south," will she hear the gunshots?

Darkness sets in. Reluctantly, she begins the long walk back. The muddy slush in the parking lot outside the restaurant is a puzzle of intersecting tire tracks. Inside, the red leather seats go nicely with the green-topped tables. A few diners—a middle-aged man in a baseball cap, another in a white Stetson—seem to be locals, but a dozen men and women—a few at this table, a few more at another—seem as out-of-place as she does. The agent who drove them to Lincoln clued Maxine in that the agents from San Francisco are passing themselves off as modern-day prospectors, rock climbers, photographers, Hollywood functionaries scouting locations for a film. Given that the prospectors, sportsmen, and Hollywood types who live here are secondhand versions of the originals, the agents are triply inauthentic.

"Hi, honey." The waitress is Maxine's age, with a graying braid and a T-shirt that shows a logger with a phallic chainsaw rising from his crotch. "I'm Debbie. You all on your lonesome tonight? Or is your hubby in the gents?"

When Maxine admits she is on her own, the waitress hands her an oversize menu with a bronco on the front. Maxine is too queasy for the steak or Cowboy Burger but doesn't want to ask for the "Oriental Salad," so she orders the quesadilla.

"What you in town for?" The waitress takes back the menu. Maxine panics.

"Just passing through?"

"Yes," Maxine says. She remembers there is a university in Missoula. "I flew into Helena. And I'm giving a lecture in Missoula." As if the only place she can be safe is a university.

"Oh, sure," the waitress says. "I could tell you weren't the hunting type. But when you get back on the road, you keep your eyes open for deer. They just love to jump in front of your car and kill you both."

After Maxine has stretched out the meal by ordering the strawberry-rhubarb pie and tea, she goes back to her room and switches on the television. The biggest manhunt in Montana history is going on a few miles down the road and the local station—albeit from Helena—doesn't know a thing about it. She watches a show about fishing, an infomercial for some hair restoration product, a late-night talk show from Manhattan. Every time she hears footsteps she prays Zach will come in. How could she allow them to take her son? Is he spending the night at the observation post? Are they testing Zach? Making him prove he isn't in cahoots with Thaddy?

She keeps the television on all night. Paces. Maintains a vigil at the window in case any of the agents staying at the hotel rush out to their Broncos and Explorers. At six a.m., when Zach hasn't come back, she changes into clean underwear, brushes her teeth, goes down to the lobby, grabs a banana from a bowl, fills a Styrofoam cup with cold coffee from the day before, and heads back out. She doesn't want to get in anyone's way. But she knows—she absolutely knows—her son is planning to do something stupid, and she is damned if she is going to sit around her hotel room while he gets injured or killed. Or ends up in prison for helping a serial killer escape a stakeout. She doesn't care how far along Stemple Pass Road she needs to walk. She can't stand being so cut off from Zach. Or Thaddy. Her husband died on another continent; she found out from a stranger's phone call. She has spent far too many hours staring at computer screens. Answering email. Updating her blog. So much of her life transpires online, via mathematical models and simulations. Just the other day, Alphred Kisbye barged into her office and demanded she put on the virtual-reality headset he had gotten in the mail from some company in California. "Just try it!" Alphred goaded her. "You'll swear you're really flying!" But the goggles made Maxine so sick she nearly vomited.

This time, when she gets to the intersection, she continues down the road she's on. The sun must be rising, but here in the woods you can barely tell. Birds she can't identify call to each other like neighbors gossiping about who got drunk at the bar the night before, who had sex with whom. The road is frozen in some spots, muddy in others. She steps across a cattle guard. She has forgotten to bring gloves and needs to draw her hands into the parka's sleeves. The scent of someone's wood fire soothes her. No wonder Thaddy loves living here. Who wouldn't be angry at anyone who disturbed this beauty, this peace, with the roar of a snowmobile, a military jet, a chainsaw?

She has no idea where along the creek his cabin might be, but she is going to get as close as she can. Without makeup, her hair pulled back in a ponytail, she doesn't look all that different from the waitress last night. If anyone sees her, she is less likely to arouse suspicion than the agents.

An engine growls behind her. She keeps walking, but the vehicle slows.

"You! Hey! Hey!" The voice is low but insistent. Special Agent Burdock leans from the driver's seat of a black Explorer. "Didn't anyone tell you not to leave the hotel?"

She shakes her head. She is not about to sit by the river counting ducks while her son gets shot trying to protect his friend.

"Turn around," Burdock orders. "Go back to the hotel. Right now."

"You're going there," she says. "Take me with you."

"I can't do that. We have twenty agents crammed in a shack above Rapaczynski's cabin. We've got motion detectors and listening devices hanging from every tree. We've got SWAT teams dug in all around the perimeter. The plan is for Shauntz to go in with a local ranger Rapaczynski knows and trusts. The ranger is going to yell to him to come out so they can ask him a question about the boundary of his property. If the plan goes right, they'll grab him before he shoots anyone or destroys evidence by blowing the place up. It's not the place for you to be."

She has the nagging sensation there's something she ought to tell Burdock. Some reason this scheme won't work. Something to do with the Conrad novel. But the word "boundary" reminds her of something Thaddy told her about his dissertation. What did he say, she could never understand the topic? She probably couldn't. But neither could these government agents who are planning to violate Thaddy's boundaries.

Burdock opens his door. She never learns what he intends to do because a blast shocks them both. Her knees buckle. Her ears buzz. She begins to faint.

Then she catches herself. Opens the back door of the Explorer and half falls, half throws herself inside.

"Get out!" Burdock shouts. "Get the fuck out!"

But she doesn't get out. Whatever she has been afraid might happen has already happened. But there still might be time to prevent something worse.

Burdock curses, guns the motor. Maxine lurches and nearly falls from the open door, then manages to grab the handle and pull it shut. Burdock accelerates down the dirt road, then up a gravel driveway, brakes in front of a cabin—surely it isn't Thaddy's?—parks, gets out, and runs. Maxine jumps out and follows—around the back of the cabin, then down a hill. She slips on some damp leaves, staggers forward, keeps running. Agents swarm from every direction. A mushroom cloud of white smoke rises above the gulley. Gasping for air, she nearly chokes on the smell of gunpowder and some nauseating stench she can't identify.

"Zach?" she screams. "Zach! Zach! Zach, where are you!" She turns full circle but doesn't see him. She has lost everything. Everything. An agent lumbers past and she grabs his arm. "Do you know where my son is? My son! Is he all right?" The agent stares at her, shakes her off, rushes toward the cloud of smoke. Maxine keeps screaming Zach's name, but no one hears or sees her. It's like the night Zach was born. She was lying there, drugged, an oxygen mask clamped to her face, demanding to know if her baby was all right. "Is it a girl?" she kept shouting. "Is it a boy?" When no one answered, she was terrified something had gone wrong. How could they not tell if her baby was a boy or a girl? But the truth was, nobody even heard her.

"Zach!" she screams again, and finally, just as she decides Thaddy has blown both of them to pieces, there he comes, up from the creek, in the direction opposite the one all the other men are running. His face is covered with soot. The canvas parka he is wearing is stained with blood and shreds of debris whose origins she doesn't want to think about. She hesitates, then throws her arms around him.

"Sweetheart! Are you all right? Are you okay?" She will never let him go. Never let him run off again. She may not be able to comfort Thaddy, but she can comfort her son.

"Go back," Zach says. He takes her by her elbows and tries to hustle her up the hill. "You do *not* want to see this."

But she does want to see. She cranes around her son's broad, jacketed shoulder. The smoke has cleared enough so she can make out a small, neat wooden structure with a pipe for a chimney, like something a child might build on his parents' living room floor. A chain-link fence encloses a plot that appears to be Thaddy's garden. A group of agents, some in padded vests, others in FBI windbreakers—out here, the agents apparently aren't afraid to advertise whom they work for—block the site of the explosion.

"Who?" she asks Zach. "What happened?"

"I was up there." He points to the cabin. "I had binoculars. None of them knew what Thaddy looked like. All they had were these old photos, so I was supposed to make sure they had the right guy." The smoke makes him cough. "The ranger, and that guy from Detroit, Shauntz? They both went down there. They were going to persuade Thaddy to come out on his own. But then I heard the snipers talking. They were going to get a shot at Thaddy as soon as he stepped outside. I couldn't stand there and watch that happen."

She starts to protest.

"I know. But I figured if I went down there I could get Thaddy to come out peacefully, so he wouldn't get shot. So I left. They weren't going to shoot me in the back. At least, I hoped they weren't.

"But Thaddy already had come outside. He was walking toward Shauntz. But then he saw me. He knew it was me, Mom. I could see his face. He must have figured out I brought them. He shook his head. But I think he was telling me not to come any closer. He motioned like I should stop? Then he held out his arms and ran. At Shauntz. He threw his arms around him. And then they just . . . they both blew up." Zach puts his sooty palm to his forehead. "Nobody could have survived that." He doubles over. "All Thaddy needed to do was wait another second and I'd be dead, too."

She imagines Thaddy wrapping his arms around Shauntz. Thaddy and Shauntz erupting in a blast of bone and blood. She has to keep reminding herself that her son is right here beside her. Her son is still alive. As to Thaddy and Shauntz, she can't bear to imagine what just happened.

Zach tries to tug her up the hill. But she sees Burdock staggering toward them, so diminished, so pale, he seems thirty years older than the man who tried to strong-arm her into his Explorer.

She touches his sleeve. "Is Agent Shauntz . . ."

He looks at her as if he has no idea who she is.

"The Professor," Maxine says. "He's a character in the Conrad novel. I should have made a bigger point of explaining. The Professor goes around with a detonator in his coat pocket. It's attached to a bomb, and if the police get anywhere near him, if they threaten to apprehend him, he plans to blow everyone up."

For a long time, Burdock remains silent. Then he says, "Shauntz read that book. He read everything on that list you gave him. In just those few days. That's how smart he was. They didn't need him out here. They could have handled the stakeout without him. He insisted on coming. He had to be here.

"So, yeah. Maybe you should have made a bigger deal about the Professor thing. But he read that book. He would have known." He bends. Puts his hands on his knees. Huffs some air. Turns and looks over his shoulder at the other agents, who are still gathered around the carnage. "I don't mean what I'm about to say. And I will deny that I ever said it. But I wish to hell you hadn't shown up. I wish you had kept your mouth shut. I wish that son of a bitch had kept living in that cabin, sending out his bombs, and anyone else got hurt, but not my boss."

. . . Spends an Eternity in Hell

In the airport in Salt Lake City—they are traveling on their own, the agent with the bowl-cut hair having handed them tickets and dropped them off in Helena—they sit awaiting their connecting flight. On the giant TV screen, Brian Williams announces the FBI has reason to believe their agents have apprehended the serial killer known as the Technobomber. In the process, the suspect blew himself up. One agent has been killed and a government employee injured. The newscaster describes events Maxine witnessed earlier in the day, which makes the carnage seem like the premonition of a tragedy she ought to have been able to prevent.

She was six when Jack Ruby shot Lee Harvey Oswald live on TV. Her mother snapped off the set, but Maxine kept asking, "Was that real? Did that one man just shoot that other man? Right on TV?" It seemed impossible that in a crowded police station no adult had been able to prevent that one man from killing that other man. Every time Maxine saw the replay she felt like shouting to warn the younger, smaller man what the older man in the hat was about to do. Or reaching into the television set and grabbing the gun from Jack Ruby's hand. Only now does she understand that most disasters do, in fact, unfold in slow motion, and even as you watch you feel powerless to prevent them.

Several of their fellow travelers look up from their phones. A few drift closer to the giant TV. Maxine squirms, as if she and Zach might be recognized as accomplices on the run.

On the screen, Brian Williams explains that the FBI has identified the now-deceased suspect as one Thaddeus Rapaczynski, a native of Oakbrook, Illinois, and the news team has dug up a yearbook portrait of Thaddy as an impossibly clean-cut, square-jawed, sixteen-year-old high-school graduate. Then the camera zooms in on the one-story brick bungalow in which Thaddy was raised by his working-class parents. Then the building at Berkeley where, as an assistant professor, the suspect taught mathematics. No mention is made of Michigan. No mention of Maxine or Zach. But the newscaster identifies Supervisory Special Agent Roland Shauntz as the agent the bomber took with him in his final destructive act. The photo shows a much younger and surprisingly less attractive version of Shauntz—he was one of those men who roughen and become manlier as they age.

Zach hasn't spoken since they left Lincoln. He left behind his coat. They haven't had time to shower, although Maxine cleaned herself up in the airport restroom. She wants to chastise Zach for having been foolish enough to put himself in harm's way to save Thaddy, who after all turned out to be a terrorist. But wouldn't she have been tempted to do the same?

Their flight is called. For the next three hours, they remain oblivious to any news. They are both so exhausted, so stunned, they say little to each other, mulling their private thoughts. Back in Detroit, they take a taxi to Ann Arbor. Zach goes up to shower and sleep. She ought to go up with him. Instead, she switches on the television, settles on the sofa, and dozes off. When she wakes, a morning news program is broadcasting shadowy footage of the crime scene. The FBI suspects that the cabin has been booby-trapped. The reporter gestures here and there, re-creating an encounter he wasn't there to witness.

After a commercial break, the scene switches to a neighborhood outside Albany, New York, where the bomber's mother lives with Thaddy's brother and the brother's wife. The brother has issued a statement that his family knows little more than what they have learned watching television. Their hearts go out to the victims and their survivors. But the family is suffering a shock of their own. Any further statements will come from the Rapaczynskis' lawyer. The brother, who looks nothing like Thaddy—he resembles a shorter, more buck-toothed version of Zach—steps inside and shuts the door.

Thaddy's mother has remained invisible. Maxine tries to imagine what she felt getting a call from the FBI. *Your son is dead. Not only that, he is the serial bomber this agency has been hunting for the past six years.* Until now, Maxine had assumed she would have been a better mother to Thaddy than his real mother. Could have made him feel more loved. Given him better advice about how to make friends or attract a girlfriend. The poor woman is probably no more to blame for her son's descent into madness, into murder, than any parent. Will she and Thaddy's mother ever meet? Shauntz promised no one would find out who identified the author of the manifesto.

But Shauntz is dead.

She goes upstairs. Zach shouts through the bathroom door that he is driving back to Ypsilanti to get Angelina. Maxine takes this to mean they will be home for lunch. By two, she realizes they will be gone the whole day. She makes a show of grading the essays her students turned in that week. Then she gives up and walks to the grocery store to get some food. By the time Zach and Angelina return home, it's almost dinnertime. But Angelina is too angry to sit down to eat.

"You promised you wouldn't let him do anything stupid!" she tells Maxine. "And you!" She turns on Zach, waving a crutch. "You think only of yourself! Was saving this killer, this crazy man, more important than saving the father of your unborn child?"

Angelina must have been railing at Zach all day—Zach is so apologetic, so subdued, Maxine thinks he will ask Angelina's permission to breathe. For which Maxine loves her future daughter-in-law even more than she already did.

Finally, Angelina consents to sit at the dining room table, where Maxine serves the Italian chicken dish she found at the corner market. They eat in uncomfortable silence, the television turned low in case an update comes on. Maxine is about to bring out the Ben & Jerry's she bought earlier in the day when they hear a clamor out front. She peers between the curtains. Cars and vans fill the spaces in front of her house and the house across the street. Two of the vans are equipped with satellite dishes, one from FOX2 Detroit, the other from the local ABC affiliate.

The doorbell rings. Zach makes a move to answer it. Maxine pushes in front of him. When she opens the door, a blonde reporter she recognizes from the Detroit news says, "Mrs. Sayers. I am so sorry to bother you, but we've been told you were the one who identified Thaddeus Rapa . . . Rapasinky? As the Technobomber? Is that true? Please, we would love to get your version of events. How did you know it was him?"

"I'm sorry," she says. "Maybe at some point. Right now I can't."

Maxine shuts the door and leans against it. Thaddy is dead. Nothing she says can harm him. But if she goes out there, if she submits to their questions, she will end up saying what she is expected to say. *He was a brilliant young man. He wasn't someone I could predict would become a murderer.* Or: *I could see even then he harbored an irrational rage.* Either way, Thaddy will no longer be Thaddy but whoever her comments freeze him into being. If she steps outside, she will stop being who she is and become the wild-haired, hollow-eyed woman in her son's sweatshirt and J. C. Penney sweatpants everyone sees on the evening news.

The landline rings. She picks up the receiver, puts it down without a word, then uses her cell to call Stuart Greenglass.

"I've been trying to get you for the past two days," Greenglass says, at which Maxine realizes the ringer has been off since she got on the military plane to Helena. "There's been a leak," Greenglass tells her, as if she couldn't have guessed. "Don't say anything until I get there." She hangs up and calls Rosa, gives her the briefest outline of what has happened. The doorbell rings. She looks out—even more reporters are crowding the lawn. Down the street, another news van blocks her neighbor's driveway.

"Please, Mom," Zach says, "let me go out and tell them to go fuck themselves." She shakes her head—she doesn't want her son to show up on the evening broadcast swearing and waving his fist. She is tempted to turn out the lights and shoo Zach and Angelina upstairs, the way she and Sam used to do when they ran out of candy on Halloween. But Greenglass arrives, pushing his way through the crowd and climbing to the porch, and she cracks the door just enough to listen as he tells the reporters the FBI has asked the Sayers family to refrain from speaking to the press so as not to interfere with the investigation. After he fields a few questions, Maxine lets him in, but he stays only long enough to drink a glass of cold seltzer, ask when the baby is due, and pick up his check.

Angelina goes up to bed. Zach and Maxine remain in the living room to watch the news, bit by repetitive bit. There is a brief interview with Arnold Schlechter, who expresses gratitude to the bomber for sparing the government the expense of bringing him to trial and executing him. There is an update on the medical status of Zach's professor, Gordon Hertz, whose condition, thank God, has been upgraded to stable. A few more shots of Thaddy's brother's house near Albany, with Thaddy's brother and mother refusing to come out and comment.

Zach excuses himself—he hates leaving Angelina upstairs alone. The coverage continues, interspersed with local news and tips from a celebrity doctor on how to avoid gluten in one's diet. Then the reporter comes up with a grainy video that shows Thaddy a few days before his death, checking out a book from the Lincoln public library. For most of the clip, Thaddy has his back to the camera. His thatch of hair—Maxine assumes he cut it himself, or hacked at it with an axe—seems like a cheap wig he slapped on as a disguise. He wears a dark shirt and oversized trousers held up with a rope. After his books have been checked out, Thaddy turns, and Maxine can see his face is coarse and lined, his beard peppered with gray. That the boy she knew has aged so drastically seems the most shocking disguise of all.

The three townspeople the newscaster interviews say they knew something was off about the man, even by the standards of the ragged recluses who populate the Montana woods. "He smelled bad," one neighbor says. "He always seemed angry at me," the woman's husband tells the reporter. "Like a time bomb waiting to go off," she adds, not seeming to notice the aptness of the analogy.

But when they interview the librarian, a different picture emerges. The woman is younger than Maxine, maybe in her late forties. She wears little or no makeup. Her hair is gunmetal gray, unstyled. "They're only saying he was a nut because he hated them. Not all of them. Just the people he thought were destroying the wilderness. Destroying his peace. With all that logging. The gold mining. All that fracking. Man, did he hate fracking! He hated the motorcycles and ATVs. He hated the jets flying over his cabin, breaking the sound barrier. He hated the real estate moguls buying up all the land. The ski resorts. Everyone letting their dogs run wild, tearing up his vegetable garden."

Thaddy—she uses that name, *Thaddy*—seemed a regular guy to her. Actually, he seemed much nicer than most men she knows. And way smarter. He used to help her son with his math homework. He said if only her kid could see how beautiful math really was, he wouldn't be afraid of it anymore and then he would understand it.

And the books he took out! They sure weren't the trash other people wasted their time reading. He did have a peculiar smell. The librarian doesn't think it was body odor. More likely the soap Thaddy cooked up from some kind of animal fat—she helped him find the recipe on a survivalist blog online. If everyone wouldn't have given her a hard time, she might have gone out with the guy. At least for coffee. Maybe he wouldn't have felt so angry and alone. Maybe he wouldn't have done what he ended up doing.

Maxine cringes. Like her, the librarian seems to believe if only she cared enough for Thaddy, she might have prevented him sending those bombs. Isn't that what every fairy tale is about? No matter how cruel the beast, if the right woman summons the courage to kiss him, his heart might thaw. He might shed his shaggy pelt. The beast might change into the prince he was meant to be.

The next morning, Zach tells Maxine his priority is protecting the mother of his child from stress. With the reporters camped on the lawn, he and Angie ought to spend the next few days with her parents.

"Of course you should," Maxine says, hiding her dread of abandonment. Zach describes an elaborate scheme in which he and Angie will drive to Norm's apartment, hang out there until the middle of the night, then sneak into the back of Norm's old van and be spirited to Ypsilanti. Zach washes the breakfast dishes. Then she watches from an upstairs window as he leads his fiancée through the scrum of reporters, shielding her from the photographers, refusing to answer any of the shouted questions, helping Angelina into his VW bug, then backing out, inch by inch, taking care not to run over any of the reporters, even as they chase the VW down the street.

She is still at the window when Rosa and Mick drive up. Rosa blusters her way inside and sets down a plate of home-made pierogies. Mick remains on the porch, giving an interview no one asked for. (When Maxine sees it on the news, she will be shocked by Mick's eloquence about the need for more resources to study and treat mental illness, which, she remembers, destroyed his own family.)

"I know everything seems shitty right now," Rosa says, "but your son is okay. He's getting married. You're going to be a grandmother. You can't go back and save Thaddy. Or save that agent. You think it's hard to predict the future? Just try going back and changing the past."

Mick comes in. She can't figure out what's different about

him until she realizes this is the first time she has seen him without his cravat. Even with the blinds drawn she can make out the thick red scar circling his throat. "Mick," she says. She touches his neck, a liberty she would have deemed impossible a few days earlier.

"My daughter," he says. "She once came at me with a box cutter. It wasn't her fault. Her voices told her I was in league with whatever government forces were trying to do away with her." He lifts Maxine's hand and kisses it. "Thank you, my dear, for caring. With most people, I would rather not explain."

"We would take you home with us," Rosa says, "but we just put my house on the market and realtors keep tromping through. We're scrambling to close on a new place. And we're on our way to meet with the EDP team at the elementary school to line up the right services for a kid with every learning disability in the alphabet."

"Go, go," Maxine says. Of course life is continuing for other people. The people she cares about the most. She and Rosa hug and kiss and promise to see each other very soon, even though Maxine suspects she and her friend will never again share the intimacies they have shared. Unlike Maxine, Rosa will no longer be a widow. She will have Mick's granddaughter, not to mention her own two sons, to care for.

An hour later, Jackson Sparrow comes whistling up the walk. When one of the reporters asks who he is and whether he has anything to state for the record, he angles his head and recites Allen Ginsberg's "Howl":

> I saw the best minds of my generation destroyed by madness . . .
> who passed through universities with radiant cool eyes hallucinating
> Arkansas and Blake-light tragedy among the scholars of war . . . .

The reporters drift off. Jackson keeps declaiming with an audience of exactly zero. Except, from behind the door, Maxine can't help but listen:

> . . . who cowered in unshaven rooms in underwear, burning their money in wastebaskets and listening to the Terror through the wall . . .
> with dreams, with drugs, with waking nightmares, alcohol and cock and endless balls . . .
> . . . illuminating all the motionless world of Time between . . . .

She opens the door and pulls him in.

"Here." He hands her a canvas tote. "I thought these might help you get through the siege." The bag contains a small bottle of whiskey, a bag of chocolate-covered popcorn, six or seven books of poetry by women and men Maxine has never heard of, and three volumes of Jackson's own verses. "You and me, we're going for a walk. Any of those assholes follow, I'll recite more Ginsberg at them. Then I'm taking you camping up north, on Walloon Lake. Hemingway country. If it was good enough to help Nick Adams recover from World War I, it ought to do you good getting through all this mess."

Jackson, she realizes, is a good-hearted man. Maybe, when this chaos dies down, she will set aside some time to get to know him. Maybe she will marry him. But when she imagines walking down the aisle, it isn't a rabbi she sees waiting for them at the *chuppah*, but the Angel of Death. Her life is over. The Institute for Future Studies has no future. She is too sick of living to study immortality. She can't summon the enthusiasm to take a walk around the block with Jackson Sparrow, let alone date and marry him.

She kisses his papery cheek, to one side of the divot the surgeons left when they removed his tumor. Surprised, he kisses her back. Now it's Maxine's turn to be surprised: this is anything but two corpses kissing.

Still, she pushes him out the door, where, despite his earlier recitation from Ginsberg's poem, he is swallowed by the reporters.

Late that night, the landline rings. She glances at the caller ID, sees the name RAPACZYNSKI, nearly crumples, then manages to pick up the receiver and say hello.

"I am Ursula Rapaczynski," the caller says. "I am Thaddeus's mother." Her English is flawless, but she speaks as if she has borrowed the language and is determined to return it in the condition she received it, no fingerprints, unsoiled, no dents. "I know very little about my son's life after he left for university," the woman says. "So forgive me for not knowing who you are. The police . . . the officers from the FBI . . . they said you knew my Thaddeus. You were his teacher. You and your son . . . they say you and your son were there when my Thaddeus . . . when he . . . when he did what they say he did. When he killed himself. And that other man."

Maxine can hear Thaddy's mother crying. "Yes," Maxine says. "I did know your son. And there were many good things about him."

"Yes!" she says. "He had *good things* in him. Many, many good things. Which he allowed so few people to see. I can tell you cared about my Thaddeus. You are one of the people who saw the good in him. So I am calling to say you should not feel too bad because of turning in my son. His brother and I, we tried to convince ourselves to do the same. But we could not bring ourselves to believe . . . We still saw our Thaddeus as he used to be, not as what he must have become much later."

Maxine tells Thaddy's mother she also found it difficult to convince herself Thaddy was capable of doing what he did. But

Thaddy's mother seems to have planned what she has to say; she won't let Maxine go on.

"Thaddeus was such a happy, happy baby! Always smiling. Talking early. Then he got a fever and a very bad rash. I took him to the hospital. In those days, they would not let me stay with my son. And when I am coming back to get him, he was a very different boy. He hated to be touched. He never smiled. He no longer spoke. He had difficulties making friends with the other children.

"Foolishly, I sent him away when he was too young. I knew only that Harvard is the best university of the world. Surely it made sense that such a brilliant boy ought to attend the best university? But they did unspeakable things to my son's mind, those Harvard professors. I am not the terrible mother my Thaddeus believes me to be. His brother tells me we did have good experiences as a family."

Thaddy's brother takes the phone. "I'm sorry. She insisted I find your number. But my mother isn't wrong. My brother did have many good qualities. I looked up to my brother. I got many of my ideas from him. And the ideas weren't all crazy. The Thaddy I knew wasn't the type of person who could build a bomb and use it to kill another human being. But he changed. I was never sure why. Maybe what my mother says about the time she took him to the hospital is the cause. Maybe what happened to him at Harvard. Or maybe none of that mattered. He blamed us. Blamed my parents. Blamed me. Because he couldn't form a relationship with a woman."

Maxine hears someone at the other end say something to Thaddy's brother.

"My wife says we didn't want to see how crazy he was, but it was right there in the letters he wrote us. We loved Thaddy.

Even when we began to suspect . . . Well, if not for you, he might have killed someone else."

Which turns out to be true. An hour after she hangs up, Maxine receives another call from the FBI. A search of Thaddy's cabin has turned up enough bomb-making materials to kill another two or three victims, plus a completed bomb, which they found beneath his bed, the address label blank except for an Oakland zip code. To whom might Thaddy have sent that bomb? Zach? Zach's housemate, Jordan, whom Thaddy had accused of selling out because he was on his way to becoming an exec at Facebook? Or one of thousands of other Silicon Valley entrepreneurs or CEOs? Whose life has Maxine saved? She is glad she will never know.

Special Agent Markham tells Maxine they also found a copy of Conrad's *Secret Agent* in Thaddy's cabin, along with the other books Maxine assigned for her class, some with Thaddy's handwriting in the margins. Maxine wants to ask why the agent is telling her this. To make her feel she is responsible for his murderous ideas? Or to prove he paid attention to what she taught him?

Shockingly, the agent also notifies Maxine that she qualifies to receive the million-dollar reward the FBI offered for any information that might lead to the bomber's capture. The agent warns her the government will need to deduct taxes from the reward, but they already have her social security number in their files.

A million dollars? For turning Thaddy in? Thaddy certainly wasn't Jesus Christ, but she can't help thinking of herself as Judas. She considers giving the reward to Thaddy's mother. But Thaddy's family will want the money even less than she does. Maybe she can use it to fund her institute. But even a million dollars will be too little, too late. Better to use at least some of the money to set up a fund in memory of Supervisory Special Agent Roland Shauntz. She will put Burdock in charge of figuring out how to spend it; hopefully, he won't commission a tasteless portrait. Maybe she will divide up the rest to pay restitution to Thaddy's victims. God knows if Arnold Schlechter will accept the money, or to what end he might put it. But that's no concern of hers.

What she would really like to do is reserve some of the money to finance Zach and Angelina's project. Zach won't want to benefit from turning in his friend. And there has to be something suspect about a middle-class white kid thinking he can save Detroit by swooping in and growing vegetables. But maybe, with this unexpected windfall, not to mention the long-delayed proceeds of her mother's lawsuit, the universe is showing its approval of the scheme.

. . . Holds Hands with Death

The Monday after Thaddy blows himself up, the provost wakes Maxine, calling to congratulate her on bringing to bay one of the nation's most wanted criminals.

"But you know," Perpetua says, "this leaves us with even less incentive to find additional sources of revenue for your institute." The fundraiser has been canceled. "We can't solicit donations for a program that will forever be associated in the public's mind with a notorious antifuturist terrorist."

Blearily, Maxine reminds the provost that Thaddy was enrolled in the mathematics department and had no real affiliation with her institute. But Perpetua has given the IFS faculty until the end of the year to clear out their offices; the following spring, the building will be demolished to make way for the new Thomas and Betsy Winkelmann Center for Entrepreneurial Research.

Maxine forces herself out of bed and sends around an email calling an emergency meeting to break the news. Rosa is using her vacation days to prepare for her granddaughter's arrival, and the receptionist hasn't returned from her maternity leave, so when Maxine arrives for the meeting, the front desk stands as empty as the prow of the *Flying Dutchman*.

She can't bring herself to unlock her office. Instead, she kills time sitting in the grungy lounge, leafing mindlessly through scientific journals that only a few months earlier promised the latest revelations and discoveries but now are shabby and stained by coffee rings. When the faculty arrives, she calls the meeting to order—and is surprised to find, for the first time in the history of the institute she founded, no one seems to resent that she is running it.

"I would never have found the courage to do what you did," Tobin Brazelton marvels.

Carleton Marius wants to know what science fiction novels were found in the bomber's cabin.

Alphred and the rest of the AI and Robotics guys ply her for details about the FBI's methods of surveillance.

Only Jackson seems to understand the reality of what has happened. "It would behoove us to remember someone died. A young man who graduated from our institution. And he took innocent lives with him. I don't know how we can call ourselves a university when we allow so many of our young people to live in so much pain. This is what happens when we focus so much on preparing them in the sciences and neglect the development of their souls."

And that ends the conversation. For once, there is nothing else on the agenda. Maxine doesn't need to break the news that they have only a few months to pack up their offices; if anything, she was the last to know. Carleton is returning to the English Department to run a program in something called the Digital Humanities. Gavin Reinehardt, who never spent more than a few hours a week at the institute anyway, will resume working full time in his genetics lab.

The only surprise—at least to Maxine—is that Alphred and the rest of the AI team have signed on as consultants at the new entrepreneurial think tank. Even Tobin will be taking a position at the Winkelmann Center, managing any new terrors that might arise to frighten consumers out of making purchases.

They beg Maxine to join them. And really, why is she so adamant about refusing? Wasn't her father an entrepreneur? How nefarious would it be to anticipate the products that might make human beings happier? Products that might distract us from our boredom? Our loneliness? Our fear of death? But she can't muster the slightest enthusiasm for the prospect.

Alphred makes a motion to thank Maxine for her years of hard work in creating and directing the institute.

"Hear! Hear!" cries Gerhard Klostermann.

"I can't imagine where I would have ended up if it weren't for you, Maxine," Alphred admits. "When I think of what a snotty twerp I was when I signed up for that seminar . . ."

They rise and clap with at least a modicum of appreciation before they toss their coffee cups in the trash and head out the door.

That afternoon, when she arrives to teach her final class of the semester, the students are dying to ask about the story they have been following in the campus daily.

"I'm sorry," Maxine says. "I can't talk about any of that. He was my student. The way all of you are my students." She hands out blue books for the exam, then sits at the front of the room and tries to concentrate on the poetry she brought to read. It's one of the volumes Jackson gave her, by Philip Larkin. Jackson has earmarked a poem called "Aubade," which Maxine thinks might mean . . . well, she has no idea what the title means. To her, "aubade" is the kind of word a person would find in the title of a poem and nowhere else:

> Unresting death, a whole day nearer now,
> Making all thought impossible but how
> And where and when I shall myself die. . . .

She rereads the poem, oddly comforted that a stranger has expressed the fear that has haunted her all her life.

> . . . Courage is no good:
> It means not scaring others. Being brave
> Lets no one off the grave.
> Death is no different whined at than withstood. . . .

She looks around at her students, nearly all of whom are scribbling in their blue books. She has set only one essay: they are to project themselves thirty years into the future and describe the ways the topics they have discussed that term will influence their daily lives. Luther van Dyke is studying his tattoos; maybe the raven is croaking out suggestions. Hideyo Suzuki writes so intently all Maxine can see is the topknot on his head. Tommy Bruce chews on his pen, no doubt attempting to figure out if baseball is still being played in the middle of the twenty-first century and, if so, how it might be affected by the increased longevity of its players. Did he make it to the pros? Will he be able to continue pitching into his seventies?

At the rear of the room, Russell Charnow sits with his eyes closed, his expression conveying that his time would be better spent anywhere but in this room. Thaddy was a fair, blue-eyed, square-jawed Slav; Russell is a tall, dark, Dostoevskian Jew. But there is something similar about these two young men. Russell came to Michigan as a physics prodigy. Like Thaddy, he gives off the air of someone studying for the priesthood who is afraid to admit he has lost his faith. He no longer rolls his eyes at everything Maxine says. But his essays still give off the brimstone stink of rage. In one paper, he theorized that if the majority of the population chooses to take advantage of medical advances that allow for extreme longevity, and if one unhappy person carries out a massacre that cuts down victims who otherwise might have lived hundreds of years, the punishment will need to be all that much greater than the system metes out now. If the penalty for murder now is death, won't the penalty for slaying a human being who otherwise might have lived forever be perpetual torture? She imagines Russell ten or twenty years from now, bearded, unwashed, poring over a wiring diagram. Sees him rigging his jacket with explosives. Walking toward the bushes where Supervisory Special Agent Roland Shauntz stands arguing with the local ranger about the boundary of his property.

She can't leave the room. Not while she is proctoring her exam. She only hopes the students won't notice she is crying.

But of course they notice. The first to finish is Obayo Stevens. He bends from his great height, lays his blue book in front of Maxine, then, tentatively, places his enormous hand on her shoulder. "You okay?" he mouths. When she doesn't answer, Obayo bends and envelopes her in a massive hug. He lets her go, and Maxine smiles up at him to reassure him what he has done is okay. He gives her a thumbs-up and leaves.

After that, every student who hands in a blue book bends for a hug.

"Thanks for everything," says Patti Querk.

"Great class," says Tommy Bruce.

Last of all, Russell shuffles up and tosses his blue book on the pile. For all she knows, he has written "FUCK YOU!" on every page. She can't hold herself responsible for the anger of every white guy who feels unloved. If she continues to teach, shouldn't she invest her energy in students like Obayo Stevens, Yvonne Switalski, or Patti Querk?

"Russell," she says. "You stay in touch, okay? Let me know how things are going."

The expression that comes over him is the expression Maxine imagines on Raskolnikov's face when he is surprised in the middle of his robbery and hacks the pawnbroker's sister with his axe. She jumps to her feet, to evade whatever blow he might deliver.

"I'm sorry I was such an asshole," Russell says. "This is the only class I felt like coming to all semester." He reaches as if to hug her, then backs away and hurries out, leaving Maxine as unsteady on her feet as if, without her student's support, she might topple from a cliff and fall.

The next afternoon, she drives to Sunrise Hills. According to the nurse, her mother has been sleeping more than usual. Refusing to eat or get out of bed. This might be the natural effect of the Parkinson's. Or her mother has seen the news on TV and can no longer bear the horror.

When Maxine goes in, her mother is lying not on top of the covers but underneath them. She is so thin she barely makes a bump. Maxine pulls up a chair. Strokes her mother's face. Kisses it. But her mother doesn't stir. Her father was dead when the EMTs carried his body past her. Her husband died on another continent. She is damn well going to be sitting beside her mother when she draws her last breath.

"Mom?" she says. She thinks of revealing the news about the million-dollar reward. But Maxine isn't even sure her mother knows who she is. "Mom?" she says again. "Do you want to get your hair done? I'll come as early as you want."

Her mother's eyes flutter open. They focus on Maxine. She shakes her head no. Then she closes her eyes and goes back to sleep.

A week later, they move her upstairs to hospice. She hasn't been conscious for more than a few minutes here and there, has eaten nothing but ice chips. No doubt she would derive great joy from holding her newborn great-grandson. But has her time on the planet really been so valuable that she should be granted eternal life? If Maxine could prolong her mother's suffering, even for a minute, would she?

"It's all right, Mom. Everything is okay. I love you."

The hospice nurse tells Maxine the end will come soon. Another hour passes. A series of rasping, throat-rattling breaths. Her mother is here, but not here. Crazily, Maxine watches for her mother's soul to escape her body. And so is thrown backward in alarm when her mother rears up and shouts, "Lennie! Lennie!," smiling radiantly, as if she sees Maxine's father at the door, bringing her a bouquet, as he often did on his way home from his appliance store. The nurse warned Maxine that when someone's brain is deprived of oxygen, she will imagine she is seeing "beloved ones from her past." And yet, her father's presence is so strong Maxine wants to find a vase to hold the flowers.

Her mother's arms shoot up to her head. "My hair! My *hair!*" As if her husband will be so put off by her appearance he will turn and trudge back to his grave in Fenstead.

"It doesn't matter," Maxine says. "Dad loves you. I love you."

Even so, she can't let go of her mother's hand. It's as if they are crossing Fenstead's busiest street and Maxine isn't sure if her mother is keeping her safe or pulling her into the path of an oncoming car.

This is how Zach and Angelina find them. The baby is due in less than two weeks. Zach and Angelina had an appointment with her obstetrician earlier that afternoon. "Stop by when you're finished," Maxine told them, thinking her mother would hold on for another day.

"Jesus," Zach says. "Is Grandmom dead?"

Yes, she thinks. Her mother is dead. She and Zach will need to drive to Saratoga to bury her mother beside her father. After Maxine dies, will Zach and Angelina ever travel to Fenstead to pay their respects to Maxine's parents? Will it matter if no one does?

Zach takes his grandmother's other hand, as if they might send the current of life coursing between them. "Goodbye, Grandmom." He leans down and kisses her cheek. Then he chides his mother for not having warned him that his grandmother was so close to dying. "You should have told me, Mom. Angie and I would have rescheduled our appointment."

Angelina, who is balancing on her crutches, seems like Atlas holding up the world, except she is holding it in her belly and not on her back. She steps closer to the bed, then, alarmingly, drops her crutches and groans. Water gushes to the floor.

"Angie!" Zach says. But he isn't quick enough to keep her from curling to her knees.

"Oh my god, oh my god, oh my god." Her breathing is ragged, not unlike the breaths Maxine's mother struggled to draw a few minutes earlier. "It hurts so much! Zach! The baby! It's coming!"

The hospice nurse, who has stepped in to see how Maxine's mother is doing, runs to press the buzzer. Luckily, one of the other nurses on the floor has experience in obstetrics. She and an aide lift Angelina to a wheelchair, then wheel her down to meet the ambulance, where, Maxine thinks, the EMTs will be pleasantly surprised to find they are picking up not an old person destined for intensive care but a pregnant young woman about to give birth.

Zach lingers to make sure his mother will be all right. "This is just so crazy." He gestures to his grandmother, then out the door toward his fiancée. "I'll text you. I'll let you know what's going on." Then he dashes out—she can hear his loping gait as he hurries to catch the elevator.

The hospice nurse flips open a clean sheet and allows it to flutter over Maxine's mother's body. Maxine wants to pull it from her mother's face and ask: *So, did that shade of mascara matter?* But she finally understands her mother's vanity. Why not look your best while you have the chance? She will give the funeral director her mother's favorite pink lipstick, her new mascara, her favorite turquoise suit and matching pumps.

The nurse is gone a long time. *So*, her mother seems to be saying from beneath the sheet, *if you're such an expert on death, is there anything you know that I don't?*

No, Maxine wants to say. *I don't know a thing.*

Except that the dead are boring. She wants to call Rosa. But it seems rude to talk on your cell phone in front of a dead person.

She calls anyway. "And please," she tells Rosa, "don't say anything about the transmigration of souls. Did my mother's essence just kind of float out of her body and into my grandchild's?"

"That isn't how it works."

"There's no other way it could work."

"I would explain," Rosa says, "but I'm here in Grand Rapids, waiting for Mick to come back from taking Risa to get ice cream. Then we're going to buy her some clothes so she doesn't look like an eleven-year-old stripper."

Maxine can hear Rosa's impatience to get off the phone. But she is reluctant to allow her to go, not only because she doesn't want to be left alone with her mother, but because she knows from now on, Rosa will have more important concerns than her. "Rosa," she asks, "what do you think of Jackson Sparrow?"

"As what, a poet?"

"As a lover."

"I don't think Mick would appreciate my taking another boyfriend."

"Is he too old for me? I think he's too old. I don't want to lose another husband."

"Ah," Rosa says. She yells something to Mick that involves "pistachio" and "chocolate chip." "I have found that if you are worrying about someone dying, that's a pretty clear sign you care about him. That's how I knew I loved Mick. I kept watching him eat those Boston crème donuts he likes, and one day, I smashed one from his hand and asked if he was trying to make sure he died before he hit seventy." More shouting. "Speaking of which, Mick just came back and said Risa threw a tantrum and tried to run in front of a truck. I have to go."

The driver from the funeral home is large and bald, his forehead dented in such a way that Maxine imagines him kneeling behind a hearse and someone yanking out a casket. She answers his questions and signs some paperwork. She tells her mother goodbye, then tempers her sadness by reminding herself that her son is waiting at the hospital with her newborn grandchild.

She takes the elevator to the first floor. She is hurrying out when the guard shouts: "Ma'am! Ma'am!"

Stifling her anger—the woman can't know her mother just died—Maxine goes all the way around the revolving door and returns to find the page in the logbook where she signed herself in five hours earlier. The space in which Zach and Angelina ought to have signed themselves out is blank. Maxine fills in the time of their departure and, in the appropriate box, her own.

Then she rips the page from the binder. Balls it in her fist. Considers throwing it at the woman behind the desk. Rushes out before the guard can get up and follow her. In the Buick, she curses and tosses the balled-up paper in the back seat, where, weeks later, installing a car seat for her grandson, she will find it, wonder what it is, unfold the sheet, and be assaulted by a flock of memories that will cause her to smooth the page and keep it as a reminder of the day something terrible happened, and something wonderful happened, although no system of mathematics provides her with a method for subtracting the losses from the gains and calculating the remainder.

By the time she arrives at the hospital, her grandson is seven hours old. The nurses have wrapped him in a flannel blanket printed with bunnies and sheep. His tiny, vulnerable head is being warmed by a yellow cap.

"It's a boy!" Angelina announces, her skin velvety against the stark white linen of her bed. "My milk hasn't come in yet." She pouts, handing their son to Zach. "But I guess my body didn't have much warning."

Maxine tries to see the baby's face, but Zach cradles him against his chest. "Mom," he says, "you haven't asked what we're calling him."

How odd, the question hadn't even occurred to her.

"I'll give you a hint. We're naming him for someone who was really smart and died too young."

For a horrible moment, she thinks he is going to say they named her grandchild Thaddy.

"Samuel," he says. "Sammy. Little Sam."

"After your father?" she asks stupidly, as if some other Sam might be involved.

"Don't you want to hold him?"

He places the newborn in her arms. Staring at the perfectly contented face, Maxine imagines everything they will do together. When she used to take Zach to the playground, she felt she was stealing pleasure from the lectures she needed to plan, the articles and books she needed to write, the tasks she needed to accomplish so her life wouldn't be considered a waste—by whoever was keeping track. Now, she imagines the bliss of swinging this baby on a swing. Pushing the pointy end of a straw into the small silver hole on the top of a juice box, then watching this rosebud of a mouth close on the straw and sip. Here she had been, if not eager to die, then willing. The possibility she might not live to see this fresh, sweet little human grow up—find out what he becomes, whom he marries, what children he and his partner give birth to—strikes her as intolerable. She wants to keep living forever.

Which means she is overcome by her old fear of dying. It's as if she has dragged herself to the finish line of a marathon, only to learn she is being forced to run another. She will need to continue worrying about global warming. The effects of technology on malleable young minds. The accumulation of microscopically small beads of plastic, mercury, and carbon dioxide in the oceans. The extinction of tigers, polar bears, elephants, and so many other species.

The child wriggles and yawns. *Sam*, she says. *My dearest little Sammy*. Love explodes from her very being. Ripple after ripple, like a thermonuclear wave expanding outward from a blast. Maxine expands outward with those waves, until, from a telescopic distance, she looks back at her grandson. Who, she now realizes, like all swaddled infants, is shaped like a figure eight. Like the mathematical symbol for infinity.

ACKNOWLEDGMENTS

Although *The Professor of Immortality* is entirely a work of fiction, in writing it I have drawn heavily on the story of the Unabomber, Theodore Kaczynski, who was a graduate student in mathematics at the University of Michigan, where I taught for a quarter of a century. Excerpts from Thaddeus Rapaczynski's fictional manifesto are quoted or paraphrased from Kaczynski's *Industrial Society and Its Future*, which was published in *The New York Times* and *The Washington Post* on September 19, 1995; similarly, the Technobomber's letter to Arnold Schlechter is a paraphrase of a similar letter Kaczynski sent to one of his victims, a Yale computer science professor named David Gelernter. The quotation about there being a little of the Technobomber in most of us is a twist on a similar quotation from an essay by Robert Wright published in *Time* magazine on June 24, 2001.

Although I have taken many liberties with Kaczynski's life and crimes, as well as the FBI's pursuit of the Unabomber, I am much indebted to the background provided by two nonfiction books: *A Mind for Murder: The Education of the Unabomber and the Origins of Modern Terrorism,* by Alston Chase, and *Unabomber: On the Trail of America's Most-Wanted Serial Killer,* by John Douglas and Mark Olshaker.

The excerpt from "Aubade" is from *The Complete Poems of Philip Larkin*, edited by Archie Burnett, copyright (c) 2012 by The Estate of Philip Larkin, reprinted by permission of Farrar, Straus and Giroux; the Canadian rights to that excerpt are granted by permission of Faber and Faber Ltd. The lines from Allen Ginsberg's "Howl," which appears in his *Collected Poems 1947-1980*, copyright (c) 1955 by Allen Ginsberg, are reprinted by permission of HarperCollins Publishers. Some of the material in this book was published in a slightly different form in my story "The Professor of Immortality Goes Swing Dancing," which appeared in *Harvard Review*, No. 53, 2019.

For invaluable information about legal and procedural issues, I am deeply grateful to Bruce C. Judge, Assistant United States Attorney, Eastern District of Michigan, and Jill Washburn, the media coordinator and public affairs specialist for the FBI's Detroit division.

For general encouragement and background details, my thanks to Jess Carroll and Marian and Marek Krzyzowski. For the hours they spent reading my manuscript and advising me on revisions, my heartfelt appreciation to Suzanne Berne, Leonard Post, Maxine Rodburg, Therese Stanton, Marian Thurm, and Douglas Trevor, as well as my wonderful agent, Jenni Ferrari-Adler, and my brilliant editor at Delphinium Books, Joe Olshan.

To Joe and Lori and everyone at Delphinium: Bless you for giving me such a warm and welcome homecoming.

ABOUT THE AUTHOR

Eileen Pollack graduated with a BS in physics from Yale and earned an MFA in creative writing from the University of Iowa. She is the author of the novels *The Bible of Dirty Jokes*, *A Perfect Life*, *Breaking and Entering*, and *Paradise, New York*, the short-story collections *In the Mouth* and *The Rabbi in the Attic*, and the nonfiction books *The Only Woman in the Room: Why Science Is Still a Boys' Club* and *Woman Walking Ahead: In Search of Catherine Weldon and Sitting Bull*. She has received fellowships from the National Endowment for the Arts, the Michener Foundation, the Rona Jaffe Foundation, and the Massachusetts Arts Council. Her novella "The Bris" was chosen to appear in *Best American Short Stories 2007*, edited by Stephen King; two other stories have been awarded Pushcart Prizes, and her essay "Pigeons" was selected by Cheryl Strayed for *Best American Essays 2013*. Formerly the director of the MFA Program in Creative Writing at the University of Michigan, she now lives in Boston.